Burned Out
and Bled Dry

MEREDITH JACOBOWITZ

For Abby, Andreea, Morgan, and Shalayne—my biggest cheerleaders!

CONTENTS

CHAPTER ONE

Tyler McCarther gazed out the window of her office onto downtown St. Louis. The view was still great. The job was still rough. After four years defending NSK Holdings, the manufacturer of a prominent men's nose hair wax, against class action lawsuits, Tyler could die happy without looking at another photo of the inside of a man's (and sometimes even a woman's) nostril. Well, everyone could probably die happy without looking at a photo of the inside of a nostril, but the point was, Tyler had looked at thousands. The nostrils were always hairless, and always either scabbed, sporting a rash, or somehow worse yet, unable to grow hair ever again. That last one seemed like the point of waxing your nose hair—a basis her firm used against participants in these lawsuits. Then, the plaintiff's counsel wised up and brought in medical experts extolling the dangers of the absence of nose hair for long periods of time. Since the injury provided Tyler with fodder for some jokes of a questionable taste level, she had no real criticisms. Plus, out of all manufacturers Tyler's law firm defended (car seats, wheelchairs, motorcycles) the photos she looked at were hands down the least disturbing.

Tyler refocused on the partner sitting across from her in her office.

"Tyler," he continued, "the point is, I've told you before that I prefer two spaces at the end of a sentence instead of one."

"Kevin, you're right, there's no excuse," she answered, shifting uncomfortably. The air conditioning was no match for the bright July sun streaming into the window, and the combination of nerves and heat had left Tyler sitting in a pool of sweat.

"There is no excuse," he told her firmly, emphasizing "is." Privately, Tyler disagreed. Out of all the partners, Kevin was the only one she knew of who still preferred two spaces at the end of sentence. It was so old-fashioned, and Kevin was a younger partner, so actually, he was the one without an excuse. Nevertheless, Tyler had no option but to agree to Kevin's face; she had recently been promoted from reviewing pictures of the plaintiffs' nostrils and legal research to actually writing parts of motions, and Tyler certainly was not going to lose that privilege over a two-space-one-space disagreement.

"I'll make sure the brief is corrected, and I'll make sure it never happens again."

"You do that," Kevin sternly said, rising from the chair, straightening his custom-made suit, and walking toward the door. He turned around. "Tyler, just remember that the definition of insanity is doing the same thing and expecting a different result." He winked on his way out, or maybe it was more of a spasm from too much caffeine and too little sleep. *Did he seriously just call me insane?* Tyler thought. But there was no time to question her sanity. The opposition to the motion to compel had to be filed by midnight, and the spaces had to be fixed immediately.

Cerene, an associate who started with the firm the same year as Tyler and who worked on car seat cases, walked by Tyler's office, perfectly pressed and perfectly coiffed. As always, Cerene was conservatively dressed in a mid-height heel and dark colors which somehow never showed lint despite Tyler having personally met Cerene's two golden retrievers. Cerene's glossy blonde shoulder-length lob—fashionable but professional—gleamed and somehow always looked freshly cut. *Shit, she probably heard the whole thing.* If they stuck around, Cerene and Tyler were bound to become competition. Both associates in the firm's products liability group, both women... only one would probably earn the coveted promotion of making partner. The other would have to wait several more years, be pacified with a promotion to "Of Counsel," or worse, shoved out entirely after being informed that after years of hard work she was failing to succeed at the firm. The women were on friendly terms for now since they were both at the bottom of wherever the phrase "shit flows downhill" refers to, but both hoped to become partner, so a competitive undercurrent ran unacknowledged through their interactions. Although Cerene was sympathetic to Tyler's plight, she probably would not be able to resist mentioning the insanity incident to a friend or two, and in an office that loved to gossip, or rather, any law firm, news of Tyler's public feedback was sure to spread among the junior and mid-level associates in a week or less. *At least I'm not important enough for senior associates or partners to be interested in anything I do*, Tyler thought glumly.

Sure enough, Cerene doubled back and pulled her mouth into an improbable expression between a frown and a smirk. "Doing okay, Tyler? Hang in there, I heard he does that to everyone."

"Fine," responded Tyler. "Thanks so much for checking in, but I've really got to turn this draft." Tyler glanced down at her wrist in a not-so-subtle "go away" signal made all the less subtle by the fact that there was no watch in sight.

"All right," responded Cerene, but she did not take the hint and walk away. "I can't imagine how stressful working with..." she glanced either direction to see if anyone was around, "Kevin" she halfway-mouthed-halfway-whispered "would be. I'm just lucky to work for Bob—he's the most relaxed." Cerene's closed-mouth smile bordered on smug.

Tyler nodded distractedly as she started adding the spaces to her draft, "So lucky," she said lightly, "but whenever I remember how many of Kevin's associates have become partner, it makes everything so much more bearable, you know? I just think it's so important to work toward an attainable goal. Don't you?" She smiled up at Cerene brightly. Kevin might talk down to her, but Tyler would be damned if Cerene did. Cerene's smile faltered slightly and Tyler thought she saw a flicker of insecurity in Cerene's eyes. Bingo. As both women knew, three of Kevin's associates had made partner in the last decade as opposed to exactly zero of Bob's.

"Well, let's grab coffee soon, once you're done," said Cerene, recovering her composure immediately, and continuing down the hall with a flick of her smooth blonde hair.

It was already six p.m., so Tyler knew she was looking at another late night at the office. She surreptitiously pulled out her cell phone and shot off a quick text to Harry, the private investigator she had been grabbing drinks with recently. *So sorry—stuck here finishing up the opposition brief... rain check on drinks?* He responded quickly, rain check was no problem, and he could even meet up later if Tyler wanted.

Tyler diligently worked to finish the draft by adding the spaces. By seven Kevin had given her his final comments, and by 9:30 p.m. Tyler had finished the draft and filed it online. Dinner was two scoops of almond butter stored in her desk for these occasions. Hit by a rush of elation at meeting the deadline and filing what she considered to be an extremely compelling motion, Tyler texted Harry again. *Hey—too late for drinks? Or just late enough?;)* She waited fifteen minutes. No response. Tyler logged out of her laptop, unplugged it from the dock, and gathered her personal items to go home.

At times like these Tyler was grateful to live in St. Louis. There was usually almost no traffic, and the city pretty much went to sleep by nine thirty—especially on a Wednesday. No one was on the roads for her short drive from downtown to her Lafayette Square townhome. Tyler drove home in a trance, re-playing in her head certain arguments she had made in the opposition brief, and re-affirming she had fixed some minor mistakes flagged earlier in the day by Brendan, the senior associate on the case. Tyler's trance continued as she parked, unlocked her door, threw her bag on the ground, kicked off her four-inch pointy-toed heels, and put out a can of wet food for Lucy, her fluffy calico cat.

"Lucy," she said, "first of all, I got the brief filed, and Kevin only said one mean thing to me." Lucy meowed. "Yeah, I know, you're sick of hearing about work. Can you believe that Harry didn't wait up to have a drink with me?" Lucy meowed again. "Me neither!" Tyler exclaimed. Lucy rubbed herself against Tyler's legs. *Maybe Kevin was right about that insanity thing,* thought Tyler, *I am talking to a cat right now.*

Even though it was now ten thirty at night, and if Tyler wanted even the possibility of working out tomorrow, she would have to get up at five thirty in the morning, the remnants of adrenaline from the office remained, and she was not ready to call it a night. She washed her face, put on some old sweatpants, threw her long dirty-blonde hair into a low bun, and poured herself a glass of bourbon on the rocks. Then Tyler indulged in a guilty pleasure—one of those real housewives shows on Bravo. The women's petty drama was a welcome change of pace from the petty drama happening at her office, and Tyler found nothing shut down the loop of office stress like watching beautifully dressed middle-aged women fight over whether one of them had accused the other's husband of having an affair in the bathroom at a charity auction or at an art gallery. Idly, Tyler wondered if she had gone down the wrong career path. If she made more of an effort with her appearance, maybe she, too, could have been the wife of someone wealthy and become a Bravo housewife. She was always up for a good argument, so she had that part covered.

One bourbon on the rocks turned into two, and by around midnight Tyler finally felt relaxed. She headed up the stairs to her bedroom and happily stretched herself out on her clean white sheets— today was the day her housekeeper had come and Tyler had recently negotiated clean sheets for an extra ten dollars a visit. Lucy was already curled at the bottom of the bed and looked up at her with annoyance as she was forced to move to accommodate Tyler's feet. Tyler set her alarm for five thirty. Probably wishful thinking, but Tyler always gave herself partial credit for trying. Head buzzing pleasantly, she passed into a dreamless sleep.

Sometime later Tyler jolted awake to a loud bang. Her head hurt and her mouth was fuzzy. Surely it was not five thirty yet. Tyler blearily looked around: the clock read three a.m. She lay her head back down. If she went to sleep immediately, she could get two and a half more hours of sleep. Unfortunately, thanks to that second bourbon, Tyler felt a gentle but insistent throbbing in her head. Tyler groaned, cursing her lack of self-control, and rolled out of bed for water. *Just as well, I can check the house alarm.* Water in hand and alarm system checked, she headed back to bed for what had now been reduced to two hours and fifteen minutes of sleep.

When the alarm clock blared at five thirty, Tyler rolled over, checked her emails, and reset it for an hour later. Waking up that early had been wishful thinking anyway.

At six thirty Tyler dragged herself out of bed and fixed breakfast. Still no emails, which was strange because normally Kevin would have copied her on an email to the client sharing the filed opposition, and he typically started working before Tyler was even out of bed. Tyler felt the familiar squeeze of anxiety in her chest that through some error in the online filing system the motion had not been uploaded. She checked the court's Electronic Case Filing page three times to be sure, logging on with Kevin's credentials instead of hers—

the last time as a separate check to confirm that her log-in was displaying accurate information. Noticing her bloodshot eyes (*thanks bourbon and five hours of sleep*) Tyler got dressed in a nicer-than-normal outfit to distract—nude heels, blue pencil skirt, white blouse, and patterned blue coordinating jacket. She freshened her hair with some dry shampoo, truly a modern miracle, although she noted the effect was more "bedhead-chic" (if Tyler was being generous) than Cerene's "fresh from the salon" hair—and spritzed herself with perfume. Tyler gave Lucy a little peck on the forehead, holding the cat gingerly half-arm's length away to avoid rubbing Lucy's furry body against her outfit and requiring a lint roll, and was out the door into the wall of St. Louis summer humidity. Opening the door to her Prius, she noticed a damp smell. Not unusual for the summer, but not pleasant. It smelled a little like the time she had forgotten Mexican leftovers in the car over a three-day weekend. The smell did not get any worse throughout the drive, so Tyler made a mental note to investigate later and get the car detailed that weekend.

Just before nine, Tyler had logged onto the firm's system, reviewed her time entries describing her work the day before, shrugging at the hours spent on "Finalize motion for filing"—let Kevin cut her time if he objected to how long it took to add an extra space after each sentence. Descriptions in order and adjusted to each partner's preference, Tyler clicked "release." Many people hated the billable hour, but Tyler was one of the few who more or less tolerated the system. She wanted to get paid as much as the next associate, and this was how the clients were charged (and, not to mention, how an associate's value to the firm was measured). The billing was an annoyance, but a necessary one.

While Tyler had been promoted from reviewing pictures of the inside of people's noses, she was not exempt from document review just yet, and she had been postponing a required review for a different case in order to get Kevin's brief filed. Document review was great for billable hours but horrible for general job satisfaction. It entailed going through tens of thousands of documents and noting which should be produced to opposing counsel, which should be flagged to prepare a witness, or which should be brought to a deposition of the other side's witness. Pluses: once an associate reviewed the documents for a particular case for twenty-plus hours, they were guaranteed to keep working on the case, meaning they maintained a steady workflow and their job, and they were set up to take on more responsibilities later, since they had become the resident expert on the facts. Minus: that associate had just lost twenty-plus hours of their life and maybe a few brain cells staring into the void of Karen the CFO's assistant's emails scheduling blowouts for her boss's yorkie.

In this case, Tyler was reviewing documents as "responsive" to discovery requests and flagging others containing information that should be redacted. Tyler efficiently clicked through the documents, sorting them into different categories and flagging where appropriate. Email from the CFO to in-house counsel shit-talking the CEO's management of some study or another: *non-responsive, but funny.* Email from in-house counsel forwarding CFO's shit-talking to the CEO: *non-responsive, but juicy.* CFO's email to in-house counsel seeking advice on something flagged by the production line: *privileged, attorney-client.* On and on it went.

In the thick of an email chain (why NSK, the manufacturer, would not thread the emails to avoid reviewing the same original time thirteen times was anyone's guess) discussing whether the CFO's insult of "douchebag" was worse than "asshole," Tyler started to zone out when her work IM pinged. It was Cerene.

Lunch? Sure enough, it was already twelve thirty.

Sure, Tyler responded, *where?*

Bread Company? Quick? Easy?

Great. See you in the lobby.

The women chatted on the quick walk to the restaurant—who had been working late recently (both) and who had weekends free (neither). While the company of someone else enduring the same stress and schedule was nice, the competitive element, somehow always about who was more miserable, crept in at the edges. "You worked four hours Sunday? Lucky you, I had a full day of work!" Gradually, between ordering and sitting down with their salads, the conversation shifted more personal. Cerene had been married for a couple years and was pumping Tyler for information on her love life.

"Oh, it's just not that interesting—who has the time?" said Tyler, almost convincingly.

"YOU SHOULD!" teased Cerene, pointing her fork at Tyler. "I know it! And I have to hear about it."

Tyler was somewhat reluctant to share. Cerene was her friend, but also her competition. It could be hard to gauge what would be well received and what would be judged. And Tyler was pretty sure that Cerene would not repeat what she shared to other coworkers, mostly because no one would be interested, but that was always a factor as well. She thoughtfully ate a piece of lettuce under Cerene's expectant gaze.

"Well, it's probably totally inappropriate, but there's this private investigator—" Tyler began when she had finished thoroughly chewing.

"Oh my god, stop! I can't believe you!" Cerene interrupted, talking a mile a minute, and in a friendly, genial way. "Although, I've got to say in my experience they've all been at least forty and going a little soft in the middle and I never thought of that as your type." The competitive atmosphere had evaporated for a few minutes, and they were just two girlfriends chatting.

Phew, not judgmental today, Tyler thought. "Okay, so his firm is one that we use regularly, they're nationwide and have excellent contacts, and he's new to the firm. His name's Harry James. Two first names... I kind of already thought that was cute, although I did expect the fortyish age range. We started using him a few months ago when we suspected the lead plaintiff in a class action was purposefully waxing his nose with overheated wax to keep it irritated. Harry somehow got pictures of the guy in his bathroom with the package on the counter, and the lead plaintiff was shit out of luck! It was so awesome. We file this—"

"Back to Harry, come on, although I know, I know the nose hair litigation is very sexy," interrupted Cerene.

"The sexiest," Tyler deadpanned. "Okay, right right, okay. So, I'd never met him, but he came in person to drop these pictures off. I met him in a conference room, but we'd spoken a couple times on the phone. Obviously, we were at work, so it would have been totally inappropriate to say anything so I just took the pics and the invoice to arrange payment. But I mean... he was *so good looking.* Basically, like the quintessential tall, dark, and handsome guy. And he was super charming. Just like, a normal person, not like us where we only know how to talk about work. I mean, he asked me about my hobbies, which is so cute, right? Of course, I haven't had a hobby since undergrad, but still. The next day, I had gotten up early for once to work out and I stopped at that little coffee shop I love that's out of the way to pick up a latte and he was there! I couldn't believe it! I wasn't going to say anything because I wanted to play it cool, but he came up and asked for my number, and I guess since then we've kind of been hanging out and talking."

"'Hanging out' and 'talking?'" Cerene said, adding air quotes to each word and a skeptically raised eyebrow.

Just then Tyler's phone buzzed. *Convenient... talking about my sex life is just a bridge too far,* thought Tyler. "Shit," she said out loud, "it's got to be Kevin... haven't heard from him since last night... so weird, right?"

Cerene nodded, slightly put out but not willing to push. "Well," she said, obviously steeling herself internally for a productive and potentially stressful afternoon, "back to the office!" As if on cue, Tyler's phone started to buzz and Cerene mockingly shook her finger at it as if it were a naughty pet. The women bussed their trays and walked back to the office.

But Tyler's email was not from Kevin. It was a routine "client entertainment opportunity" from the marketing team for tickets to see the Cardinals baseball team play. Tyler continued the document review but was starting to feel a little worried. Kevin took exactly one and a half weeks off every year to travel somewhere fabulous with his picture-perfect family (the well-maintained wife and adorable twin son and daughter stayed on several additional weeks wherever they traveled), but that happened in September, and it was July. Other than his trip, Tyler could not think of a day she did not see Kevin in his office, and that included Saturdays.

At around five Tyler's phone buzzed with a text from Harry. *Rain check today?* Tyler was still feeling disquieted due to Kevin's radio silence, and responded, *Not feeling like going out—wine and cheese at my place?* Three dots popped up on the screen, then disappeared, then popped up again. *Okay, sure. You get the wine, I'll bring the cheese. 7:30?* Tyler responded with the cheese emoji and the champagne emoji.

It was almost seven by the time Tyler hopped into her car. The smell was definitely worse. She checked under all the seats—*weird, nothing is there*—rolled down the windows and hoped it did not get caught on the upholstery and her clothing. This was not ideal for meeting up with Harry, to say the least. Tyler had been planning on picking up wine on her way home, but luckily, she had a bottle of chardonnay in her fridge, so she could drive straight home and change to avoid contamination. Whatever was going on with her car would also be easier to face after a glass or two of wine.

Tyler quickly changed into a breezy linen matching set and added a few extra spritzes of dry shampoo to her hair, which was pushing the limits of the product's capabilities after the drive home with ninety-five degree, wet, humid air streaming into the car. After a second of further scrutiny, she pulled her hair into a ponytail. She was also sweating just from the quick walk from her car to her door. At this time of year just looking outside could get someone sweating. If she took a shower, Tyler would have to wash her hair though, and she did not have time for that, so she flapped her shirt to cool down. She tried to wait for Harry, but after a few minutes, she cracked open the bottle of wine and poured herself a generous glass. As an afterthought, she got two glasses of water, too. Tyler had read recently that lack of hydration could cause deep, premature wrinkles, and given how stressed she was all the time, the last thing she needed to do was add to the problem with a lack of hydration. Fifteen minutes later Tyler heard a knock at the door. She opened the door to Harry, who held a small paper bag and greeted her with a kiss. Tyler shrugged apologetically with her glass in hand.

"I started without you..."

Harry laughed, "As long as you saved me some! Where can we put this cheese? Also, are you having sewer problems? Something is not smelling good outside your house." He sniffed the air as if he could smell it inside, too.

Shit, Tyler thought. She was mortified. She stepped backward and tried to sniff the air to see if the smell had clung to her. She was pretty sure it had not.

"Harry, it's my car! I looked all around the seats and I couldn't find anything! I don't know what the smell is!"

"The seats... hmm... did you check the trunk?"

"Well, no," Tyler furrowed her brow, "but I never use it so why would anything be in there?"

"Just a thought," Harry responded. "Maybe we should check."

"I'm sure nothing is in there, and the stench is really bad, maybe we should just... proceed with our evening," Tyler said, hoping to change the topic. She waved her wine glass toward the kitchen, trying to direct Harry that direction and away from the front door.

"Tyler, if there's something wrong with your car, it's probably going to get worse overnight. I really think it won't hurt to check. I promise I won't judge you. I'm a PI, I've seen some seriously weird shit, I doubt whatever is in your car can compete."

Tyler sighed, took a swig of wine, and walked purposefully toward her front door. *Annoying. Drink the fucking wine,* she thought. She was not in the mood to deal with this issue—which was sure to be disgusting—at this time. Tyler grabbed her keys and slammed the glass down, stretching the structural limits of its delicate glass stem. Anger growing with each step, she consciously controlled herself to avoid stomping like a child. Harry followed close behind. Since Harry had arrived the sun had gone down and the street was illuminated only by street lamps. And she was sweating again. *Fucking perfect.*

"Stay there!" she snapped irritably, "You may have seen some weird shit, but not in the car of someone you're sleeping with. I'll deal with it myself, just *please* go inside." Harry went back up the steps waving his hands in surrender but lingered on her front patio.

Rolling her eyes, Tyler popped the trunk, then stifled a scream as a wave of putrid air wafted out. *Kevin* was in her trunk. And Kevin was very dead. Tyler had only ever seen dead bodies in photos from discovery in other attorney's cases, never in person, but she knew immediately that Kevin was clearly, unmistakably dead. He was pale, and disturbingly, his eyes were open. He was wearing the same suit as when he implied that Tyler was insane. Tyler slammed the lid of the trunk closed, hoping against hope that she had not seen what she thought. But, she'd slammed the trunk too hard and it bounced back open, slightly jostling Kevin's body, which shifted unnaturally and wafted more of the putrid smell toward her, driving home that he was indeed dead.

"Well?" Harry called, "what's the damage?"

"Fuck fuck fuck fuck fuck," Tyler whispered under her breath. What had Harry seen? Why was Kevin in her trunk? Why was Kevin *dead?*

"Tyler," Harry said again, "what's the deal, do you need a trash bag?" The idea that she thought she had left Mexican food in her car, or that she could simply drop Kevin into a trash bag and go about her evening seemed laughable.

"No," Tyler said, stifling a hysterical laugh. "Just give me a second." Tyler's mind started racing, hardly finishing a thought before jumping to another one. She knew what she should do: call the cops. But she also knew that this looked *really, really bad.* Primarily, of course, because her boss was dead in her trunk. On top of that, Tyler did not have a conflict-free relationship with Kevin. Just the day before, he had chewed her out. If Tyler was honest with herself, that happened more days than not. The cops would assume Tyler had killed Kevin. Shit, *Tyler* would assume she had killed Kevin if she heard about this from someone else. She glared at Kevin in the trunk, willing him to blink and get up. Tyler could feel her heart pounding faster and faster, and the edges of her vision started to spin. She breathed deeply in through her nose, trying to regulate her pounding heart, and gagged again at the smell. She needed more time, she just needed a little time to think of what she would say to the cops, how she would explain that she apparently had driven around all day with her boss's corpse in her trunk. *I WILL call the cops,* she thought, *I just have to think about how this could have happened in the first place.*

She slammed the trunk down again, taking care to keep contact until it clicked into place. Tyler looked up toward her patio where she could see Harry's shadowy figure standing on her porch and wondered how much of her face was illuminated, how much of the panic and horror he had seen on her face. Tyler hastily rearranged her face in a fake smile she hoped looked natural.

"You know, on second thought I think maybe the smell is coming from another car," she croaked. "But boy does it smell bad." She dramatically waved a hand in front of her nose and walked back to her front stairs and to her front door. She was pouring sweat by now and her heart continued to pound.

"I told you I never put anything in my trunk," she told Harry. "You don't listen to me. I'm the one here who's knowledgeable about what I do. Not you." She shot him a sharp look, "Wasted time. My favorite thing." Some of her shock and fear seemed to be mixing into anger toward Harry just for existing and being present at this particular moment.

"Sorry..." he started.

"Your apology isn't needed," Tyler snapped, "and I think you may not be tonight, either."

"Seriously?" he asked, looking at her as if he expected her to laugh it off as a joke and continue the evening.

"Yes. No." She grabbed her glass of wine from the table and finished it in three swallows. She needed to think through where she had been all day, when someone could have put Kevin into her car, *who* could have put Kevin into her car. She needed to call the police.

"Look," Harry said, opening his hands out in surrender, "I really just thought I was helping. I'm honestly confused about how my encouragement to take potentially rotting food out of your car morphed into a commentary on my character."

In some small section of her brain, Tyler knew she was being unreasonable, knew she should tell Harry what was going on and call the cops. But her heart was still pounding, she could feel the bottoms of her feet sweating, and the rest of her mind was whirling so fast she felt like she might pass out. Tyler had done nothing wrong, and now she was going to be arrested for her boss's murder. Even if she wasn't charged, she would never be able to keep her job. The stink (*haha*, she thought grimly) of the scandal would guarantee no one would want to work with her, attorneys and clients alike. Tyler's hopes and dreams for the future were ending before they had even really begun. And why was she thinking about herself—Kevin was dead. What about Kevin's hopes and dreams? *Selfish*, she thought. She was a mess.

"Hello?" Harry said. Tyler had been standing with the empty wine glass in her hand, eyes glazed.

"Hello," she answered sarcastically. "Or rather, goodbye. I'm obviously off tonight, I've known you for all of two months, I'm not going to get into a fight with you. Please go." She had to get Harry out of her house, *then* she could call the cops. Tyler plastered the fake smile she had mastered while responding "thanks for your feedback" to Kevin's more harsh criticisms and gestured Harry toward the door.

"Fine," he said, in a way that made clear he was not, in fact, fine. He grabbed his keys and the bag of cheese off the counter and stalked out, slamming the door.

Tyler walked to her living room and sank down onto her couch. Her eyes stung and her nose started running. Lucy jumped up, sensing something was wrong. Somehow, in the sixty seconds it took Tyler to walk to her car and open her trunk, her whole life had gone to shit. Her career, living in her chic townhouse, was done. She had not killed Kevin, but who had put him in her car? She poured herself more wine. She would have to call the cops but waiting a couple more minutes to collect herself would not make anything worse for Kevin.

She looked blankly around the living room she had so carefully decorated and drained the second glass of wine. Lucy eyed her from a stool in a corner. She seemed to look at Tyler sympathetically, if that was possible for a cat. Tyler had no appetite. She looked toward the kitchen and saw Harry's unfinished glass of wine. She would have that, too, and then she would call the cops. Draining her third glass of wine and stalking toward the table by her entryway where she left her cell, Tyler caught a glimpse of herself in the round mirror hung over the entryway table. She looked rough. She looked drunk. She shook her head quickly and looked back. Still drunk. Should she call the cops in this state? She looked down at the phone in her hand and started to unlock it. It took three tries. Tyler let out a frustrated shriek and flung the phone back down on the table. It skittered off the edge and landed on the floor with an ominous thunk. She could call in the morning. It was not as if Kevin was going anywhere.

Tyler stumbled up the stairs and turned on her shower. As the hot spray of the water stream hit her skin, the sob she had been holding in came out, and she wept in the shower until the hot water ran out.

CHAPTER TWO

The next morning Tyler woke up late. She was visibly hungover, beyond what she could compensate for with a put-together outfit. And on top of it, her eyelids were swollen from the tears in the shower. Worse, they had swollen unevenly, Tyler's right eye was distinctly more puffy than the left. Tyler had not washed her hair in the shower or brushed it afterward, so it fell limply over her shoulders in a tangled heap. She surveyed her disheveled appearance in the mirror and felt like crying all over again. What had she been thinking the night before? Lucy silently watched her from the end of the bed with a distinctly judgmental air. In the sober light of morning Tyler could not believe she had considered not calling the cops. She could be selfish, sure, but even she was not so selfish that she would not report a murder due to personal inconvenience. Tyler threw on a pair of slides and grabbed her phone off the floor, which she noticed now had a cracked screen and twenty-five unread email notifications. Her car keys were not sitting in their proper place, a silver dish. Instead, they were lying on the ground next to Tyler's kitchen table. She must have inadvertently knocked them down. Tyler walked out to her car, noticing that the smell seemed to have dissipated almost entirely.

Tyler dialed 911 and popped the trunk, to reveal... nothing.

"Nine-one-one. What's your emergency?" said a calm female voice.

"Um, um, I'm so sorry, this was a misdial. There's no emergency." Tyler hung up. *What the fuck?* Had she imagined Kevin's body? She'd had only two sips of wine at that point, and Tyler had never found wine to cause hallucinations.

Tyler's phone pinged. It was the office manager sending a firm-wide email: "The St. Louis office is closed today due to an incident in the garage and will be re-opened tomorrow." That was wonderful news at least, as Tyler's hungover appearance precluded her going into the office. Her phone pinged again: a text from Harry. She deleted it without reading it. While getting into bed might have been a blur, her anger toward Harry, mostly just for being in the wrong place at the wrong time, remained cold and clear.

Tyler decided to begin work immediately, and firmly told herself to move past the last twenty-four hours. Either her boss had been murdered, placed in her car, then moved, or Tyler was literally losing her mind. Tyler was not sure which option was worse, but it seemed more likely that she was losing her mind. If that were the case, Tyler figured she might as well rack up a few more billable hours before she lost the plot completely. She grabbed her work laptop and started the dual-step login process in the kitchen as she started the coffeemaker. While she waited for the coffee, she ate three pieces of dry toast washed down with Pepto Bismol. After catching another glimpse of herself reflected in the glass door at the back of her kitchen, she showered again—this time washing her hair—and put on a lounge set. Hangover contained and coffee in hand, Tyler headed upstairs to her second bedroom where she had installed a small desk facing the window. Back to doc review. Even though Kevin might or might not be around anymore, his cases still were.

An IM popped up from Cerene:
So what's the deal with the garage today?
No idea... no complaints though!
My guess is someone hit a pipe and it's flooded again.
Tyler sighed. Normally she would love to laugh with Cerene about whichever idiot flooded the garage, but today she could not get the image of her trunk bouncing closed and open and Kevin's stiff body staring up at her out of her head. She really must have had a mental break. *Maybe,* she thought hopefully, *if I repress the memory it will just be a weird blip I'll never have to discuss with anyone.* Tyler shook her head and opened up the document review software. She should stay on top of her work and maintain her reputation for billing a lot of time in case she had to find a new partner to work for now. Despite her best

intentions, Tyler had an unproductive day. She googled Kevin's name several times to see if any news articles had been published. Her nausea slowly crept back, overpowering the toast and Pepto Bismol combination, and Tyler could not tell whether it was caused by the hangover or the on-edge feeling that emanated with greater and greater force from the base of her stomach. Tyler ate some more toast, threw it up, then retreated to bed with her computer so she could at least monitor her emails. That night, as she mindlessly continued reviewing documents, now simply attempting to catch up, the email came in. Tyler had seen countless others like it, but not for someone she directly worked with.

> *Colleagues,*
>
> *It is with great sadness I announce that Kevin Stevens, Partner, has passed away. Kevin began his career at this firm and was very successful. Funeral announcements will be shared when they become available.*
>
> *-PP*

Tyler felt cold trickle down her spine and fill up her stomach. It was too much of a coincidence to have a psychotic break in which she hallucinated seeing Kevin's body, and for Kevin to also have died. An even worse thought struck her: *what if I killed him?* She brushed the thought away. Obviously, there was no mental break; Kevin had really and truly been in her trunk for around a day. Because there was no mental break, there was no chance Tyler had killed him then forgotten. Right? Several more questions popped up: What was Kevin's body doing in her trunk? Why was it put there, and why was it moved? Was Tyler now involved in a murder? Was a temporary sighting of a body in her trunk (Tyler still had not entirely ruled out a psychotic break) something she should call the cops over? *Probably...* But now the whole thing seemed murkier. How on Earth could Tyler explain her panicked binge drinking, decision to wait until morning, and aborted 911 call? Putting herself in the shoes of an outside observer it looked a little unhinged and definitely suspicious. On the other hand, how would Tyler ever be tied to Kevin's murder? The only person outside of herself who knew about the body in the car was the person who put it there. And that person was presumably a murderer. At the very least that person was involved in moving a corpse, which had to be a criminal violation. Either way it seemed unlikely that this unknown person would report to the police, since any explanation would reveal their own involvement. Despite her rationalizations, the nausea bubbled up worse than before and Tyler ran to her bathroom, dry heaving. Not having eaten a real meal all day, she threw up pink-tinged water and bile and rested her forehead against the cool tile of the floor for a minute.

Mentally steeling herself, Tyler crawled back into bed and entered her password to unlock her computer again. She checked her time entries for the day—she had managed to bill nine hours, not too shabby. There was no way she could put up hours like that and also be involved in a police investigation. And without billing a lot of time Tyler would not remain staffed on the nose hair wax cases. And without being staffed on the nose hair wax cases, Tyler could not advance at the firm. The progression would have been inevitable.

Tyler had noticed her first year that the true "rock stars" of the firm were people who routinely billed 2,200 or 2,300 hours each year. Tyler billed 2,000 to 2,100 and felt exhausted and stressed all the time. She often felt caught in a catch-22: caring about success but not enough to actually do what she had to do to reach it. Since the billable hours included active time working (not meals, long bathroom breaks, getting set up, etcetera), hitting that brass 2,200 ring entailed six or seven days of work a week. It simply was not going to be possible to be the subject of a police investigation, or even to assist with one for that matter, and bill those hours. Shit, she was hardly billing those hours now and she did not even have a spouse or children to distract her. However creepy it had been seeing Kevin's body, maybe it was for the best that things had turned out the way they had. *Mistakes were made*, Tyler thought, wryly noting the use of passive voice in her train of thought.

As she made some minor changes to her time entries, Tyler put on mindless reality television and ate a frozen pizza. After finishing the entire pizza she frowned angrily at her stomach and thighs, which were a bit looser than she would like. Same trend, different topic: wanting a toned body but unwilling to do what she had to do to get it (on the short list of action items was (1) not eat pizza; and (2) work out regularly). Body positivity, for women at least, had not hit big law firms yet—being anything but thin was seen as a sign of lack of self-control which might bleed over into job performance. Mentally shrugging, Tyler acknowledged that her failure to take action now was in itself a decision, but she was determined to go back to business as usual. Let the cops do their job.

Tyler woke up at five thirty the next morning, noted the all-firm memo that the office was open again, went to her Pilates class, and made it into the office by eight. She resumed her normal work schedule—and miracle of all miracles, it was Friday. She was even in a good enough mood to ask Cerene out for happy hour. Cerene gladly agreed (*weird week, drinks definitely in order*) and the women met up at their favorite wine bar to split a bottle of Sancerre.

One glass in, Cerene turned to Tyler with a sympathetic look.

"So, how are you holding up? Do they even know what happened to Kevin?"

"Honestly," Tyler answered, "it's been surreal, and so so weird." She gave herself a little internal assurance that she was being truthful, just not specific. Feeling a little falser, she went on, "Nobody knows what happened, but he was young, right?"

Cerene gravely nodded. "Young, and with a family. I wonder when we'll learn more details."

"Same." Tyler nodded. "And... I wonder who is going to take over his cases."

"Time and tide wait for no man," Cerene intoned dramatically. A former English major, she was well-read and never let anyone forget it. "Chaucer *was* referring to the billable hour, right? Enough of the depressing topics though, I seem to remember we got interrupted by an email from Kevin JUST as you were about to tell me about your hot private investigator 'friend.'" Cerene winked and leaned her face on her hand eagerly.

"Oh, is that how you remember it?" Tyler laughed "I seem to remember the email coming in at the perfect time to avoid spilling my guts! But you know, I thought it was going well but I think it's over... *" because he was over at my house when I found Kevin's dead body in my trunk, and then the body was gone and I have no clue what's going on.*

"That's too bad, what happened?"

For a split-second Tyler worried she had spoken her thoughts aloud. She blinked at Cerene, trying to collect herself. "What happened with the private investigator?" Cerene looked at Tyler expectantly. *Right.*

"Well, we basically got into this nasty fight, and he's still kind of new. I don't think he'll stick around to resolve it."

"That's a shame. You sounded really excited about him."

"Yeah, but you know, things happen," Tyler shrugged, *like finding your boss's body in your trunk and maybe having a psychological break... STOP*, "but what's the latest with you and Brian?"

Cerene winced. "It's... okay... honestly, I've been working so much I kind of don't even know! But he's been too. What are you going to do, though?" Brian worked at a similarly sized firm in the corporate department.

"I'm sorry, that's really hard," Tyler said. "But you guys are so great together, and you both get that you have to work a ton."

Cerene nodded her agreement but looked a little sad, like she was not fully convinced. "Time, tide, and the billable hour stop for no man."

Later, sitting in the bath, Tyler thought more about the argument with Harry. She was lonely, and despite the challenges Cerene described, the thought of having someone—and not just a cat—to come home to, or just to sleep beside at night was appealing, and seemed objectively better than Tyler's current isolated existence. Here she was looking at another weekend alone. Tyler had tried using dating apps, but without any success. It was hard to date anyone when you might have to cancel your plans at any minute due to work responsibilities. Tyler dried herself off with a fluffy towel and slipped on her pajamas. Maybe she should text Harry and apologize. Maybe every time she saw Harry, she would only be able to think of her mistake/psychotic break though.

Her phone pinged... Harry? It was her mom. *Sweetheart, hope you are well. We haven't heard from you in a while, and don't forget your grandma's birthday tomorrow.*

Fuck, Friday night texts from Mom? Not great.

Thanks for the reminder, Mom, got it! Doing well, just very busy as always.

You work too hard, you should come home and see us.

Okay, let's talk about a date tomorrow.

Conversations always went that way. Her mom would never actually call to set the date to go home to Indianapolis and neither would Tyler. While she thought of her family fondly, she mostly just saw them at Christmas and Thanksgiving. She glanced over at Lucy... was a cat really the closest living being to her? When had she become such a loner? She vaguely remembered circles of female friends from college and even law school, but for the most part any closeness had subsided to occasional friendly-but-surface-level text messages and, as with her family, empty promises to visit and catch up.

Sighing, Tyler clicked on another meaningless reality TV show and picked up her phone. Scrolling through the suggested news articles as two women dressed to the nines discussed whether one of them was late to lunch or the other one was early, she gasped and nearly dropped the phone.

UP TO HIS NECK IN WORK? LOCAL LAWYER SLAIN IN ROUGH SEX GONE WRONG?

Gripping the phone tighter, she tapped the article.

> *Normally, lawyers are known to bleed their clients dry, but one individual flipped the script against local lawyer Kevin Stevens of Cloose and Elkman, who was discovered dead in his own vehicle early on Thursday morning by a coworker. Police have classified Stevens's death as a homicide, but declined to provide any additional details. Sources report that cause of death was blood loss. Marks indicating restraints were found on Stevens's wrists and ankles. Police have not ruled out the possibility that Stevens's death was an accident following a sexual game gone wrong.*
>
> *Stevens is survived by his wife Melissa Stevens and his twin sons Drew and John, his brother Gene Stevens, and his mother Jane Stevens. Melissa has asked for privacy for her family during this trying time. The investigation is ongoing.*

Tyler felt a sharp stab of anxiety in her chest at the conclusion that Kevin had been moved after he died. *Although, didn't I kind of already know that?* Tyler re-read the article more slowly. A strange mix of relief and trepidation took over as she zeroed in on the word "ongoing." Relief at the thought that her failure to call the police would result in someone getting away with murder, but trepidation that she could be involved in the investigation. Tyler poured herself a bourbon and kept watching the show, forcing herself to focus on the inane entertainment.

Tyler went about her regular activities throughout the weekend: cleaning, grocery shopping, Pilates. She called a friend from law school to catch up. Another engagement, another bittersweet moment of happiness for her friend and uneasiness for herself. Lying in bed Saturday night, she saw Kevin's lifeless face every time she closed her eyes and despite some stern internal pep talks, Tyler was unable to shake the worry that she *had* suffered a psychological break. Although she was fairly confident there were no large chunks of time missing from her memories, her days admittedly blurred together with the sameness of reviewing mountains of documents, watching the familiar beats of reality television, and attempting and failing to make it to Pilates class.

With a groan, she rolled over, grabbed her laptop from her bedside table, and logged on. Pulling up her emails, she identified ones sent automatically from her firm's system designed to help attorneys keep track and bill their time. The program sent an email providing a rough picture with time stamps of how long was spent on the legal search engines, writing emails, reviewing docs, and other tasks and made a rough log of her time in an Excel document for Wednesday, when she estimated Kevin had been killed based on when she found him in her car. Thinking back to the smell in her car, Tyler realized Kevin was probably already in the trunk on Wednesday morning, so she reviewed Tuesday's time as well. Next, Tyler reviewed her online records from the Pilates studio, although, predictably, she had not taken a class on either Tuesday or Wednesday. Still, between work and when she presumed she was sleeping, Tyler had no more than forty-five minutes of time unaccounted for. Her suspicion of a mental break decreased, and she fell asleep almost as soon as her head hit the pillow.

On Sunday evening, Tyler got a text from Harry. *I'm sorry. I'm still not really sure why, but I want to see you so I'll say it.*

What a crap apology. On the heels of her friends' engagement though, Tyler was not so confident in her knee-jerk reaction to brush Harry off. Should she do the "nice" thing and accept his apology despite its inadequacy? That might be how everyone was finding husbands. She sent back the eyerolling emoji. If that was how she had to get a husband, she would die alone and be eaten by Lucy. Annoyed, Tyler threw her phone to the other side of the couch and resisted looking at it to see if he would respond. Just before bed her phone buzzed:

I'll try again. I want to see you, let's start over. Dinner next Friday?
Okay. Talk later this week.

Tyler still felt vaguely annoyed, but his persistence had won her over for the moment.

CHAPTER THREE

A week passed in a blur. Tyler was still sleeping poorly and had increased her few-times-a-week bourbon into a nightly event, which seemed like a bad habit to be getting into. Her appetite had deserted her, so she was practically on a liquid diet of coffee and bourbon, and it was showing in the bags under her eyes. Billing was at an all-time low because she was obsessively searching for any updates to the news stories covering Kevin's murder throughout the day. Tyler felt a bit fraudulent about even the small amount of time she managed to bill because she was so scatterbrained it took her roughly twice the amount of time to complete tasks as usual. Even googling Kevin's name was taking twice the usual time, since Tyler was out of cell phone data, which she had been using in case IT was paying attention to her Internet patterns at work. With each passing day, Tyler felt a little more confident that she would know if she had suffered a mental break, but that meant her uneasiness grew over not knowing who had put Kevin's body in her trunk, then removed it, not to mention why they had done so.

If that were not enough cause for stress, Tyler knew she had to snap back into productivity as well. Someone, the new Kevin (as she had been thinking about that person), would eventually want to know the status of the doc review, and there was really no way to explain the sudden drop in pace. On the plus side, Tyler was pretty sure she had lost weight, and she had not eaten any more frozen pizzas. On Friday morning she remembered she was supposed to see Harry. Still feeling annoyed and not sure how she would react to seeing him again, as he had become inextricably tied to her discovering Kevin's body, she canceled, making an excuse about a late filing. Fully expecting him to give up (it was not as if she had been great at keeping plans with him and she definitely did not have enough goodwill built up yet to account for her outburst), she was pleasantly surprised when he suggested two weeks out.

The following week, all hell broke loose. It started on Monday morning. Peter Parisi announced the hiring of a new partner: John Delaware. The usual email regarding a new partner hire followed. John came from another large firm and was pleased to make the move; John would be taking over Kevin's book of business (*In case any of us forgot just how replaceable we are*, Cerene noted via IM in response to the firm-wide email). John had started that morning and word through the grapevine was that one, he was unsettlingly good-looking with a thick head of salt-and-pepper hair in a movie-lawyer-villain type of way, and a tan that had to be fake given the lack of daylight hours attorneys at the firm were free to be outside doing recreational activities; and two, he had already reamed a paralegal for using Times New Roman instead of Garamond in an entry of appearance for one of Kevin's cases. "FIRST IMPRESSIONS COUNT!" he was supposed to have yelled.

Tuesday lunch was "team bonding" with John and his new team of associates over drab sandwiches slathered in condiments during which John made a surface attempt to inquire about the associate's lives in a loud, self-assured voice that screamed, "I'm used to being carefully listened to" before getting to the real reason for the lunch: the current status of their work. If Tyler had thought Kevin was bad, John made him look like a fucking Care bear.

"Tyler. Status," he said, fixing her with an ice blue gaze.

Tyler blinked rapidly. "Well, we've just submitted our reply to the motion to dismiss in the Newman class action so we'll have to wait for the district court in Minnesota to rule. We've been doing a rolling production in the Brosby class action, and I've been reviewing materials provided by the client."

"And how far along are you on that review?" He gave little pauses in unusual places, unfortunately giving Tyler extra time to realize how badly he was likely to take her slow progress.

"A third? Halfway?"

"And you've had it... how long?" He glanced down at a pad of paper sitting in front of him. Something in his tone sounded just a little bit too casual and made Tyler suspect he knew exactly how long she had been reviewing the documents and was about to make an example of her.

"We've had the documents several months."

"Unacceptable. While I'm managing these cases we'll be turning around all documents within one month. How many hours did you bill last month?"

The other associates on the team shifted uncomfortably. This was a taboo question, firstly because the partners could just look up that information on their own time and render their own judgment and second because associates typically did not talk about their exact hours outside of their close work friends.

"I can't remember exactly," Tyler said.

"Well, more or less than one eighty?" That came out to forty-five billable hours a week, a.k.a. fifty hours of time spent working at minimum.

"... less?" Tyler kicked her past self for looking up "the Kevin matter" as she had been referring to it in her head instead of doing something productive with her time.

"That's going to change... if you're interested in staying on the case at least. You're the junior associate on these cases. When we have documents, you review them. Quickly."

"Understood," Tyler choked out. The room had filled with tense energy. Tyler glanced around uncomfortably and caught the eye of Brendan, the senior associate. He looked sympathetic and shot a barely-there "WTF" look in John's direction before his face returned to its typical neutral-but-tired look.

"Well, I hope you do. I've heard good things about you but if you're going to continue on these cases, we're going to need you to be a team player." John looked at Tyler with barely disguised disgust. Things were seriously going down the tubes.

John's cross-examination was just a harbinger of things to come. Thursday, two detectives came and set up shop in a conference room. John emailed out to the team:

Team,

Detectives are here to interview you re: Kevin. Of course, providing the detectives with any and all information they ask for is important, but please remember that your time is billable and be concise.

-JD

Tyler's hands felt clammy and her head swam. She nervously took a sip of water. *This was to be expected,* she told herself, *the body had apparently been discovered at work, so it was not unusual for detectives to want to interview Kevin's colleagues.* She tried to keep reviewing documents, but just ended up re-reading the same sentence from a production-line procedure guide again and again. What would the detectives ask her? What would she say? An hour later, with no good answers to either question, Tyler got a call from the receptionist, Martha.

"Hi, doll. Detectives Armstrong and Myer are ready for you. They're in the Oak conference room on twenty-six." Tyler could hear the sympathetic look on Martha's face in her voice. Martha had been the receptionist for a decade and knew all about how important it was for attorneys to remain productive during the workday.

"Okay. Thanks, Martha, be right up."

Tyler grabbed a hairbrush from her desk and furiously yanked it through her hair as if brushed hair would make her look like a mentally stable employee who had not seen her boss's corpse in the trunk of her car. She rolled her eyes at her own stupidity. Although Tyler had convinced herself that she had not murdered Kevin and blacked out a large chunk of time (partially due to three reviews of her time entries precluding a large chunk of time spent not working), she felt panicked at having to talk about the incident and ashamed that she had not called the cops as soon as she had seen the body. Her palms were clammy and damp, and she wiped them nervously on her skirt, straightened her posture, and headed to the conference room.

The Oak conference room was a smaller conference room with a window to the rest of downtown St. Louis. The table could hold up to six people, and the room was equipped with glasses branded with the firm logo, soda, water, and coffee. Detectives Armstrong and Myer sat on one side of the table with half-drunk cups of coffee. Both were tired-looking, middle-aged white men. One was balding but clearly worked out. His biceps bulged against his button up shirt as he rested his elbows and forearms on the table with his hands loosely clasped. Upon further inspection, the second was younger than he appeared at first—early to midthirties—and had a deep wrinkle between his eyebrows and a beautiful head of thick curling brown hair. There were no biceps in sight on the second detective, but Tyler thought she saw a slight paunch. The detectives were having what appeared to be an intense discussion but stopped speaking abruptly as the door opened.

Tyler softly knocked as she entered even though they were obviously aware she was there.

"Hi. Tyler McCarther." She gave an awkward rainbow-shaped wave with each of her clammy fingers stuck together and formed her mouth into a toothless smile. *Please don't shake my hand,* she thought, stiffly holding it back down against her side. The well-built detective sitting closer to the door stood up with a friendly smile and reached out his right hand.

"Detective Myer, thanks for your time today, Tyler."

Fuck. She took his hand and gave her best firm handshake, hoping he would not notice the clamminess. His friendly smile did not waver as his own dry and warm hand encircled her wet, cold one.

The other detective, Detective Armstrong by order of elimination, remained seated. He looked up with trustworthy brown eyes, *like a golden retriever,* Tyler thought immediately, and gave her his own closed lip, toothless smile.

"Afraid I'm coming down with something, so no handshake... Detective Armstrong." He gave her a slight upward tilt of his chin instead. His voice was distant and almost cold. Tyler recoiled internally. She had expected a warm and friendly voice to match the face.

"So," Detective Armstrong continued, "as Detective Myer said, thanks for your time today. We're here to ask you a few questions about Kevin Stevens, who I'm sure you've heard was found dead in his vehicle in the garage last week."

Tyler nodded. She still had no idea what she was going to say. As little as possible, she figured.

Detective Myer shifted a small, black electronic device Tyler had not noticed until that moment to the center of the conference table. "We'd like to record this conversation, Tyler. So far none of your colleagues have had a problem with that." He looked at her to see if she would object.

Tyler nodded and felt her hands go clammier by the second. Detective Myer smiled. "So, that's a yes?"

Tyler coughed, "Yes."

"That's great, thanks." Detective Myer pressed several buttons on the recorder and stated the day, time, and that Tyler had consented to being recorded.

Detective Armstrong cut in, "All right. So, Tyler, tell us about the last time you saw Kevin."

In my trunk, dead? She blinked rapidly. "Well, it would have to be last Wednesday. He gave me some comments on a draft." This, she told herself, was true if "seeing Kevin" assumed he was alive.

Both detectives sat in silence, staring at her.

"And," she continued more nervously, looking above their heads, "while this wasn't in person, around seven that evening he emailed me about the draft again. If I can just..." she pulled her phone out gestured with it, "I can see the exact time."

"Thanks," said Detective Armstrong.

"Yep," she said, "Six fifty-two p.m., Central time, Wednesday... I'd show it to you but it's got confidential client information so..."

The detectives continued to stare at her. Tyler tried to wait them out. She felt a drop of sweat trickle down her back.

Nervous energy taking over, she continued, "Well, you know, as an attorney, I have to protect the client's confidential information. I can't just show you this email, right?" She addressed herself to Detective Myer.

"So, we've heard," sighed Detective Myer. Detective Armstrong rolled his eyes and said to Detective Myer, "add this one to the list." To Tyler he said, "Don't delete that email, we're working with the firm to get these emails, with client information redacted."

Tyler nodded.

"So, how would you describe Kevin?" continued Detective Armstrong in his cold voice.

"Ummmm," Tyler said, "he's very smart? He started at the firm as a summer associate sometime in the nineties I believe and he's been handling quite a bit of products liabilities business."

"How was he as a boss? You should know we've been talking to your colleagues all morning. We've heard he could be difficult."

"Well, I don't know if I would say that," Tyler said slowly. "He was committed to providing the clients with the best work product possible."

Detectives Myer and Armstrong shared a meaningful look. *What did I say?!?* Tyler was freaking out internally. It was surreal. This time last week her biggest worry was spaces at the end of a sentence, and now she was pretty sure she was in the middle of an interrogation regarding the murder of her boss. *Which I did not commit*, she reminded herself.

"You know... if you don't have any more questions, I should probably better get back to work. Billable hour and all, you know?" Tyler said, trying to smile with her teeth this time but making more of a grimace. The detectives were non-plussed.

"Tyler, we'll tell *you* when we don't have any more questions," said Detective Armstrong.

"And all of you, in my opinion, are way too obsessed with this billable hour." *Wrong*, thought Tyler and mentally rolled her eyes. Seeing the expressions on the detectives' faces, she realized her thoughts had been written on her expression.

"I'd heard it twice in my life before today," Detective Myer said, seamlessly taking over for Detective Armstrong, "And now everyone we've spoken to today will not give it up. Anyway, we have been told by several different sources that Kevin could be difficult to work with, very demanding. Is that true?"

Tyler flashed back to her last interaction with Kevin with the two-space one-space controversy, but she applied the same advice she had heard Kevin give a witness before a deposition and waited until she had a full sentence planned before carefully speaking.

"I really think the best way to put it is that Kevin is, or was, committed to excellent, efficient, work product. And, like any boss, he wanted things to be 'just so'—to be the exact way that he preferred. I'm sure he would say... I'm sure he would have said that his way was the one correct way, though."

"Fair," said Detective Myer. "Now, we want to go back to last Wednesday night. Could you tell us about what you were up to?"

"Well, as I mentioned, I was here until around seven. I had plans that I had cancelled because I wasn't sure how long I would be wrapping things up. So... I just went home, watched TV and had a drink."

"So, no one was with you?" said Detective Myer looking down at a pad of paper he was writing notes on.

It seemed overly casual, indicating to Tyler that it would be much better for her if she had been with someone else, but unfortunately there was only one individual who came to mind, and that individual did not speak English. "Just my cat... ha ha." *Oh my god shut the fuck up*, she thought.

"Okay... just you and... the cat," said Detective Armstrong adding an emphasis on "the cat" to demonstrate how sad and weird he thought that was, "and that was from seven in the evening until when you arrived at work the next morning?"

"Yep," said Tyler, bordering on aggressive. She had always disliked passive aggression, and had only become more sensitive to it during her time at the firm, where it was the primary mode of aggression between the attorneys.

"Okay. So, switching gears, did you know of any enemies that Kevin might have had at work or in his personal life?"

"Well," Tyler began, "I hardly knew anything about his personal life. He was pretty focused on work when he was here, and whether you like it or not, we operate on a billable hour, so time at work not spent working for a client is few and far between. Chit chat about your personal life isn't a revenue generating activity and Kevin was definitely focused on client work and revenue generation. So, I pretty much only heard about kid birthday parties and that kind of thing in passing. At work I can't think of anyone who would physically harm him."

"Harm him physically," Detective Armstrong mused, picking up on Tyler's choice of words. "How about harm his business, or want to harm him personally?"

"This is confidential, right?" Tyler asked.

"We do our best to keep sensitive information confidential, but I'll remind you that we're working on solving a man's murder. That means that we might have to act on something you tell us if it leads us farther in the investigation. That also means that if you don't tell us something you know that might lead to finding Kevin's murderer, you will be interfering in a police investigation, and you wouldn't want to do that, right?" Detective Armstrong smiled in a way that made it seem like he looked forward to arresting anyone who might interfere in his investigations.

Tyler shifted back and slightly to the left and looked Detective Armstrong up and down. "You're not the friendliest, you know that? Here's the bottom line, though. We're at a large law firm, and the business that partners bring in and support determines how much power they have around here and how much money they make. Everyone wants more power, and everyone wants more money, right? So... who would want to harm him professionally or personally? Anyone who thought it would further their interests without harming the firm's. I mean, someone would probably hesitate to harm him personally... we don't get so personal here as heart-to-hearts are *not* a revenue generating activity as I already explained... but professionally, more people than not would take the business he brought in given the opportunity." Detective Armstrong's combative attitude was triggering her own competitiveness. Plus, it seemed clear that the detectives did not think she was tied to the murder, which made her feel entitled to some righteous indignation. *And,* Tyler reminded herself, *you're really not tied to anything. You didn't kill him, and you only PROBABLY saw him in your trunk for like thirty seconds.*

Detective Armstrong looked at her sharply. "You're not the most forthcoming, you know that? If you know of someone, an individual, who specifically had a problem with Kevin, you should tell me... right now."

Tyler narrowed her eyes. *This asshole.* "And here I was, trying to help explain it to you. *Pick any partner in the firm.* Okay? Jesus. That being said, I heard from my secretary Gina—and she's Kevin's secretary too so I'm sure she's on your interview list—that Kevin had a rub with Peter Parisi, our managing partner. Gina's discrete so she didn't say anything more really. I got the sense that it had to do with comp. There's no way Peter Parisi would do anything to Kevin, or anyone else though, he's got a good reputation around here."

Detective Myer nodded thoughtfully. "That's really good, Tyler. Thanks."

Annoyed now, Tyler just nodded. "Now really, I've shared what I know about Kevin, I've shared rumors that I heard about Kevin... I have no additional relevant information to share." Tyler privately worried she had shared too much already. The firm was like a dysfunctional family. Internally, gossip was practically a competitive sport, but externally the implied expectation was that everyone presented a happy front and said only positive things.

Detective Armstrong looked like he had something to say, but Detective Myer cut in, "That's all we wanted, Tyler, thanks for your time."

Detective Myer now, "We may have more questions for you, could you give us the best phone number to call if we need to reach you again?"

Tyler gave her cell phone number to the detectives and went back up to her office. She closed her door and felt the sharp squeeze of anxiety where her rib cage met in the middle of her chest. The feeling, which she used to experience several times a month, was becoming her new normal. She tried to squeeze a tear out because it seemed like the thing to do and it might relieve her anxiety, but Tyler could not even manage that. Numb, she continued reviewing documents still discussing the drama between the CEO and the CFO. At five thirty she left and took her Pilates class. Talking to the detectives had made everything seem somehow more and less real. More real than seeing Kevin's body—which until this point had seemed almost like a dream—but it had definitely happened and it seemed possible, if unlikely, that it might come out that his body had been in her trunk and she had not said anything. For the first time, Tyler wondered if she had committed a criminal offense. She should have paid closer attention during law school, although it was not as if her introductory criminal course would have covered something so specific. Tyler could tell she was starting to spiral and gave herself a mental shake and decided to keep avoiding the issue and do a few more hours of work this evening. Maybe that would improve her standing with John.

As Tyler pulled up to park in front of her house, her heart sank. Detective Myer was sitting smoking a cigarette on the front steps while Detective Armstrong leaned against a railing.

"Hi, again," said Detective Armstrong. "Turns out, we had some new questions sooner than we thought. Can we come in?"

Tyler shrugged, "You know, it's not a great time because..."

Before she could think of an explanation for why it was not a great time, Detective Myer interjected, "Well, we can always take you into the station." He raised an eyebrow.

"Take me into the station?!" Tyler repeated, feeling like someone had punched her in the gut. "What for?" How could they know what had happened? Tyler assumed if they had suspected her of anything it would have been brought up at the interview at the firm, so what changed? Her breath started to become shallower and she silently counted to ten as she breathed in, held for ten, and breathed out for ten, as she had read she could do to stave off a panic attack. She had googled this advice following her most recent attack, which hit her after she woke up on a Saturday morning to five urgent emails from Kevin demanding to know why she was not responding.

"Like we said, we would like to come in," said Detective Myer. His voice now matched the coldness of Detective Armstrong's and had a triumphant air of someone who had gotten their way.

"Do I need a lawyer?" Tyler asked, clutching her bags.

"Well, I don't know... do you?" said Detective Myer. "You know, they're typically for the guilty. Plus, I thought that you were a lawyer."

"Well, I'm a civil lawyer so I don't deal with criminal matters. I think I really should get one."

"Okay, great," said Detective Myer with what seemed like inappropriate excitement that Tyler had not expected based on his removed attitude the last time she had seen him. He pulled handcuffs out of his pocket with a flourish. "You're under arrest, and you can call your lawyer from the station."

Tyler took a step backward in panic. "No!"

"Well," said Detective Armstrong, mildly now that he could see he was getting his way, "in that case we would like to come in and ask you a few questions." He gestured toward Tyler's front door with the hand holding the cuffs.

Tyler nodded mutely and walked up to her front door. She could not open the door with her shaking hands and after a few tries threw the keys at Detective Armstrong. They bounced off the unsuspecting detective and clattered onto the brick entryway. Detective Armstrong looked surprised, and Tyler glared at him silently until he picked them up and unlocked the door. The three walked in, and Lucy sauntered up expecting only Tyler, then quickly retreated upstairs at the sight of two new strangers.

Tyler sat down at her kitchen table, and Detectives Myer and Armstrong assumed their position from their earlier interview across from her.

"So, earlier today, we asked you about Wednesday night," Detective Myer said. "Isn't there more that you think you should add?"

"N... n... no?" Tyler stuttered.

"Fine," said Detective Armstrong, "as it seems that we should have been asking you about Thursday night, or rather Friday morning, instead."

Tyler felt a sharp pain in the center of her rib cage and started crying involuntarily through shallow breaths. How was this happening? She really was not involved, and now it seemed like these detectives thought she had murdered Kevin. *You are experiencing a panic attack,* she told herself silently. *Focus on breathing and the physical symptoms will dissipate.* She felt a flash of disgust at herself. The panic attacks had started in law school and though she had never sought treatment, which was a blessing in disguise when it came time to disclose any psychiatric treatment she had received while applying to the state bar, Tyler regularly convinced herself she had moved past them. Tyler tried circular breathing but ended up gasping in front of the detectives.

The detectives shared a sidelong glance. Detective Armstrong leaned forward, and his eyes, which had looked warm and brown earlier, looked black now.

"Are you okay? Do you have asthma or something?" The detective was clearly annoyed to be getting sidetracked; Tyler could see him resisting the urge to roll his eyes.

Fuck you, she thought. "I'm fine, I'm experiencing a panic attack, but it's an outsized physical response to stress, not a medical event," she said, quoting her favorite google source on the topic.

Detective Armstrong smirked. "Okay, so I'll ask you again. Where were you on Thursday night and Friday morning last week?" Tyler had never seen a shark in person, but she imagined she must feel like the fish after the shark caught a whiff of blood.

The circular breathing really was going incredibly poorly. "I... I was here! I was here at home!" she gasped. Her left hand clawed ineffectually where each side of her rib cage joined together.

"Here... and where else?" said Detective Armstrong. His cold voice came out calmly and softly, but two spots of pink had appeared on his cheeks.

"Nowhere else!" said Tyler. Her voice rang out loud and higher than its normal pitch. The yelling seemed to help the panic. Tyler redoubled her circular breathing efforts as the color in Detective Armstrong's cheeks deepened. *Fuck you,* she thought again. That seemed to be helping as well.

Detective Myer reached his hand out halfway across her kitchen table as if to pat her arm and Tyler recoiled. "Look, Tyler, we know that's not true, okay? We've gotten the records from the parking garage at your office building."

"What? That can't be. I was drunk! I wasn't driving!" Tyler said before she could stop herself. She clapped one hand over her mouth to stanch the verbal diarrhea. "I think a glass of water sounds great right now, how about you two?" She tried to throw it out casually to try to delay the impending discussion. The words had released some of the internal tightness though, and she felt her breathing ease up slightly more. She started to stand up.

"NO!" said Detective Myer and slapped his hand down on the table and Tyler flinched back into her seat. "You will sit down, and you will answer our questions. Cameras or not, the garage keeps track of who swipes in when. And guess who swiped in at three twenty-three a.m. last Thursday night?"

"She doesn't have to guess," said Detective Armstrong with a crooked smile, "do you, Tyler?"

Tyler's mind raced. Obviously, her badge had been used on Thursday night and somehow returned, because Tyler had used it to access the garage and her office earlier that day. There was no way *she* had used it though, she had spent the night drunk-crying in the shower, which was embarrassing, but definitely not a criminal act. Should she tell them about seeing the body? What would someone advise their client? Why had she paid so little attention during criminal law in law school?

"You said cameras or not... are there cameras?" Tyler asked slowly.

"Now why would that matter?" said Detective Armstrong. "Your badge was used. We understand that it's company policy to report a stolen badge, but we checked and you have not made any such report. You were in the parking garage around three thirty a.m. the day that Kevin's body was discovered in his car."

"No, it wasn't me, though! That's why I'm asking about the cameras. If there were cameras you could see who it was." Tyler still hadn't completely ruled out the psychotic break theory, so she *had* been very slightly wondering whether there was footage of her driving into the garage. "Look, I was pretty messed up that night... I drank almost a bottle of wine and had some bourbon on top of that, I didn't drive anywhere."

"And why was that?" said Detective Myer.

"I wasn't aware I needed a reason." Tyler pressed her lips together. Now that she was feeling more in control of herself she was not going to say any more than she needed to.

"So, you have your badge? It didn't go missing at any point in time? It's not lost?"

Tyler grabbed her purse and pulled out the badge, "Yeah, it's right here... I used it today. I used it on Thursday too, but just to go to the office for work, I left around six!" As she showed it to the detectives, she remembered with a sinking feeling that she had been using a temporary badge for the last week and a half or so, when she had not been able to find hers in any of its usual spots. "Shit. This is a temporary badge. I totally forgot, I have actually been using this one, I'm not sure where mine is."

Detective Myer looked annoyed. "That's convenient, isn't it. How long have you been using that temporary badge?"

"I think about a week and a half? You can check the records, though. I signed it out with Barbara Thompson. I can give you her extension?"

"We can, and will, contact her ourselves, thanks. Is that company policy to use a temporary badge when yours is lost?"

Tyler frowned. "Well, no, but I didn't think mine was lost per se, just that I couldn't find it. In the short term, you know? Not like permanently. Shit, was it used to get into the office too?" If the badge was used to get into the office, confidential client information could have been accessed. Clients might have to be contacted, and the firm would look bad. Tyler had never heard of that happening before, but she was sure it would not help her career prospects if her badge was used to breach the firm's security.

"I have no idea, Tyler. Look, we've heard Kevin was a hard boss. We even heard about the disagreement between the two of you earlier in the week. We understand, you just have to be honest with us."

"No," Tyler shook her head, "no... it wasn't like that. It was worth it to work with him. He might have been harsh, but he made his associates good attorneys and he made them partners. Regularly. If you ask around a lot of people who work with him have stuck around for a long time. Kevin was tough, but he made it worth it. And plus, if I lost my badge, how could I have used it that night?"

"Come on, to be pushed and pushed by someone who, as you said, demanded excellence? Did it drive you to drink? Did it drive you to do more?"

"No." She threw it out forcefully. "Well, I mean," she paused, "yes to the drinking but that's plenty of us at the firm. No to anything else. It wasn't me who drove into the garage. I couldn't drive. I didn't kill Kevin ... I swear. And if I was involved *at all* why would I use my badge, or allow my badge to be used? Wouldn't I use the temporary badge? Or find a temporary badge that I did not personally sign out? Something that would not immediately point you back to me?"

"You tell me," Detective Armstrong said. An ominous silence descended over the table. Detective Armstrong turned to Detective Myer. "I say we arrest her."

Detective Myer looked thoughtfully at Tyler. "I agree, unless you have anything else to add..."

"Fuck! Fuck you!" Tyler said. "I don't have time to be arrested! I absolutely had nothing to do with Kevin's death! So, someone used my badge to swipe into the garage at a horrible time? That proves nothing about where I was or was not. Can't you like, use my cellphone to see where I was? I thought the cellphones link up with towers or something." She had seen this mentioned in multiple true crime documentaries.

"Well, that would be assuming your cellphone was with you. You could have left it here and driven without it," pointed out Detective Armstrong.

"I'm a lawyer! I get emails all the time! I ALWAYS have my cellphone with me." Tyler was getting desperate.

Detective Armstrong turned to Detective Myer. "We gotta arrest her, right?" he reached down to unhook his handcuffs. Tyler let out some sort of garbled screech. "NO!" she gasped "No, I CANNOT be arrested. Absolutely not. I don't have the time."

"You might be surprised," Detective Armstrong said, "to find that most people feel they cannot be arrested, although not having the time is a new explanation."

Tyler put her head in her hands. Her panic had turned into fury. She absolutely *could not* fall behind at work. She knew John had taken an initial dislike to her, so now was the time to be doing more, not less. It was certainly not the time to be getting arrested, as she, Tyler, was almost certain she would not be allowed to bring her laptop and work remotely from jail. "Okay, okay. Something really weird happened that night, but I don't think you guys are going to believe me. And I'm not proud of what I did, so I didn't say anything before."

Detective Myer eagerly brought the same tape recorder out he had used during the first interrogation at the office and pressed record. Detective Armstrong put the handcuffs on the table in front of him.

Eyes fixed down at her hands, Tyler briefly outlined the events, from the wine with Harry to the rotten Mexican food that had actually been Kevin, to her utter panic, to the body's disappearance. Saying it out loud made it somehow worse. She was a smart girl, she had graduated near the top at her law school class, what the fuck had she been thinking?

Detective Armstrong looked at Detective Myer and said, "Myer... I know I'm not really supposed to say this... but what the fuck?" He turned to Tyler. "That's fucking weird enough that maybe it actually did happen. But let's summarize. No alibi for last Wednesday, and you saw the guy's body last Thursday and lied to us about it. But," he glanced down at his notebook, "*someone* moved the body out of *your car*, but it wasn't you, and also, you *didn't* kill him." His mouth twisted into a sarcastic half smile.

"Well,... may I please clarify? Also, I do think we have it all on your tape recorder there," she pointed. "I never lied, I answered each of your questions today truthfully." Tyler was surprised by Detective Armstrong's sudden use of profanity. Not that she was sensitive to it, but he seemed to be in perfect control of himself until then.

"Fucking lawyers!" exclaimed Detective Armstrong, standing up from the table and pacing around Tyler's kitchen. "Fine, maybe you technically didn't lie because we didn't specifically ask you 'hey, Tyler, did you happen to "find,"' he added air quotes, "'your boss's lifeless body in the trunk of your car, not call the police, and then continue about your regular business and keep this information—which you knew would be crucial to a murder investigation—to yourself when the body mysteriously disappeared?'"

Detective Myer, who had been sitting quietly since before Tyler began her story, calmly interjected, "Tyler, let's say I do believe you, which I want to make clear is not necessarily what I am saying at this point. Why not call the police as soon as you found his body?"

"Well, I knew how it looked, I knew I would get arrested, and I mean, did you ever watch *Making a Murderer*?" Even to Tyler's ears this sounded horrible.

"But if, as you insist, you didn't kill him, that would have been clear almost immediately. Come on. We're in St. Louis, not rural Wisconsin, and logistically, you don't seem large enough to kill an adult man."

"But this stuff all takes time, too." Tyler tried to explain more, "For example, how long have we spent talking so far just today? An hour? More? And you know, all of us are under a lot of pressure to bill at the firm."

"You have got to be joking," Detective Armstrong said to Detective Myer. "This man, who she worked with every day, with a beautiful family, is dead, and she's worried about her job."

Detective Myer kept his eyes on her. "If that's true, that's pretty despicable. You found the body of someone you knew well in your car and your thoughts immediately turn to you, your job, and if I'm getting this right... the *inconvenience* that assisting a police investigation would cause you."

Tyler stared back at him. It sounded terrible the way he put it. And it was selfish. "I agree," she said finally. "It was despicable. But I still did not kill him."

Detective Armstrong shifted the handcuffs on the table in front of him impatiently. "We should book her."

"If you're going to do that, I'm definitely going to need a lawyer." She could call the person who had presented a CLE on fixing traffic tickets, maybe he knew about murder too.

The three sat in tense silence, Tyler with her arms crossed tightly in front of her, Detective Armstrong vibrating with barely contained fury, and Detective Myer with an unreadable expression.

"I think I believe her," Detective Myer said finally, and gave a sideways head nod to Detective Armstrong to put the handcuffs away.

"We will, however, be taking your car for testing at our lab though. Let's see if it backs your story up."

Tyler could not believe her luck, or lack thereof; she could not decide which. She nodded and tried not to cry. Detective Armstrong reached out for Tyler's keys sitting on the table next to her. Slowly and gently, he detached the car key from the ring and softly set the remaining keys down on the table. Tyler looked up to meet his eyes. He still looked furious. The slow movements had been deliberate in order to stop himself from losing his temper. He set down a business card next to Tyler's keys. "If you have any questions, you can reach me here."

She looked up at him. *Fuck you.*

Detective Myer looked at Detective Armstrong intently, clearly seeing the anger, and the effort to control it, and nodded. He turned to Tyler. "It's your lucky day. Don't leave town."

They walked out.

For the millionth time, Tyler wondered about the psychotic break. For the third time, she logged onto her computer to analyze her hours. This time, instead of just a rough estimate, she broke the spreadsheet out by fifteen-minute intervals. She was not missing any large chunks of time. She nodded. *So, I didn't kill him.* Unbidden, another question entered her mind... *so, who did?* Tyler was desperate for a drink, but she was out of bourbon and wine and now she did not even have a car to get more. Maybe this was for the best. In her current mental state, she knew she would have had about three drinks too many, which seemed like it might be becoming a pattern. Not sure what else to do, Tyler sat on her couch and stared at her blank TV on the opposite wall. Lucy came and sat with her, just out of arm's reach.

CHAPTER FOUR

Tyler woke up the next morning feeling rested for the first time since "the incident," as she had been thinking about it. The momentary sense of optimism that flooded in subsided almost immediately as Tyler remembered the looks of, well, disgust on the officers' faces when they realized that Tyler had withheld information that could have helped them because she had prioritized her nose hair wax lawsuit document review over helping to solve a murder. And she had suffered a panic attack.

Tyler stared up at the ceiling and shook her head. She thought she had gotten her panic attacks under control. Trying to come up with some positives to start the day, Tyler noted that it was Friday, which might mean happy hour, and which absolutely meant wearing jeans to work. Even better, Tyler would not be expected to be available for emails or meetings early in the morning for two days straight, and the limited interruptions would help her catch up on the document review. And Tyler really *did* have to catch up on her document review. That was a simple fact, and if it made her selfish to want to contribute to her team and keep the case moving forward, so be it.

Tyler quickly got dressed, ultimately selecting a seersucker pencil skirt which would keep her cooler than jeans, and took her coffee to go in a firm-branded Yeti cup. She spent fifteen minutes looking for her car keys before remembering that they, and the car, had been taken by the detectives. *Duh.* She called an Uber and arranged for a rental car pickup that evening.

At the office, Tyler found she had all but reached the end of the internal emails regarding the internal dispute between the CFO and

CEO, and she moved on to reviewing pages upon pages of nose hair wax product specifications and internal quality control checks. After looking at the same page (relevant, but boring) for the third time, Tyler clicked open the Excel document containing the log of her time. She stared at it for several minutes, as if the numbers might rearrange themselves into something that would absolve her of her selfish behavior rather than what was, maybe, possibly, strong evidence of an unhealthy level of self-involvement. In her mind's eye, Tyler flashed again to the faces of the detectives as she tried to explain the pressure to bill. They really had no idea of the pressure she was under, but still, maybe she *should* try to help the investigation. First, however, Tyler had to make sure the police were convinced of her innocence. She could hardly help with the investigation, or bill, from a jail cell. Struck with an idea, Tyler saved the Excel as a PDF and pulled out Detective Armstrong's card.

Detective Armstrong,

Please see attached above a log of my time for last Wednesday evening, when you have told me that Kevin was regrettably killed. I use timers in our billing software when I log my time each day, and if you obtain access to the records stored in our billing software system, you will see that these times line up with what is recorded in the above-referenced Excel document. I am unable to share those records with you due to client confidentiality, however, I expect you can request access to these records through whatever means you are requesting access to our emails. The software may also track whether we are logged onto a computer at the office or at home, too. Using that information, and any location information you are able to obtain from my cell phone, you should see that my time is accounted for. My Pilates instructor can also verify my attendance in class.

-Tyler

Tyler hit send. She obviously had not been thinking clearly when she said she had no alibi. This should set the record straight.

In what Tyler now thought of as her prior life, also known as the time before her identity as an associate at a large law firm had swallowed up all of her hobbies and free time, Tyler had watched a lot of *Law and Order.* Especially SVU, but also the original. Although it was a TV show, it had to be based in reality to at least some extent, so Tyler tried to remember how the detectives in the show went about solving murders. It seemed they spent a lot of time questioning and confronting potential suspects and witnesses, which was obviously totally inappropriate for Tyler to do. And in terms of suspects and witnesses, Tyler really only had access to attorneys and staff at Cloose & Elkman. Tyler could not name Kevin's friends or acquaintances. For that matter, Tyler was only medium-confident she could name Kevin's children, although she was familiar with their faces smiling down from the shelf in Kevin's office.

Another factor to consider—Tyler figured it would likely make her look worse than she already did if she started questioning people connected to Kevin and those actions got back to the detectives. Not to mention that the whole endeavor, identifying then tracking down who knows how many people and trying to get them to answer questions, seemed like it would be a major time investment. Of course, Tyler wanted to help and prove her unselfishness, but she saw her help happening more from behind her desk in between document review and briefing versus eating away into her billable time. Tyler opened a new Word document up and started listing categories for motives: personal, professional, accident. Under "Personal" she added: affair, impending divorce, debt, secret (self), and secret (discovered someone else's). Under "Professional" she added: money, career advancement, secret (self), secret (discovered someone else's), and malpractice. Malpractice was a stretch, so she italicized it. Under "Accident," Tyler listed rough sex and affair. Tyler's cursor blinked its familiar beat as she eyed her list.

She jumped involuntarily when she heard a knock on her door. "Come in!" she called as she frantically minimized her windows and pulled up the document review software. Her invitation ended up being unnecessary as the knocker was John Delaware and he had opened the door as he was knocking. Looking just as freshly starched and pressed as when she met him, and in a full suit, he smiled at Tyler, or rather, displayed his perfect, even white teeth in the shape of a smile. His eyes did not change shape at all. *Is he Botoxed? And are those veneers?* wondered Tyler. Belatedly, she realized she was staring up at John with her mouth hanging slightly open, and she quickly put a smile of her own on her face and stood up. Teeth (or veneers) remaining on full display, John pulled out one of the chairs on the opposite side of Tyler's desk. She sat back down in her chair.

"Tyler, do you have a minute?" he asked unnecessarily, since he was obviously going to discuss whatever he wanted with her even if she said no.

"Of course," Tyler said, trying to sound like an upbeat junior associate who was eager to help however she could, and not like someone embroiled in a murder investigation. Tyler was no actress, and she saw John's eyes flicker almost imperceptibly in response to the false tone in her voice. He had obviously seen something off-putting, but whether it was the fact that Tyler was in the midst of a mini-mental breakdown or whether it was her puffy tired face and un-blown-out hair (Cerene would never), she did not know.

"Fantastic." He placed his hands on his knees and leaned forward. "I've been following up with everyone on my new teams and today you're up."

"Wow, that is so thoughtful of you," said Tyler. She sounded just as fake as before, and pinched her leg under the table both in punishment and in an attempt to snap herself back into authenticity. Quickly, Tyler reached back up to grab a legal pad and pen from the side of her desk to take notes. John inclined his head slightly as if to say, *of course, I am the most thoughtful and smart man in the world.*

"I really want everyone to get off to a strong start with me, which means understanding expectations," he went on. Tyler nodded and tried to look thoughtful. Internally, she began to feel lightheaded and was glad she was sitting down. Although she had only been working with John less than a week, Tyler had a strong suspicion she was about to be informed she was not meeting expectations. "Because," John continued after a dramatic pause, "you can't entirely fault someone for failing to meet expectations they don't know about. But then once they know, and they fail to meet clear expectations..." he trailed off, spreading his hands out in an expansive gesture and raising his eyebrows. Of course, Tyler knew what happened to associates who failed to meet expectations, known or unknown. A warning period of being frozen out followed by being informed that they were not succeeding at the firm and would be best served by finding a new position, preferably in the next couple months. The warning period was really only for a lucky few, too. In theory, if there was enough to do on a case and the partners were desperate enough for help anyone could be failing to succeed but remain busy.

Tyler nodded emphatically. "So, I really hate to get into this level on my cases," John continued, leaning forward, "but we absolutely must keep discovery moving. Must." Again, John paused dramatically. "As you must know, we are on a schedule, and even though we agreed to rolling production, that's no excuse to neglect the doc review. We need to know the documents out there both so we can produce, but also so we can prepare our own case." Tyler nodded again. "I expect that we won't spend more than a month reviewing any set of documents that comes in from the client. And I'll cut to the chase, in the course of familiarizing myself with my new case load, I had some statistics pulled from the doc review software, and I can see that you've had some documents for two, or even three months." John looked down and shook his head dolefully, then made eye contact with Tyler to make sure she understood the dire situation.

Tyler glanced over to her computer screen, where, as John had just pointed out, the document review software listed thousands of documents yet to be reviewed. Although it was horribly insensitive to think ill of the dead, Tyler peevishly remembered asking Kevin for permission to add other associates to review the documents, and that Kevin had denied approval, "the client doesn't like to see more than one junior on the bill." She moved her hand back down under the desk, gave herself a firm pinch and said, "I'm really sorry, John. I want to succeed. I want to meet your expectations, or even exceed them. I understand and I absolutely will not let things get to this point again."

"Well, that's great to hear, Tyler. Really wonderful. We all want you to succeed. If you have any other questions, please do not hesitate to ask." John stood up and strode deliberately out of Tyler's office. As he rose, his suit obediently smoothed itself out. It clearly understood and met his expectations better than Tyler. John's head popped back in. "Open or closed?"

"Closed, thanks. Better for focusing!" Tyler said. John gave Tyler half a nod and left.

Tyler leaned forward and gently banged her head against the desk twice. *Pull up your doc review software and get your shit together,* she told herself. Instead, almost involuntarily, she opened up her list of motives and refocused on the first category. Personal: affair, impending divorce, debt, secret (self), and secret (discovered someone else's). Impending divorce... she could potentially figure out through public records whether Kevin was getting a divorce. Tyler opened a new tab and pulled up Missouri Casenet. Casenet was the website where Missouri courts housed their dockets, which were essentially the timelines of cases along with filings available for viewing by registered users. Dockets were searchable by party name, among other categories.

Tyler searched for Kevin Stevens under party last and first name. Hundreds of results popped up. *Predictable*, Tyler thought, *it's a common name*. She refined her search, limiting it to the current year. Fifty plus results. Her computer pinged, alerting her to an email. Tyler flinched internally, as if John might have magically known she had not taken his warning to heart and had taken it upon himself to redirect her.

> *All,*
>
> *John would like the team on his cases to refresh themselves on our office policies, attached above. Please contact him with any questions.*
>
> *Suzie*

Suzie was John's assistant, but what office policies could this be referring to? Tyler opened up the attachment. It was the firm's manual, with the dress code and the firm's open-door policy highlighted. Tyler rolled her eyes. Obviously, her "door closed" response had been a mistake. She looked down at her clothes... clean skirt (and on a casual Friday nonetheless), clean shirt (wrinkled), pumps (heels were completely torn up from walking on the downtown sidewalks but she had yet to figure out how anyone kept theirs any other way). Fine, she was a little scruffy, not quite as polished as she should be, but she was certainly within the dress code. That section must have to do with some other unlucky team member. Tyler smiled a little to herself with the thought that she was not the only associate in John's crosshairs.

She forwarded the email to Cerene and messaged her a minute later. *When you request 'door closed' after getting chewed out... this is a LOT for a Friday afternoon.* While sympathetic, Cerene predictably expressed surprise that Tyler was not turning the documents around more quickly, and gently suggested that might be why Tyler was still on documents at all, unlike Cerene who only supervised first-year associates in their document review. *Asshole*, Tyler though. Tyler closed out of the chat window without finishing the conversation. It popped back up again with Cerene asking to grab drinks soon. *I'll be working all weekend on the MSJ so thinking I might just sneak out at five thirty today!* Well, la di da for Cerene and her superior, more substantive assignments, and her unflagging work ethic. Tyler closed the chat window again without answering. *Okay, now seriously pull up the document review software.*

Tyler opened up the document review software. *Now start reviewing the documents.* Tyler reviewed three documents outlining production line procedures (relevant, but boring). Then she pulled up the Casenet window again. Striking a private bargain with herself, she reviewed two more documents, for a total of five, then ten Casenet entries. Tyler was looking for divorce only (so, a case in family court) in the last calendar year. She had Kevin's home address from the firm directory and also from the time she had to deliver deposition preparation binders to him at three in the morning (even the office runners had not been working). Now, Tyler planned to use the address as a cross-reference to see if any potential divorce involved Kevin Stevens of Cloose & Elkman. Once Tyler finished reviewing the Casenet entries—the bargain fell to the wayside after the first twenty Casenet entries—she italicized "impending divorce" to indicate its less-likely status and added notes underneath:

- No results found for last calendar year
- Very recent still possible
- Older? Trying to work things out, unsuccessful?
- To do: Check last three calendar years.

Before she knew it, she was back on Casenet. When a window popped up informing her she had been logged out of the document review software due to inactivity, she realized it had been forty-five minutes. But with less than fifty results left to check, it seemed silly to stop at that point before finishing the task. Several minutes later Tyler updated her bullets to indicate the last three calendar years had been checked with no results. *Most likely, no divorce.* Tyler leaned back in her swivel chair and slowly circled around 360 degrees.

She highlighted the remaining "personal" categories, affair, debt, secret (self), and secret (discovered someone else's). Tyler figured she would be unlikely to find anything about debt, then shaking her head at her stupidity, she checked Casenet again for bankruptcy under Kevin's name, or with someone with Kevin's address as a defendant. No hits. She added a quick note to that effect under "debt," indicating that no bankruptcy actions or other suits had been found. Both of the "secret" categories would be tough to find anything about, since by definition they were, well, secret. Affair would also be tough. Maybe it should even be a sub-category under secret. Tyler moved it back and forth a few times, before leaving it as its own category.

Tyler also wondered how Kevin could have had time for an affair with the hours he put in at the office. He would have had to meet someone, convince them to sleep with him, and then meet them somewhere and fuck them, and maybe he would have to buy them presents, and wine and dine them as well. And presumably he had some facetime with his family too. The idea that all of this, and twelve-plus hours of work, could be fit into a day seemed unrealistic. *But... what if some of it overlapped?* A work affair! As far as Tyler knew, there had not been one in the Cloose & Elkman office in years, so maybe the office was overdue.

Tyler could think of two people who might know about an office affair involving Kevin: his secretary Gina and Brendan. Tyler determined she would start with Gina and go to Brendan only if she really needed to. Brendan was nice, but every conversation with him always turned into him assigning Tyler work, which she never had time to complete, and always ended up doing between midnight and four in the morning. Now, she probably did not even have those hours, since there was so much document review to catch up on. Plus, she still had to work on the reply brief from the motion she had filed a few weeks earlier once plaintiffs filed their opposition, do some personal investigation into Kevin's murder, and then figure out how best to present the information to the cops. And she could still be arrested, which would certainly take up a lot of time. Not to mention Tyler should really try to keep up with the Pilates. *Speaking of which,* Tyler thought, realizing that it was already six. If she was going to make the last class of the day she was going to have to rush. Reaching for her keys, Tyler remembered again that she had no car, and now she was late to pick up her rental. Secretly relieved that she did not have to work out, Tyler called another Uber and picked up her rental car, which she drove straight to Total Wine. She would definitely cut back on the bourbon, but Europeans drank wine every day, right? So maybe that was not such a terrible habit after all. Maybe drinking wine every day was not problematic and could even be considered sophisticated. Convinced, Tyler decided she was only drinking wine on weeknights going forward. But for weekends, she also purchased a bottle of bourbon.

Later, feeling invigorated from skipping Pilates and thinking more about her investigation outline, but feeling a little guilty about how much time she had spent on it, Tyler logged back onto the firm's system around nine to review some more documents. She opened up the review software and was horrified to see that ten thousand more documents had been added by the client. She also saw that John had emailed her. She started to panic thinking about adding additional work to her list when she saw that the email was actually just the document load notification forwarded to Tyler with the message, "To review in 1 mo. Thx." *I guess he was serious about setting expectations*, Tyler thought. She wondered why he was even emailing on a Friday night—he seemed like the type to have plans. Most people did, after all. Well, the same could be said for Tyler, she realized as she responded with the only acceptable message, "Will do!"

Despite her chipper message, the idea that she personally would review ten thousand documents (plus the several thousand she was now aware were past due) within one month and also perform any other work that came her way was laughable. It was so overwhelming, in fact, that Tyler almost shut the laptop then and there because the task was too big to even begin. Tyler told herself to break the problem down. Surely it was doable. In fact, whether or not it was doable was irrelevant because she was either going to review every document or be kicked off her cases and probably have to leave the firm. So, she would get it done. It was now August 15. Tyler saw that in fact, 10,351 documents had been added. That was added to the 2,563 documents Tyler had not yet reviewed. Tyler figured she had until the end of the month to review the 2,563 documents (sixteen calendar days), and until September 15 (thirty-one calendar days) to review the remaining 10,351. Doing some quick math, she saw that she would have to review about 415 documents every day. More if she was not going to review on the weekends. Specifically, about a hundred more a weekday. *Okay, deep breaths. Of course, I'll be working on weekends, and 415 documents a day is* totally *doable.* And as a bonus, Tyler had not counted today, August 15, so anything she did right now would just be getting ahead. Diving back into a sea of emails, Tyler put on a *Law & Order SVU* re-run on the TV, settled into her couch, and reviewed for several hours. Although, worryingly, only 150 documents which meant the total time to review every document would be... Tyler cut herself off and fell into bed.

The weekend could not be classified as a success by any measure. Tyler went to Pilates only on Sunday, meaning the prior week she had gone only twice, three trips below her five-workout-a-week goal. And Tyler reviewed only 350 documents each day, meaning in only two days she had essentially used up her bonus Friday night review. Worse yet, on Sunday night, worrying about her lack of document review while watching Bravo, she had eaten another entire frozen pizza.

CHAPTER FIVE

The next morning, Tyler made sure to put on what she considered to be an "A" outfit and curled her hair. She planned to approach both Gina and Brendan, and it always seemed like favors came easier when you were looking your best. Swiveling back and forth in her office chair, she wondered the best way to approach Gina.

Back when Gina had started working at Cloose & Elkman, around twenty years ago, each lawyer had their own secretary, and the secretaries kept track of time for the attorneys, typed up handwritten briefs, and often managed their personal appointments. While Gina was now a proud new grandmother with sweater sets in every tasteful neutral imaginable, Tyler had been floored to see an old picture of Gina from around when she had started. In spite of her giant perm, Gina had been a fox.

Anyway, now, each secretary was responsible for about five or six attorneys of varying seniorities. So, Tyler's secretary Gina also happened to be Kevin's secretary, but Kevin relied on Gina much more than Tyler, as he had started working with her before computers were quite so ubiquitous. Gina was a notorious gossip and pretty much never had time to help Tyler with anything, but Tyler was the most junior attorney assigned to her. And, unless Tyler was the rare associate who stayed at the same firm for her entire career, Gina would be there long after Tyler left. All in all, Gina and Tyler both knew that Gina had been at the firm a lot longer than Tyler and would probably keep working at the firm after Tyler left. But despite Tyler's second-class citizenship, Gina *did* always find a way to assign Tyler's tasks out to other people so Tyler did not have to do them herself, and Tyler liked to think their relationship was on the warmer side.

Tyler thought back to the first, less disastrous, interview with the detectives when she told them the gossip she had heard about Kevin from Gina. When had Gina said that, and how had it come up? It had been about a month earlier, maybe three weeks or so, but it felt like much longer given recent events. Tyler remembered she had heard the rumor by chance. She had been on her way back from a Starbucks break and had walked by Gina's desk to find another secretary leaning over toward Gina whispering furiously. Both women had been sending darting glances out that clearly indicated they were discussing something they did not want overheard, which was an excellent sign it was good gossip. Tyler had made some joke about not eavesdropping and Gina responded, "Do you want the tea?" (something her youngest son had recently taught her to say and Tyler herself had only recently learned about on Instagram). Tyler responded that, obviously, she wanted the tea, and she had gotten the gossip. So, it was pretty unlikely that Tyler was going to engineer that scenario again to find out about an office affair. Or be that carefree. She allowed herself six minutes to languish in the nostalgia for a time before she was involved in a murder investigation, and then she resolved to try and flesh out Section I.A.1 (Motives→personal→affair) on her murder investigation outline. Deciding to replicate her prior gossip-gathering experience as much as possible, she headed down to Starbucks, where she saw two partners in the litigation department (two more than she wanted to see, but at least neither was John, who she suspected might maul her for not being at her desk reviewing documents) and assured everyone she was quite busy and having so much fun, thanks so much for asking, while internally panicking at the possibility of being given more work.

Starbucks in hand, Tyler returned to her floor and slowly walked up to Gina's desk. Gina was alone. This seemed like a bad sign, because it did not match the last time, but maybe a good sign too, since Gina would likely not be eager to gossip about her recently-murdered boss around a group.

Telling herself to just be casual, Tyler approached. "Hi, Gina. How was your weekend?"

Gina jumped and let out a small scream. "Oh, Tyler, hi, you scared me!" *Great*, Tyler thought sarcastically, *I'm off to an amazing start.*

"Gina, I am so, so sorry. I just ran out to Starbucks and I wanted to check in and see how you were."

"Oh, Tyler, don't worry about it. What can I help you with?" Gina was starting to breath more evenly, although she was holding her right hand to her heart. Tyler wondered how she could have scared Gina so badly with a simple greeting on a Monday morning. Kevin's absence must be affecting Gina more than Tyler would have thought.

"Well, nothing really, I was just grabbing some Starbucks and I wanted to check in. Did you have a nice weekend?" The question was wrong, Tyler could tell as soon as she said it.

"Nice? Well, I'm not so sure that's the word to describe it. You know Kevin's funeral was this weekend?" Gina looked at her with faint disapproval. Tyler vaguely remembered seeing an email about funeral arrangements and mentally kicked herself. Outwardly, she sadly nodded. "Tragic," Gina continued. "I didn't feel it was my place to go, but I heard it was a nice ceremony. I take it you didn't go either." Tyler shook her head and tried to put an appropriate sad expression on her face.

"Like you said, I just didn't feel it was my place," Tyler lied shamelessly.

"Well, anyway, now we've got the 'new' Kevin," she added the air quotes and nodded in the direction of John's office.

"We sure do," Tyler glanced around to make sure no one was around to overhear, "I have to say though, so far I'm really missing the *old* Kevin." Gina looked like she was about to agree, but then looked up, startled. "Tyler, it's my pleasure to get this letter out, and I'll make sure the mailing room emails you the tracking number." Tyler made a face, then turned around to see the "new" Kevin, himself, John, standing at Gina's desk.

"Tyler, how are you?" She felt sweat break out all over her body.

"I'm good, how about you, John?" She backed away from the desk. "Gina, thank you *so* much." She narrowed her eyes meaningfully to indicate she understood that Gina had just totally covered her ass and made her look productive when actually she had been wasting billable time. Tyler was pleased to have been proven right in thinking she had a good relationship with Gina, but unfortunately fleshing out murder investigation outline Section 1.A.1 would have to wait.

"I'm well." Slight emphasis and eyebrow raise on the "well." Of *course*, he used perfect grammar in everyday conversations. And of course, he judged others for not doing so. Tyler smiled at him as if she did not register the correction.

"Well, I won't keep you, I know how busy we all are." She started to walk away, then before she could stop herself turned back. "I'll be in my office and you had better believe my door will be open!" She gave a little salute, winked and booked it back to her office before John could react.

Back at her desk, with the door open, Tyler relayed the entire exchange to Cerene via the internal messaging system. Cerene called her immediately.

"You *didn't*. Tyler, WHY?"

"I HATE passive aggression."

Cerene continued to express her disapproval passive aggressively. Tyler mentally shrugged.

"Thanks so much for the call, pal, I appreciate the backup. Talk to you soon!" Tyler rolled her eyes and hung up the phone before Cerene could continue.

Tyler decided to revisit the murder outline in light of her unsuccessful Gina interaction. She had really been hoping to cross something off her list or at least flesh out part of the outline. Drumming her fingers on her desk, Tyler wondered about the professional category. Again, she was not sure what to do to investigate the "secret" category, especially if she was not going to go around asking intrusive questions. She supposed she would just go ahead and do her actual job. The day passed by surprisingly quickly, and without any interruptions, Tyler was able to review 500 documents before leaving for Pilates. She also noticed on her calendar that the opposition brief for the motion she had filed under Kevin's supervision (for another class action in Texas—the DiNinno case) would be filed on Wednesday. They would have two weeks to file the reply from there.

Post Pilates, shower, and salad, watching TV with Lucy, who again was sitting just out of arm's reach, Tyler's phone started to buzz. Tyler looked down to see: *To review in 1 mo. Thx. -JD*

Well, at least she had gotten a signoff this time. Tyler turned the volume down on the TV and pulled her laptop out of her bag. She felt her stomach drop as she saw that another 4,000 documents had been loaded. And she had just one extra week to review these along with the 415 per day she had to review to catch up. Another email notification popped up.

Tyler,

Need binders for depos of Brian Brosby & P's expert witnesses in the Brosby case. - JD

Tyler's stomach dropped further, if that was possible. At least the binder prep would be more interesting than document review. Deposition experience was elusive for associates at a large law firm, since the name of the game for most of the clients was to settle the case out of court without spending a fortune on litigation. Hearings and depositions, which required extensive preparation and travel, were costly and avoided when possible. Not to mention they were considered more fun, and therefore handled mostly by partners. Tyler sent two more quick "Will do!"s. She had no idea how she would finish all of this work, but that was a problem for the Tyler of tomorrow, the Tyler of today was going to bed.

Tyler woke up before her alarm went off feeling uncharacteristically refreshed and decided to go to an early Pilates class. After the class she decided to just go home and work from there. She thought she would knock out the document review in the morning, then assess what had to happen for the binders in the afternoon.

At 10:30, feeling she was off to a productive start, Tyler got an IM request from Brendan, who she had only ever emailed with.

Brendan: Tyler, where are you. I see that you're online but I just walked past your office and its empty.

Tyler: I'm working from home, I'm knocking out the doc review!

Brendan: You need to get here. Now. JD came by your office to discuss depo prep binders and you weren't there.

Tyler: Okay, be there ASAP! Thanks so much for telling me! So so sorry.

Tyler rushed to get dressed and drove to work. There was no way John could be too upset, right? The unofficial firm policy was that working from home was permitted a day or two a week as long as you had plenty to do and were productive. Tyler definitely had plenty to do, but she could maybe see where productivity could be seen as an issue both from a document review rate perspective and an hours perspective, since both had definitely decreased in the last few weeks. Tyler sped down the spiral drive in the garage, almost rear-ending the car in front of her at the barrier where employees swiped their cards, and narrowly avoided flattening someone walking to their car (luckily not someone she recognized). Tyler jumped out of her car and got to her office as fast as she possibly could without running. Once she was logged onto her work computer, she grabbed a notepad and a pen and walked down to Brendan's office, panting and sweating. Brendan was sitting at his computer looking tired.

"Brendan, do you have a minute?" Tyler asked, modulating her voice despite feeling her heart pounding in her chest.

He nodded. "Close the door." Tyler closed the door and sat in one of the two "guest" chairs that were in every associate's office.

"First of all, I'm so sorry—I was just on a roll at home reviewing these documents." Brendan nodded. Tyler could not tell if that meant he thought reviewing documents at home made sense or whether he was simply acknowledging her apology. "So..." she continued, shifting uncomfortably in the guest chair and feeling her shirt stick uncomfortably to her back, "how bad was it?"

Brendan grimaced. Tyler quickly said, "I take it back. I don't want to know."

"Well, to be fair none of us have much experience with John, and I think he's a yeller, so it's hard to say how bad it was, really," Brendan said. Tyler pressed her lips together. It was clear Brendan thought the situation *was* pretty bad and was just trying to make Tyler feel better, but she guessed that was nicer than the alternative.

"Ugh. So stupid. Well, obviously going forward I will make sure I'm in the office every day. This never would have been an issue with Kevin though, you know? As long as you came in most of the time he never seemed to have any issues. And, of course, as long as he could reach you."

Brendan nodded again. He was too professional to agree with Tyler outright, but she thought he would have said something in John's defense if he thought she was wrong. Suddenly, something clicked in Tyler's mind: *flesh out Section I.A.1 (Motives→personal→affair).*

"I just really find myself missing Kevin, don't you?"

Brendan nodded. Brendan had never been one for small talk, so Tyler suspected he was starting to get a little impatient.

"I was just so shocked to see what happened to him. And all these rumors about it being, you know, an *encounter* gone wrong..." she trailed off in the hopes that Brendan would take the bait.

Brendan stared at her a few seconds without blinking. His eyes were bloodshot and bleary. Tyler hoped he was thinking about sharing something about Kevin, but it looked like he might actually be about to go to sleep.

"I think you said you wanted to talk to me about something?"

Tyler realized she should have tried to bring this up at a time when Brendan was not trying to bill time. But that was probably never, not to mention bringing it up at another time might end up with him assigning her more work, so she tried to give it one last shot.

"Right, I'm so sorry. I just find the whole thing to be so upsetting, and now I've gotten off on such a bad foot with John. I just can't imagine what Kevin's family is going through right now. I mean, we've all seen the wife and kids, they are such a cute family and to do something like that just didn't seem like Kevin." Tyler realized she was babbling but kept it up for a couple more seconds while helplessly watching Brendan's eyes drift from her face back to his computer, which had started pinging rapidly, at what sounded like ten to fifteen emails arriving. Tyler stopped talking and sat in silence until almost a minute later when Brendan seemed to realize she had stopped.

"Well, anyway." Tyler knew she was the most junior on the team, which made her the least important. On top of that, she was now probably the worst member of the team from John's perspective, which would have made her the least important team member even below anyone junior to her, but still, it seemed like Brendan could pay *a little* attention to her being upset that their old boss had just been murdered. And he did not even know that Tyler was trying to investigate—she might have really been upset! *No, you are really upset. You're so upset you're investigating, and the detectives were wrong to say you were selfish*, she told herself.

"What I was hoping to talk to you about was these depo prep binders. When I used to do them for Kevin you always sent me the depo outline and we discussed what should be flagged, then I took it from there. So, I'm wondering if we're doing it the same way here?"

"I don't know, I've been in the weeds on the Smith discovery dispute. Kevin had been pretty looped in on that one, but John basically told me to handle it and leave him alone. The client's freaking out, plaintiffs are asking for twenty years' worth of data—the client would have to go into some moldy old closet in deep storage and scan it all, if it's even still there!"

"Shit," Tyler said. She saw Brendan blanche slightly. She always forgot he was not a swearer. "You've got it, though—you're a discovery star! Remember in DiNinno when plaintiff's counsel took issue with our responses and you got the judge to almost sanction *them* for harassing and intention to cause embarrassment with the discovery requests. And our client is a corporation... I didn't know until then that corporations get embarrassed!" That got a slight smile.

"Tyler, come on, corporations are people too." She smiled back at Brendan, more broadly. She loved when he made jokes—a rare occurrence. The jokes made Tyler think Brendan might actually like her and not just tolerate her.

"On these depo prep binders though, what I was telling you on the chat is that John wanted to discuss them with you, so you probably want to catch up with him ASAP. I don't know for sure but he seems to have quite a different style from Kevin so I'd venture to guess that we will not be handling them in the same way. I'm sure it will be a good learning opportunity for you to see how someone else handles depo prep, and maybe to take more ownership over the process." Tyler saw this as the cue to leave that it was, but she tried to press her luck.

"I just wanted to ask you about one more thing, if that's okay," she said. Brendan nodded.

She launched into her document review sob story, complete with the daily document review count, the addition of the depo prep binders, and the upcoming reply brief, then looked at Brendan expectantly. "I just think I need some more help. Don't we have first-years or the document review specialists to jump in on this kind of thing?"

"Well, Tyler, there are a few questions that you need to ask before making that kind of request." Tyler nodded. "What have you been billing per month?"

"180."

"Hmm."

Tyler could see that number was unimpressive to Brendan and felt her heart sink.

"Are you missing deadlines?"

"No!" Missing deadlines was a cardinal sin. "Well, actually... yes! I mean, I didn't *know* I was missing deadlines, but you were in the same meeting as me—John wants things turned around in a month, and I haven't been that fast! I am totally missing those deadlines."

Brendan nodded. "He did say that. But you didn't know the timeframe. Now you do. Bottom line is, if you are not missing deadlines and you haven't been consistently billing 200 plus, you are not overwhelmed, and you do not need help."

So, no help. Tyler felt panic rising at the thought of the hours she would have to work just to get done what she already had on her plate, not even taking into account other things Brendan or John might need help with. And whatever was going on with these binders. She heard a soft knock on the door behind her and whipped her head around to see Cerene.

"Oh hi, sorry, am I interrupting? I thought your calendar showed you as free, Brendan."

What was Cerene doing here? Tyler and Brendan worked exclusively on nose hair wax cases, and Cerene worked exclusively on *not* nose hair wax cases. Tyler felt her hackles rise—was John trying to replace her with Cerene? She thought Cerene would warn her if that was happening, and Cerene certainly had enough of her own work to stay busy, but at the same time, it was foolish to ever think you could fully trust anyone at the firm.

"I'm on my way out, thanks so much, Brendan." *For nothing,* she added silently as she smiled sweetly at him. Tyler stood up and eyed Cerene suspiciously.

"See John," Brendan said, "and good luck." Tyler showed crossed fingers to Brendan and walked out. Cerene immediately shut the door. Tyler bristled and made a mental note to investigate what was going on there later. Tyler walked by Gina's desk on her way to John's office, and caught Gina's eye.

"Time of death, five minutes from now. Is he in a meeting?"

Gina laughed and shook her head, "No, Tyler, his calendar shows as free."

John's office door was closed. Tyler leaned in to try to hear if someone else was in there, or if John was speaking on the phone, and at just that moment the door was yanked open and John walked out. He walked straight into Tyler and she almost fell down, dropping both her notebook and her pen.

"John! I'm so sorry! I'm so sorry I missed you this morning." She scrambled to pick up the notebook and pen. Gina, who was sitting across the hallway, discreetly picked up a few files and walked back into a recessed storage area, presumably to avoid seeing Tyler make a total fool of herself. John had started walking down the hall so Tyler trotted after him. "I saw your email about the depo prep binders and I was just hoping to go over the timeline and what you are looking for in the binders. I used to coordinate with Brendan, but he mentioned that he was focusing on discovery in another case, so I wanted to check in."

John nodded and kept walking.

"So, do you have a minute to talk?" Tyler asked.

John shot Tyler a withering look. "Does it seem to you like I have a minute to talk?" he asked. "No."

"Um, oh, okay. Should I look for some time on your calendar? We could go over it in person or we can do a call if you prefer, too. Whatever's most convenient."

"What's most convenient, and what I desperately want, Tyler," pause, "is for you to take care of this simple task that I've assigned you, like I already asked you to do." They were at the elevator bank now and John had rapidly started pressing the "down" arrow. "I'm heading to a client lunch now, so please excuse me." Feeling a potent mix of panic and rage, Tyler stood with her notebook and pen in hand and tried her best to keep her face in a friendly neutral expression. As the elevator doors slid closed, John saluted Tyler. *Damn*, she thought. She really should not have done that when she was already on John's bad side.

Tyler slowly walked back to her office, closed the door (no John around to notice for at least an hour), and stood staring at a wall. The rage had faded quickly and Tyler felt so overwhelmed she wanted to cry. She now had all the documents to review, plus she had to somehow identify when Brian Brosby and his expert witnesses were scheduled to be deposed, who was making the depo outline, and what set of documents were needed. She felt tears welling up and shook her head quickly. She really did not have time to cry. She emailed the team in charge of calendaring case deadlines and asked if anyone was aware of when the depositions had been scheduled. She forwarded the email to Gina and asked if Gina had seen any deposition notices come through. *Okay*, she thought, *I can do this. I've got two choices here, I can get it all done or I can get kicked off these cases and leave the firm. I'm not leaving the firm, therefore I'll get it all done.* A new email came in from PACER—the opposition in the DiNinno case had been filed... a day early. Not for the first time, Tyler wished for a pillow to scream into. Instead, she forwarded the email on to Gina and the calendaring team and asked when the reply would be due. Gina would download and distribute the opposition brief, plus the original motion, to the case team in a separate email.

Tyler reviewed documents for a few more hours before she started to feel her eyes cross. Against her better judgment she opened up the murder outline. She highlighted Section I.A.1 (Motives→personal→affair) and decided to take another run at Gina. If she was lucky, John would be at the client pitch for a long time, which would serve dual purposes: Tyler could avoid seeing John while she was not working and John would return in a slightly better mood if the pitch went well.

Following her original plan, she went back to Starbucks (ordered iced tea because she was already on edge), got Gina a hot chocolate, and walked back by Gina's desk.

"Hi, Gina," she said ruefully. Gina, thankfully, did not jump this time. "How much of that disaster did you pick up?"

"Oh, Tyler, honey, how are you?"

"I'm okay," said Tyler, "but I feel like I keep doing the wrong thing with John and I'm not sure how to stop. Also, I got this for you." Tyler set the hot chocolate down on the desk and slid it toward Gina, "It's hot chocolate, you can give it to someone else if you don't like it. But it *is* a bribe... do you have any advice on dealing with John? You're sitting here across from him and you must have seen all kinds of personalities over the years, so if you have any ideas, I'm all ears."

Gina took the cup. "Thanks, honey. But I'm not sure I can help. John's just as new to me as he is to you. It's too soon to get a good idea of his personality," Gina unhelpfully explained. "Its not like Kevin. You know I was his secretary from the time he started as a first-year associate?"

"Really? I actually never knew that," said Tyler, spotting an opportunity to get more information about Kevin. Gina had told Tyler several times that she had been Kevin's secretary since the time he started. "What was he like?"

Gina smiled a little at the memory. "Nervous! And a terrible dresser. Always in suits two sizes too big, and with a terrible haircut."

"Well, that definitely does not sound like the Kevin that I worked with," observed Tyler, "at all."

"Well," Gina said, "you adapt to fit in, don't you." She smiled encouragingly at Tyler. Tyler did not want to change the subject off Kevin.

"You know, Gina, I've been feeling so terrible about how I scared you yesterday, and especially after you covered for me with John. I owe you one, well *another* one there, by the way."

"Don't worry about it," Gina said, and started to pick up and shuffle some files. Tyler could see she was losing Gina's attention. What did she have to do to get people to finish a conversation with her?

"So, tell me more about Kevin when he started!" Tyler said a little too loudly. "Was he already married to Melissa? I miss him and I realize the more I think about it I barely knew anything about him because we just talked about cases."

Gina thought for a second. "Probably not right when he started, but they were college sweethearts. I think they got married after a couple years."

"I just feel so terrible for her..."

Gina nodded and looked sad. Tyler could see that bringing up Kevin's potential affair would probably be in pretty poor taste. How had she not realized that earlier? Yet, here she was at Gina's desk. *Too late now*, Tyler thought, and decided to go for it.

"Have you seen any of the articles about ... it?" she asked.

Gina frowned. "Well, I suppose I have."

"Some are pretty sordid to say the least." Tyler looked expectantly at Gina, but Gina was looking more and more displeased by the minute, which could either mean Gina thought Tyler was being inappropriate or Gina did not want to discuss this topic. "I just couldn't believe what I read, but then like I said I never heard about Kevin's personal life. Either way, disgusting to write about it."

"Lies, all of them," Gina said with finality. "Disgusting to write about or talk about."

Tyler took her cue. "Well, he is so missed. I learned so much from him. And at least he told you clearly what he wanted up front..."

"I think that one step forward with John might be by billing a lot every day," Gina suggested. She was clearly ready for Tyler to leave.

Tyler smiled, "Right as always, Gina—I can take a hint! Thanks again for yesterday."

Tyler walked back to her office. She almost shut the door but thought better of it and left it ajar but not completely open. She was not sure whether Gina's response was her honest opinion or her desire not to speak ill of the dead. Nevertheless, under Motives→personal→affair, Tyler added a short summary of Gina's response and Gina's report that Kevin and Melissa were college sweethearts who married when he was a junior associate.

CHAPTER SIX

The next few days passed in a blur—Tyler was waking up at five in the morning to get a few hours of work done at home, then staying at the office until about seven when she would return home, eat dinner, then work again until midnight or one. Somehow, Tyler was still falling further and further behind on the document review. She had been left on her own to draft the reply brief, which was due in only two weeks, and Tyler did not dare to ask John to consider whether they might ask for an extension. On top of that, Tyler was supposed to prepare materials for the depositions, and since John would not speak to her about them, she had to reach out to a variety of paralegals to figure out who was being deposed and when, then try to guess what kind of materials John would want when questioning the witnesses, and what the plaintiff was likely to use in their own questioning. As a result of the other tasks, Tyler now had to review 500 documents every day (up from 415), and that number continued to grow as she failed to meet the quota and new documents were added to the queue.

While her work life was a total disaster, to Tyler's surprise, on Wednesday she received a text from Harry confirming that they were still on for dinner on Friday. Not only had she lost track of the fact that she had agreed to dinner, Tyler had expected and maybe even hoped Harry might not follow through. She blocked out some time on her calendar on Friday night so she would not forget about the date and work through dinner. Harry had chosen a Mexican restaurant, which reminded Tyler of how she thought she had forgotten Mexican food in her car before discovering that the smell was actually Kevin's body. Again, Tyler allowed herself six minutes to feel bad for herself, then kept working. She was not really sure she should be going out to dinner at all, but figured she could at least take two hours of a break before resuming work.

On Friday, Tyler changed into a sundress and flat sandals in her office bathroom, and attempted to freshen herself up as best she could before heading to meet Harry at the Mexican restaurant. Harry had offered to pick her up, but she explained the work situation and he seemed understanding. She felt trepidation at seeing him again—would Harry want to talk about her outburst? Tyler had no energy for that.

Harry had beaten her to the restaurant and was sitting in a booth with chips and salsa. He was facing away from her as she walked up, and Tyler unsuccessfully tried to read his body language based on the three-quarter profile she could see as she approached. God, she was tired. Why had she agreed to this if it was going to be awkward? It was not as if she had the time. For a split second she thought about turning around and leaving, but instead she steeled herself and walked up to tap Harry on the shoulder.

"Hey." It felt very weird to see him. In the last few days, she had not had a chance to think about Kevin and everything that had happened the last night she had seen Harry, and was surprised to feel a lot of the panic coming back. Plus, she had acted totally crazy and inappropriately, which was embarrassing to her privately, even if she was not prepared to apologize out loud. Tyler realized she was standing to the side of the booth, once again behaving inappropriately, when a waiter rushed past her, giving her a dirty look for blocking the walkway.

"Hey you!" replied Harry. He seemed to be ignoring her weirdness and greeted Tyler warmly, as if their last interaction never happened. He got up and wrapped Tyler in an embrace. Tyler stood stiff for a moment, before relaxing into the hug, and surprised herself by feeling tears welling up in her eyes. She realized she had not touched another person since shaking the detectives' hands the week before. Harry hung on for a long moment, long enough for Tyler to collect herself and blink the tears back, then held her out at arm's length and smiled down at her. "I'm really happy to see you."

"I'm happy to see you, too," Tyler responded, smiling as she realized the words were true.

A waiter came by to ask if they wanted anything to drink. "Definitely!" Tyler responded, perhaps a little too eagerly. They split a pitcher of margaritas. Tyler was pleasantly surprised that Harry made no mention during the entire dinner of the last time they had seen each other. He asked her about her work and listened intently as Tyler explained that Kevin had been murdered, that John was the new Kevin, and that John hated her guts and she was more overwhelmed than she had ever felt before.

"I did actually see that in the news. That's terrible. You must have known him really well from working with him so closely."

Tyler nodded. This was circling dangerously close to the entire incident that had incited her prior extreme reaction.

Harry looked thoughtful. "You know, we kind of have Kevin to thank for meeting."

"We do?"

"Well, yeah, he's the one who hired me to investigate the man with the nose hair that 'wouldn't grow back.'"

"That's right." Tyler smiled sadly. She felt disconnected from the person who met Harry in the Oak conference room.

"But of course, that was really just the one phone call. Not really enough to get a sense of him at all. Then I worked with you."

"Yes," she answered noncommittally, not sure where this was going.

"You worked with him every day though, how are you doing?"

"I'm fine," Tyler said. "I don't want to get into it."

Tyler saw Harry's face fall at her standoffish response. She knew she should say more, try to be more accessible, but she was still so tired. She took a big sip of her margarita while thinking of a way to sidestep this conversation.

"Hey," she pointed her fork at him, "you kind of inspired me over the last week or so."

Harry made a noncommittal noise but seemed slightly less put out.

"You know, all your investigative stuff! So, right after, you know, Kevin was found in the garage and everything, these cops came to the office and they talked to everyone who worked with Kevin." Tyler paused. Was that true? She should check who John's email was addressed to. Tyler pulled out her phone. "Well, I think they talked to everyone Kevin worked with, at least. They talked to me. I'm checking now, John emailed everyone. Of course, John's email made sure to tell everyone to cooperate but keep in mind that our time was billable." Rolling her eyes while she quickly scrolled through her inbox, Tyler opened up the email and saw that it included all of the associates staffed on Kevin's cases. "Okay, so they interviewed all Kevin's associates—that's who was on the email, but maybe they talked to others, too." Tyler could see she was losing Harry's interest. "So, anyway, things were already going badly with him, John that is, so I *really* did my best to have a quick interview, and the cops put this whole guilt trip on me about how this man, with a family, had died, and we were all still worried about work, and basically that our priorities were fucked up." Tyler paused to breathe. She was on a roll, and mentioning the later conversation with the detectives was on the tip of her tongue. She did not want Harry thinking she might be a murderer though, so she skipped it. "And, you know, it really got to me, the guilt trip, and I thought, here I am, right where Kevin spent almost all his time, I should see what I can find!" Tyler found herself liking this narrative. When she just left out the fact that she had withheld important murder investigation evidence, she was looking like a thoughtful empathetic person.

Harry looked amused. "See what you can find? So, what have you been up to?"

"Oh, well, mostly just public record searches. But I kind of tried to brainstorm what might have caused... you know... and then I did kind of try to ask his secretary and Brendan about it. But that really didn't work at all, especially Brendan."

"Well, I think you better not quit your day job in that case," Harry teased.

"Seriously, though, you find out so much about people, and so quickly. How do you do it?"

"It's my day job," Harry deadpanned. "But actually, when you have time to follow someone and see where they go, who they talk to, what they buy, it's a lot easier to learn about them. And you pick up the knack of talking to people."

"Are you saying I can't talk to people?" Tyler asked. She tried to phrase the question as a joke but it came out with a more offended tone than she intended.

"Of course not, but come on, you have less practice than me, you sit in front of your computer morning, noon, and night."

"Yeah, I guess so. So, what would you do, if you were trying to figure out, purely as an example," Tyler winked, "if someone you knew who had been murdered had any secrets like... say, an affair."

Harry sat thoughtfully. "Well, truthfully, I would just ask people directly. You can tell a lot from their reaction. But I would not... hypothetically... have to work with them or see them every day."

Tyler nodded. "And what, hypothetically still, might you think about in terms of a motive for murdering someone who was maybe a little difficult but overall a nice person."

"Oh, I'm not in the motive business. I'm a private investigator, not a detective. I might find out someone's secrets or information about them, but I don't wonder why or ask too many questions."

Tyler pursed her lips.

The waiter came by with the check, and Tyler went to take it. Harry looked offended.

"It's a date—I got it, and I didn't realize you were in a rush."

"It's just... you know, I told you how upset John has been with me? Well, I have all these documents to review, and this motion to prepare, and these depo outlines, and I thought I'd get a little more work done tonight."

"So, let me get this right, you're going home now," Harry made a slightly exaggerated show of looking down at his watch, "at nine o'clock on a *Friday night*. And you're going to work."

"Yeah," Tyler answered. What was there to be confused about? Sure, she had slept with Harry before, more than once even, but she was under no obligation to do it again. She was exhausted, and she really had to work.

"Well, can I at least walk you to your car?"

"That would be great, thank you!"

In the parking lot Harry looked confused as Tyler walked over to her car, which she belatedly realized was a rental with Massachusetts plates.

"Rental," Tyler said shortly. Then she kissed Harry to cut the conversation off. It was nice, but again she felt like she was going to cry at the physical contact. She was a real mess, but at least she was a productive one.

"I'll text you, have a great weekend."

Tyler went home and had another margarita, then only reviewed about a hundred documents. She did not have the heart to recalculate how far behind on her review she was now, and she studiously avoided thinking about how she now seemed to be so isolated that any human touch made her cry.

CHAPTER SEVEN

Tyler did not leave her house the rest of the weekend. She got food and groceries delivered and sat in a variety of spots around her townhouse working while her hair became progressively greasier and more tangled. Cerene was online on Saturday, and Tyler made a half-hearted attempt to chat with her. Once she started the conversation Tyler could not shake the suspicion that Cerene had been trying to take her cases, and Cerene seemed a little off, too. Her answers were short, and she seemed uncharacteristically cranky about working during the weekend, a dramatic departure from Cerene's usual annoyingly chipper, firm-can-do-no-wrong self. It threw off Cerene and Tyler's whole dynamic and left Tyler feeling unsettled. Tyler was accustomed to being talked out of crankiness by Cerene, not the opposite. Brendan was online as well, but only messaged Tyler to check in on her progress on the depo outlines. Tyler typed out a response asking if she was being replaced on the cases, then deleted it and assured Brendan that the outlines and binders would be ready well ahead of time (a lie, Tyler knew she would not finish until the last minute). Harry texted wondering whether Tyler wanted to grab a drink on Saturday, but she pushed him to the following weekend. Late on Sunday, Tyler realized that Officer Armstrong had never responded to her email. Miffed, Tyler forwarded the email to keep the attached time log included and wrote:

Detective Armstrong,

I am emailing to follow up on the below email. Please advise if further information is needed.

-Tyler

Satisfied, Tyler clicked the power icon to log off when her eye was drawn to the murder outline saved on the desktop. Tyler double-clicked the outline and thought about her notes under Motives→personal→affair while Microsoft Word took what felt like a lifetime to open up. Specifically, Tyler thought about what Harry had said about asking direct questions. Tyler could not afford to lose Gina's help by offending her with disrespectful questions, and if Brendan was already trying to replace her on her cases then it certainly was not the time to upset or offend him either. Maybe if Tyler had a little more goodwill built up she would be in a different position... it all came down to professional performance again, or lack thereof. Tyler let out a small, frustrated sigh.

But maybe there were others she could talk to. She highlighted "Professional" on her screen. She had told Detectives Armstrong and Meyer that Kevin was in conflict with Peter Parisi, the office's managing partner. Tyler assumed that had to do with money, since everything at the firm had to do with money in one way or another. But maybe that was too simplistic. The issue could have been power, namely professional advancement. Tyler did not know the ins and outs of what additional power or titles were up for grabs after someone became partner because she had not stopped to think what she would do if she happened to make it that far. But surely there were certain partners who were more important than others, certain partners who wore custom tailored suits while other ones wore suits from off the rack at Saks. Now she was back to money, but Tyler thought there could be something to the idea of a power struggle. Tyler added Peter's name under both "money" and "career advancement/power." Thinking further, Tyler added John's name under "career advancement." She realized she did not know much about John prior to his arrival at the firm. Had it been a big move up for him?

Tyler performed the requisite LinkedIn and Google searches without getting a good sense. John had come from another well-regarded St. Louis firm, so his move did not seem to be such a step up from that perspective. And he had been a partner at the old firm, so it was not as if he received a promotion. Tyler noted both of these facts in the outline. In terms of a career advancement motive, John did not look promising.

Still, something about the timing of the move bothered Tyler. For one thing, Tyler wondered why John, apparently a successful partner at his old firm, had been able to take on Kevin's full load of cases—a workload that had kept Kevin away from his family every weekend and made him leave his family vacations early every year. Had John brought his own clients with him? How could he manage Kevin's caseload, which was completely new to him, and his existing clients? And how had he been able to transfer over so quickly?

When Tyler had observed partners leaving C&E, she noticed that they usually gave a month notice at the very least. Partners were always scrambling to take as many clients with them as possible, thus the month notice period allowed them to notify clients of their impending departure while toeing the line of their non-compete clauses and the Missouri Bar Association's ethical rules. Regardless, Tyler did not get the sense that John had brought any clients. She had not heard about any new cases from Brendan, and as the resident senior associate helping John, he would definitely have heard about them. Certainly, none were mentioned in Peter's welcome email. For that matter, John had brought zero staff or associates with him from his prior firm and had arrived seemingly with no plans to do so down the line. Although, thinking about the tenor of the interactions with John and the mounting pile of documents, Tyler wondered if that might change. Still, it seemed a little unusual that John did not arrive with any thought of bringing his own associates with him, even if he changed his mind later on.

The more she thought about it, the less the timing of John's arrival made sense. In order to change law firms lawyers had to pass a conflicts check—basically, a cross-reference ensuring that a lawyer changing firms would not go from representing a plaintiff to representing a defendant in the same case, or otherwise bring inside knowledge about a client to a case where that would provide an inappropriate competitive advantage. Tyler did not know how far back the check would go, but for a lawyer practicing as long as John, there had to be hundreds of clients that would need to be checked. Those clients, and their parent corporations and all related subsidiaries, would have to be cross-checked against Cloose and Elkman's clients. If there was any whiff of impropriety—even his old firm's client's parent on one side of litigation and Cloose and Elkman's client's parent on the other side, John would have to be screened from the offending matter and the both clients (the one from his old firm on the one side of the litigation and Cloose and Elkman's client on the other side of the litigation) would have to sign a waiver that they consented to the arrangement. It seemed impossible that the whole conflicts check could be completed and resolved in a week. In fact, Tyler's old law school acquaintance had changed firms after only a year and a half of practice, and the acquaintance's conflict check had taken seven weeks. Apparently, John's had been completed had been obtained in only one. Tyler wished she knew someone in conflicts she could ask about how John's check had gotten done so quickly.

All Tyler had for reference was Peter's email welcoming John to the firm. It, of course, said nothing about conflicts checks, anyone accompanying John from his old firm, or why John had wanted to make a change in the first place. She copied it into the outline with the date included and highlighted as a reminder. Tyler wondered whether she had any classmates who worked at John's prior firm who she could ask. As she mulled it over, her phone rang with a private number.

"Tyler McCarther."

"Detective Armstrong." She heard ambient office noises in the background.

"Hi, Detective Armstrong, did you get my email?"

"I did."

"So, you're up to date, you see that I can't have... you know..."

"No, Tyler, an Excel document is not an alibi."

"But, did you see I referenced other things, like my time logs which I think you can get."

Tyler heard a heavy sigh.

"We'll take a look, Tyler, but as I told you, no law enforcement official would accept an Excel document as an alibi."

"Well. Fine." Tyler was disappointed and slightly annoyed— the Excel that the detective was shitting on had taken valuable time to put together—but she figured it was worth one last try to convince him. "You know best, of course, although I really do think that if you take a look you'll see that I simply did not have the time to commit any crimes. And it's not *just* an Excel document, because you can cross-reference what I'm saying with outside sources, so it's more like a guide or an outline as opposed to just an Excel document. I'm just trying to point out here that I am not asking you to accept *only* an Excel document as an alibi." A long pause. "Hello?"

Detective Armstrong grunted.

"Okay, fine! Message received. If you're not calling about my carefully documented timetable slash reference manual to other evidence that would likely be accepted as an alibi, then why *are* you calling me?"

"Your car is ready to be picked up. Actually, it has been for several days, but we haven't had a chance to let you know." *Yeah right*, thought Tyler, remembering Detective Armstrong's rage at not arresting her.

"So, what did you find in the car?"

"That's classified."

"Well, it's my car."

"Well, it's a murder investigation."

"Well... am I under arrest?"

After another long pause, "No."

"Did you pause because you're still deciding whether to arrest me or not or because you didn't want to tell me I'm not under arrest?"

"You can pick up your car at the office on my business card. Ask for Jeannie and she'll help you." He hung up.

Tyler stared at her phone, perturbed. Detective Armstrong was obviously missing the point about her Excel document accounting for her time. She would have to try to explain the concept to him again. She went to call Detective Armstrong again but was reminded by the call log the number was private. She called the number on the detective's business card instead and was sent straight to voice mail. Remembering the ambient noise, she called the St. Louis City police department non-emergency line and was told Detective Armstrong was out of the office, but she could leave a message, which she did.

"Hi, Detective Armstrong, it's Tyler McCarther. I think our call was cut off, but I had a couple more questions. Please call me when you get a chance."

Sighing, she turned back to her computer to assess her plan for the week. As always, Tyler had gotten less done on the weekend than she intended to, and now she was going to have to go to the police station to get her car. Tyler had been renewing her rental car week by week, and it was not due back until mid-week. Since her car had already been sitting unneeded in the police lot for several days, she figured a couple extra would not hurt and decided to pick up the car on Thursday after she returned the rental. Hopefully no one at the office would be looking for her.

The next several days passed uneventfully. Tyler continued to fall further behind on the document review but finished her brief draft and the first depo outline. The brief draft was surprisingly well received by John, so much so that Tyler had some doubts he had actually read it. The depo outline had significantly more comments. As Tyler might have guessed, John did not like the format of the outline or the order of questions. It would have taken John ten minutes maximum to explain his strategy or preferred format to Tyler, but because he waited to tell her what he wanted until after she had completed drafts, she ended up working until two in the morning on Wednesday night updating the outline and re-ordering the exhibits for Thursday.

The next morning, Tyler went to work, confirmed via email with a paralegal that John had what he needed at the deposition and continued her document review. In the early afternoon, hearing nothing from John or Brendan and figuring there would still be a couple hours left in the depo where no one would miss her, Tyler left the office, returned the rental, and Ubered to the police station.

The station was a far cry from the cool marble lobby of Cloose & Elkman where security guards greeted you upon entry, and someone was always mopping the marble floor. The police station had carpeting that might have been patterned at some point in time. It was dingy with an unpleasant musty smell. No one came up to greet Tyler. She looked around and noticed several people, at least one who appeared to be in dire need of a bath, sitting in chairs to the left of the entrance in what seemed to be a waiting area. A cop walked in leading a handcuffed man with a face tattoo and Tyler involuntarily recoiled. She continued to look around, more discreetly now, for the front desk, or someone who might be named Jeannie. Spotting a middle-aged woman in a chest-height desk facing the door, Tyler made her way over.

"How can I help you?" the woman asked in a bored voice, picking up a pad of paper and pencil.

"Hi, are you... Jeannie?"

The woman pointed down at a nameplate on her desk with the word "JEANNIE" printed in large white letters. Tyler felt herself blush.

"Right. Thanks. Well, I'm here because I am hoping to get my car. Detective Armstrong mentioned you might be able to help me. He took it the other week because he wanted to look for evidence?"

"Last name?"

Tyler spelled it.

"All right, one second." Jeannie got up and disappeared into a doorway off to the side of the reception area. Jeannie returned a few minutes later with a paper-clipped packet. "Sign this, hon."

Tyler rummaged in her bag for a pen and leaned over the corner of the desk to sign the form at the top of the packet, which reported the date her car had been taken, a case number, but regrettably no information on what had been found in the car. A uniformed cop walked up to Jeannie with a cup of coffee and asked after her kids. Tyler surreptitiously slid her phone out of her bag and snapped a picture of the form. She glanced over at Jeannie and the cop, whose children seemed to be part of the same youth soccer league, then removed the paperclip from the packet and started taking pictures of each page while pretending to look around the room. She hoped her camera was in focus but could not risk looking down. Tyler had nearly reached the bottom of the stack of papers when she stopped hearing the cop's voice. She quickly shuffled the papers back together and handed them back to Jeannie, smiling.

Jeannie narrowed her eyes, leaned over, and slowly picked up the paperclip Tyler had left on the desk. Willing herself not to start sweating or blushing, Tyler said, "Okay, anything else?"

Jeannie looked down at the packet, which of course now did not have Tyler's signed form at the top. Tyler felt a stab of panic.

"Dropped them, so sorry! The pages must have gotten mixed up, I didn't look I just grabbed them from the floor." Jeannie looked at her with increasing suspicion and quickly flipped through the pages to reorder them. Tyler tried to keep a friendly smile on her face. Jeannie snapped the papers on the desk to align their corners while staring at Tyler, then reached into a drawer in her desk and pulled out a blue slip of paper, copied some information, and signed.

"All right. Take this down to the impound lot and they'll get you the car back."

"So sorry, but where is the impound lot?" Tyler's question was swallowed up by a hearty "Jeannie! My favorite lady!" Tyler whirled around to see Detective Armstrong, wearing a full suit and looking the happiest she had ever seen him.

She and Jeannie spoke at the same time "Tommy!" "Detective Armstrong?"

Detective Armstrong happily greeted Jeannie, then turned to Tyler.

"Did you get my message?" Tyler asked.

Detective Armstrong's face visibly darkened.

Jeannie jumped in, "Ms. McCarther, the impound lot is at Jefferson and Cass." It was a short drive away or a medium walk. That is, if the walker in question did not mind being drenched in sweat in the summer humidity. Tyler had hoped the car would be at the police station and she could get back to work before John was out of the deposition. She glanced down at her phone and saw it was already three thirty and that she had four email notifications. No time to walk.

"Okay, thank you so much for your help, Jeannie." Although Tyler wanted to ask Detective Armstrong more about what he had found in her car, and whether he had her time and cell phone records, she wanted Jeannie to forget the disordered packet more, and she would have to rush to get back to the office by five, when she predicted John would be out of the deposition.

Tyler turned away with the blue slip in her hand and went back outside of the station to call an Uber. As she left, she heard Detective Armstrong telling Jeannie about a trial. It sounded like he had come straight from providing testimony that had gone over well with the jury. Outside, it was sweltering hot and Tyler felt her shirt stick to her back immediately. She wished she had opted to wait in the lobby and run out once the Uber arrived, after all, she had called the Uber to avoid sweating on the walk, but Tyler figured it was better to sweat it out outside than risk additional scrutiny from Jeannie, especially in front of Detective Armstrong. Tyler refreshed the Uber app. Her ride was fifteen minutes away. The drive was five minutes, the walk would be twenty. How was it possible that the closest driver was that far away? Tyler rolled her eyes and started to open up her email application.

"Hey," it was Detective Armstrong again, "I did get your message." He was wearing aviator sunglasses with his suit now. Tyler, who had become somewhat of an expert in men's suits based on what she saw at the Cloose & Elkman office, could see that the material was cheap, but that the suit had been either carefully selected or tailored to fit the detective well.

Tyler looked up at Detective Armstrong, squinting, and crossed her arms, feeling a drop of sweat trickle down from her hairline down her back. "Yes, I had a few more questions, I think our call got cut off, when you hung up on me." Tyler had started the sentence intending to ignore that Detective Armstrong had hung up on her but gave up halfway through. Why bother to be polite? He had done the hanging up, and tact had never really been Tyler's strong suit anyway.

Detective Armstrong smiled, seeming happy at the memory. "I thought you were going to the impound lot," he said, ignoring Tyler's commentary.

Tyler rolled her eyes again. "No car."

"I'm in a good mood, I'll give you a ride, come on."

Tyler hesitated, "I want to sit in the front." That way she could make sure that this was not some sneaky way of putting her under arrest. Tyler wanted very much to ask Detective Armstrong more questions, but his friendly attitude was putting her on edge. Things felt more genuine when he had been barely containing his anger and disgust.

Detective Armstrong had already walked down the stairs of the building to where his car was parked, and he opened the passenger door and gestured dramatically. "Come on down, princess." He still sounded nice, like he was joking with a friend. Tyler narrowed her eyes and flipped her hair over her shoulder, then pressed cancel on the Uber app.

Detective Armstrong was driving a normal Toyota sedan, not a cop car. Tyler glanced to see whether the car contained anything personal, but saw nothing, not even a phone charger. Knowing she had about five minutes until they arrived at the impound lot, she turned to Detective Armstrong. "Can I ask you a couple questions?"

"You can ask."

"So, not to beat a dead horse, but *did* you receive the time logs?"

logs?"

Detective Armstrong shrugged.

"Well, you know, I have my computer right here. I can't show you privileged information, but I can show you times when I was logged into the software."

"We have the records."

"And, you know, I'm happy to sign whatever I would need to for you to see my phone location."

"That's not like what you see on TV, we can't track your phone's location continuously."

"Well, even still..."

"We looked at that, too."

"So... was it helpful *at all?* Was it at least *not harmful?*"

Detective Armstrong sat in silence. Tyler fidgeted, she figured she had two or three minutes left in the drive.

"Look, I just want to know if I'm a suspect still or not."

"It's not 'suspect,' its 'person of interest.'"

Tyler rolled her eyes. "I don't really care about the terminology—am I still a 'person of interest?'"

They sat in silence a bit longer. Tyler saw a sign for the lot coming up.

"You're not." Relief flooded Tyler's body. She had become so tense that she forgot what being relaxed felt like.

"Oh my god, *thank you.*" They were pulling into the entrance to the impound lot. "So, it looks like you did use the Excel as my alibi after all, huh," she added slyly. Detective Armstrong rolled his eyes. Tyler reached for the door handle, but the detective reached over and took the slip of paper from her instead.

"It's a big lot, I'll see where your car is and drop you off there." Detective Armstrong walked over to the kiosk, briefly chatted with the attendant, and came back with Tyler's keys. Tyler reached her hand out and he dropped them in. They drove in silence to Tyler's car. Tyler felt unexpectedly nervous upon seeing the car again.

"So, there's nothing you can tell me about what you found in my   car?"

"It's an ongoing investigation, so no."

"Okay." Tyler opened the car door and swung her legs out. "Hey," she said twisting back. "I've been asking some questions around the office. People don't really want to say anything, but I don't think Kevin was having an affair. And you probably know this, but there's nothing filed online showing either financial troubles or a divorce. Do you know anything about John Delaware taking over all of Kevin's business, though? That happened very quickly. Well anyway, thank you so much for the ride, this was... unexpectedly pleasant!" As she moved to get out of the car Detective Armstrong reached over and grabbed her wrist. Tyler instinctively shook his hand off.

"Why are you asking questions around your office?"

Tyler shrugged. "I guess I felt kind of guilty about Kevin being in my trunk and not telling you about it?" Tyler could not read Detective Armstrong's expression under his aviators, but she thought maybe he was considering changing his evaluation of her. "And you know, I thought also if I could figure out what happened, then you wouldn't arrest *me*. I'll let you know if I hear anything else!"

"We have it under control, leave the investigation to us."

"Well, if you need somebody 'undercover,'" Tyler made the air quotes, "you know where to find me, a non-person of interest, or would it be a person of non-interest? Doesn't matter, I guess."

Detective Armstrong looked like he might say more, but Tyler slid out of the car and closed the door before he had a chance.

Tyler drove back to the office, and made it before John got back from the deposition. She noticed him look into her office out of the corner of her eye as he walked by to see if she was there at six. Luckily, Tyler was reviewing documents and not looking at her phone. When she saw John, she furrowed her brow and clicked randomly on her screen to appear more focused. *Killing it*, she thought, and immediately regretted her word choice.

Later, over a celebratory glass of wine, she told Lucy about the day, explaining, in conclusion, that she had really demonstrated to Detective Armstrong how *not* selfish she was, and how generous with her time she had been—even though she was very busy—not only to ask questions about Kevin around the office, but also to pass it along to the detective. Lucy appeared dubious.

CHAPTER EIGHT

The next morning, despite having two glasses of wine and falling further behind on her document review, Tyler felt energized and light due to no longer being a suspect, or rather no longer being a person of interest. *Who cares what it's called*, she thought, *it's finally some good news*. Her newly energized state powered her through a pre-work Pilates class and Starbucks drive-through. She greeted Gina with a hearty "Happy Friday" and plugged her laptop into its station. As she was waiting for her computer to boot up, Tyler's phone lit up with a call from John.

"Tyler McCarther," she answered brightly.

"Tyler, it's John."

"Morning, John! How did the deposition—"

He cut her off, "See me in my office. Now."

Tyler felt a cold pit open up in her stomach, and the coffee she had drank started to churn unpleasantly. She smoothed down her hair, grabbed her notebook and a pen, and slowly walked around the corner to John's office. John's door was open, so Tyler leaned in and knocked on it to get his attention. John gestured her in from behind his desk, remaining seated.

"Close the door." Tyler cringed but closed the door. John had already moved into Kevin's old office—a Persian carpet in deep shades of red covered up the majority of the firm's neutral carpeting, and several large, extremely healthy-looking houseplants sat next to the floor-to-ceiling windows. It was a little jarring to see the office look so different so quickly, but Tyler had to admit it was quite tastefully decorated.

"So, how did the depo go?" Tyler suspected something bad had happened but was clinging onto the hope that if she remained positive, she could minimize any damage.

John remained silent and stared at Tyler angrily. After a beat, he passed her a couple email printouts. Tyler looked down and tried to remember where she had seen the emails before. They were emails between NSK personnel, and they were Bates-stamped, so the obvious conclusion was that Tyler had reviewed them and marked them to be produced to plaintiff's counsel. The emails concerned an issue flagged by the nose hair wax production line. Tyler vaguely remembered the issue, which had never been spelled out. To her recollection this issue had only been referenced in documents that she had marked "privileged," and therefore that should not have been produced. There were only two possibilities for these documents then: first, either Tyler had missed a mention of the issue in non-privileged documents and had failed to investigate; or second, she had mistakenly coded privileged documents and produced them. Feeling her stomach drop, she started scanning the emails for any attorney names. If she had directed privileged documents to be produced at least she could try to try to claw them back. But if opposing counsel had seen them, the damage was done. Worse, if the documents were privileged, Tyler could have actually waived privilege which would inadvertently allow even *more* documents to be shared with plaintiff's counsel... Tyler breathed a sigh of relief seeing that no attorneys were mentioned or included in the emails. Unfortunately, this meant that Tyler had missed these emails during her document review. She slowly stacked the documents on the edge of John's desk and adjusted them until the edges lined up perfectly.

"Why didn't I have these in my prep materials?" John asked.

Tyler apologized stiffly. She was internally panicking and struggling not to show it. However, she wondered why these documents had come up in the deposition, which she had not anticipated covering anything near that topic.

"No, Tyler, I didn't ask for an apology. I asked, *why didn't you include these emails in my prep materials?*" His voice was starting to rise.

"I guess they didn't seem important for the witness?"

John let out one loud, disbelieving, "Hah!"

"Weren't you deposing the company's former accountant?" Tyler asked quietly. She was struggling to understand how a production line issue might have anything to do with profit earned on nose hair wax.

"An accountant," John paused meaningfully, "whose father worked on the production line."

"So, these documents were brought up?"

"They were, Tyler. Plaintiff's counsel seems to think this issue on the production line is quite important. Imagine my utter humiliation." He paused for dramatic effect. "Utter. Humiliation." Tyler thought he was laying it on a bit thick. "That I had not been made aware of them before the fact. And worse, it's all recorded for posterity in the transcript." John glared at her. Tyler was still trying to deduce how bad the situation had actually been. It seemed extremely unlikely that this witness would have a lot to say about an NSK business unit with which he had no relationship.

"Well, did your witness know anything about it?"

"Irrelevant." John's face remained calm, but he was yelling. The mismatch made Tyler wonder if John had Botox. He seemed vain enough to go for it. John slapped his hand on the desk as if he were in court making an objection. Tyler jumped. She was in a ridiculous situation. Admittedly, she had forgotten about these documents and she should have investigated further when she noticed attorneys were brought in to consult on the issue later on in the thread, but there was no way an accountant testifying about the company's financials and tax returns knew anything about production lines. In other words, Tyler had kind of messed up by failing to investigate the earlier emails in the chain and flag them for Brendan, who handled questions to the client on this sort of thing. But that mistake was not what had John hot under the collar. His complaint made no sense.

"It won't happen again." Tyler had no way of guaranteeing this, and she actually thought it was more likely than not that something like this would happen again seeing as it was an unpredictable occurrence that she could not have prepared for in the deposition outline. However, promises to never make a mistake again were always the right thing to say to an angry partner, and John was clearly not interested in her point of view. John stared at Tyler in silence. It looked like he was doing some kind of breathing exercise.

"See that it doesn't." He had stopped yelling but was obviously still furious. John got up, so Tyler did too, but instead of going to the door as she expected, he walked around the desk to lean against it, facing her. Tyler glanced at the door.

"There's one more thing."

Tyler felt a cross between utter panic and utter annoyance. There was no way for her to prevent random occurrences like not including documents that she still did not think were relevant to the witness's testimony. But whether or not the random occurrences were in her control was irrelevant: if John decided she was off the cases, she would get kicked off, and no one would care whether the reasons made sense or not. She could try to explain her point of view, but from what she had observed during her time at the firm, that was seen as "not taking responsibility" or "deflecting." And, obviously, John was already displeased with her, so he was even less likely than the average partner to take her point of view into account. At the end of the day, John thought she showed incompetence by not including the documents, and her only real choice was to agree, apologize, and do whatever was necessary to avoid the same thing happening again (so, apparently, googling witnesses' family members' occupations).

Reluctantly, Tyler sat down. John sat down on the other visitor chair so that he was angled toward her, and cleared his throat.

"As I'm sure you recall, I asked you that we review documents within a month of receiving them."

Tyler nodded.

"And I'm sure you also recall that I explained that I do not want to be involved on this level in my cases."

Tyler nodded again. The question style made her feel like she was being deposed. Tyler had not technically missed any of her new deadlines, but to be fair that was only because she had not had the opportunity to do so since it had been less than a month since she agreed to turn the documents around within a month. *Off on a technicality*, she thought. Still, Tyler was woefully behind on her review, and she was sure if John had looked at how many documents she reviewed he would know that, too.

"Well, I had some diagnostics run on the Brosby documents, and there are still thousands of documents that we have had more than a month. I thought we were in agreement that you were not going to let documents sit for more than a month."

What? Tyler sat in silence. This was not exactly what she had expected—it was a request as ridiculous as Tyler including the production line email in the depo prep materials. Tyler had agreed to review the documents in John's timeframe, and she admittedly was behind where she would need to be to make that happen, but John had discussed this with her only a few weeks ago, since that time several thousand documents had been uploaded for review, she had written a reply brief, and she had done all of the preparation for John's deposition the day before. This comment, combined with the deposition preparation complaint, was a lot to take in especially when she had already billed sixty-five hours for the week and it was only Friday morning. It was preposterous to expect her to have completed so much work in such a short amount of time. However, since John had now identified two issues, and Tyler still had not forgotten about Brendan's mystery discussion with Cerene, she knew her only choice was to apologize, again, if she wanted to continue working on her cases.

"I'm really sorry, John, I've been pulled in a few different directions with the reply brief, deposition prep, and these documents, but you're right, I agreed to review all documents in a month and it hasn't happened. I'll make sure I catch up as soon as I can."

"You know, this is the second time I've raised this issue with you, Tyler. I don't like to repeat myself. It makes me wonder if I can count on you, and I can't work with associates that can't be counted on."

Tyler continued to sit completely still. She had apologized, for frankly ridiculous complaints, and now it looked like she was going to be kicked off her cases anyway. She felt tears fill her eyes and blinked rapidly. She could not add a very unprofessional meltdown to her list of existing offenses.

"Do you have anything to say?"

Tyler shook her head. She was going to cry if she said anything. She was going to have to try to find another partner to work with or leave the firm. *Humiliating. You're a fucking loser*, she thought. Perfect Cerene would get Tyler's cases. Perfect Cerene would review all documents in a month, magically guess which emails would be brought up in a deposition, and do it all with perfect hair and a can-do attitude. Tyler quickly gathered her phone, notepad, and pen. Before she could get up, John reached out and took hold of Tyler's lower arm. Instead of withdrawing it once she had stopped moving to leave, he kept a firm grip, sliding his hand down to Tyler's wrist. Tyler looked down at her arm as if it belonged to someone else, then up at John, confused.

"I was just thinking," he moved his arm to her knee, "that maybe, this one time, I could look the other way."

Tyler nodded. Something felt wrong, but she could not put her finger on it, and she was still internally catastrophizing about ruining her career by failing to read John's mind.

"Given certain, circumstances," John paused and looked down at his hand, which remained on Tyler's leg, "I could be *convinced* to ignore your mistakes."

"Wait," Tyler was catching up. "Is this like a 'me too' moment?"

John looked confused.

"Are you... propositioning me... to look the other way from me not reviewing thousands of documents in less than two weeks and not identifying a document that you *still* haven't said the witness knew anything about?"

John squeezed her leg a little bit, where his hand remained, but did not say anything.

"Seriously? Is this why you left your old firm so fast? Scratch that... how exactly do you see this going?" She gestured down to his hand, then picked it up between two fingers and removed it. Tyler could not believe this turn of events. While she doubted that anyone at the firm would take her side if John expelled her from the cases she was currently staffed on based on her failing to meet his arbitrary expectations, they absolutely would if she was expelled following her refusal to go along with some kind of fucked up quid pro quo sexual harassment. Especially in today's climate. "Come on, I really want to hear your answer," she continued, "were you thinking like, some light groping, a hand job, a blow job?" John still had nothing to say, and his hands were now folded in his lap. "Sex?! And in exchange for *you looking the other way on a document review?*" John's gaze dropped. Tyler started to giggle. Obviously, what John had tried to do was disgusting, but it was also incredibly stupid, and Tyler knew immediately she could use it to remain on the cases.

John abruptly got up, and after a moment of hesitation, picked the cup holding pens on his desk and threw it against the wall. Tyler flinched and stopped giggling.

"You bitch."

"Okay," Tyler said, with a half-smile. "Whatever. I'm a 'bitch.' But I'm a 'bitch' who you just tried to get unidentified sexual favors—which I'd still like some more detail on to see what value you place on 'looking the other way' for frankly ridiculous non-offenses—in exchange for you ignoring two mistakes. And by the way, I don't even agree that those were mistakes."

John looked like he was searching for something else to throw, and Tyler backed toward the door. "I don't know what you think happened, but it didn't. I provided constructive criticism to you," he pointed at her, "and you are now baselessly accusing me," he pointed back at himself, "of something vile."

"No," Tyler said, drawing out the "o." "We both know that's not true. If that's your story, it's going to be your word against mine." She backed further toward the door in case this set John off again. John seemed to be deflating, so Tyler continued, "Your word, a.k.a. the word of a middle-aged male partner, against mine, a.k.a. the word of a young, vulnerable female associate. In the midst of a general public outcry against this type of behavior. You know, the whole 'me too' movement?"

John leaned his forehead against the wall.

"And my word also happens to be the truth." Tyler paused to make sure no more outbursts were imminent.

"So, here's what's going to happen. *I'm* going to look the other way and pretend that this attempt at sexual harassment didn't happen." Tyler pointed at herself in a parody of John. "In exchange, *you* are going to either let me take the time I need to review the documents, or you are going to allow me to staff two first-year associates to perform the review. Up to you. You can let me know on Monday. Got it?"

John didn't react.

"I'm taking that as a yes." Tyler grabbed the door handle triumphantly, then turned around. When she had noted John's arrival at the firm, she had been thinking only about his move being motivated by professional advancement, but maybe that had been wrong. Maybe John had been moving away from professional ruin and not toward a new book of business. Tyler thought about Harry's advice on asking direct questions, and realized this was possibly the only situation where she could put that advice into practice.

"You're also going to answer some questions. Going back to the beginning of our conversation... did you have to leave your old firm because of similar issues?"

John shook his head.

"John, pretend it's a deposition, I'd like verbal answers. A clear 'yes' or 'no,' please."

"No."

"But I mean, this isn't the first time you've done something like this..."

A pause, "no."

"Maybe somebody more junior, or pre 'me too,'" Tyler mused aloud. "Regardless, you came over to the firm so quickly after Kevin passed away. How were you able to do that?"

"Why do you care?"

Tyler felt her pulse quicken.

"I liked Kevin. I feel bad about what happened to him."

"What happened to him is irrelevant to me joining the firm." Maybe she was onto something here. Why else would John be so reluctant to answer the question? If anything, Tyler would have expected this to be a welcome topic change.

"What? It seems highly relevant. You took over Kevin's cases because he died! If he didn't die, there wouldn't be any cases to take over!" John said nothing. Tyler shot him a nasty look. "Fine, so I guess I will just go back to my office and inform HR of what just happened." John glared at Tyler. "So how did you pass conflicts so fast? How were you prepared to come to C and E so quickly?" John paused again. Tyler was about to get up when John started speaking. She was glad, because she wasn't keen to give up the advantage she had just won over John, which would benefit her professionally, in service of her unofficial murder investigation.

"From my perspective, it wasn't so fast. Kevin's passing was interesting timing." Tyler waited expectantly as John slowly walked back to his office chair and sat down. She wondered if she should be taking notes for her murder outline. "I'd been discussing a move with C and E for several months. I was contacted by someone in recruiting and she told me the firm was looking for someone to take ownership of a sizable block of product liability class actions involving minor injuries. They preferred that the candidate bring their own book of business with them, but the important thing was that the candidate be a lateral partner available to come over by the end of the year, manage the cases well, and make the client happy. It was similar work to what I had been doing, and I wasn't seeing a promising future at my current firm. I was offered equity partnership here, and I was just a salaried partner at the old place, so I went through conflicts and had some quiet discussions. To be clear, I had not accepted the offer yet—we were still negotiating— and the plan was that I would come in at the end of the fiscal year, meaning not until next month. Well, then Kevin passed and Peter Parisi is calling me three times a day and wants to know when I can start. Hell of a negotiating position. With the timing being what it was I brought no clients over, although I'm speaking to a handful now and expect we'll get a few by the end of the year. Meanwhile, I became equity partner at a peer firm."

Tyler digested this information. "So, you were going to take over Kevin's cases even before he died? Why?"

"Because it was a better opportunity for me here. Although until Kevin actually passed, I wasn't sure I would come."

"No," said Tyler impatiently. "Why were Kevin's cases up for grabs?"

"I don't know."

"You didn't ask?"

"You don't look a gift horse in the mouth."

"That doesn't follow. You were offered an opportunity to take over someone else's business. To do so you would undoubtedly burn bridges at your firm. You didn't wonder why this offer existed at all? What if the client was completely unreasonable, or the firm was going to plug you into the cases until the next, newer, more exciting person came around, then kick you to the curb?"

John sighed. "Sure, I wondered. And I asked. Actually, that was one of the things holding me back from accepting the offer to begin with. I never got a straight answer. I was told Kevin had decided to make a career change. I never knew Kevin well, but obviously we've both been in the industry a while, and it's a small market here. That didn't seem like him."

"That doesn't sound like him to me either."

"But we can't ask him anything now. I'm here now, and the cases are mine. As far as I'm concerned, that's that."

"So, you haven't heard anything since you came over? Any gossip?"

John scoffed. "Of course, I've heard gossip, but nothing about Kevin leaving the firm."

Tyler sat forward. "What gossip?"

John waved his hand. "Oh, this and that. Nothing I'd pay too much attention to. And really, it's all in poor taste, the man is dead for Christ's sake."

"Well, I haven't heard anything."

"Of course, you haven't. It was more partner level."

"Come on, what did you hear?"

"Well, I'm sure you've seen the headlines, how they've presented the murder in a... lurid... fashion. It's been things like that, maybe a couple questionable things he did at a partner retreat in Vegas. I wouldn't pay much attention."

"So, like... sexual misconduct?"

"No, that would be going too far. I guess he went to a strip club and did some questionable things in a champagne room, but of course that's just a rumor. And, obviously, it's not a reason to leave the firm."

"No," Tyler agreed. "So, you never asked anybody once you were here? If they knew he was leaving?"

John shook his head.

"And what did Peter say once you accepted?"

"Just that he was happy it worked out and that he was looking forward to having me at the firm."

"Aren't you worried now, that you don't know the full story?"

John spread his hands out, in a *what-do-you-want-from-me* gesture. "No. Tyler, I'm here now, I'm happy with the position I'm in, and I'd very much like to get back to work."

Tyler pursed her lips. "Fine. So let me know what you choose on the document review question. I look forward to hearing from you."

CHAPTER NINE

Back in her office, Tyler quickly typed up notes from her conversation with John, and highlighted Peter Parisi's name. Why would Peter want Kevin to leave? And if Peter wanted Kevin to leave and Kevin wanted to stay, could Peter force him out? Tyler really wished John had gotten more of an idea of why Kevin was leaving. Although, she realized, that was just John's story, maybe Peter would tell a different one. Unfortunately, Peter, as the managing partner of Cloose & Elkman's St. Louis office, was so far above Tyler on the food chain that she rarely even saw him. And if she did see Peter, she certainly could not ask him about why Kevin had been leaving because obviously, she would want to take the opportunity to highlight some of her professional achievements instead of dig up drama. Tyler wondered whether there was any way to fact check what John had told her. Tyler tapped her fingers on the desk while wishing for the second time in a week for a good friend in the conflicts department.

Struck with inspiration, Tyler looked up the matter identification number for one of Cerene's cases, then dialed the conflicts department.

"This is Michael."

"Michael, it's Tyler McCarther. I sit in the St. Louis office."

"Hi, Tyler, how can I help you?"

"Thanks so much, Michael. So, I'm helping John Delaware with some deposition outlines, and he wanted some internal samples to take a look at and maybe use as a starting point. I've found some great ones under matter number 3578.11114690, but John said I should run anything I wanted to use by you to make sure he isn't screened."

"Could you read that one off again?"

"3578.11114690. I think I got the right amount of ones," Tyler laughed.

"Nope. I'm showing no screens. Thanks for being so conscientious."

Shit, thought Tyler, who was going to ask the date that the screen began to see whether it was before Kevin's murder. "Actually, I'm so sorry, its 3578.11114698, I misread that last number. The ones weren't the problem for me after all!" Tyler crossed her fingers.

"Hang on. Okay, that's a merger... I think you had it right the first time, I don't think there will be any deposition outlines associated with that one."

"Oh, you must be right. It looked like an eight! Well, I don't suppose you could just send me a report on John's screens, then I wouldn't have to call every time I want to use some internal materials?"

"Sure, that's no problem, just have him send an email in with that request and we'll get the report over to you right away."

"Okay, thanks so much, I'll definitely do that!" Tyler hung up. She briefly considered asking John to send the conflicts department a request while he was at her mercy but decided not to press her luck. She did not want to risk John calling her bluff about going to HR if she asked for too much, and she also did not want conflicts to mention her earlier call and reveal she had gone behind John's back. Maybe she could try to call again tomorrow and see if she got a different conflicts team member.

Tyler opened up the document review software to continue her review and idly coded a few spreadsheets reporting statistics for the production line (relevant and boring). She mused that she must be an extremely fear-motivated person, because the second that her month turnaround deadlines were no longer looming over her, she had lost interest in reviewing the documents quickly. Tyler took a sip of her Starbucks but gagged when she found it cold and somehow congealed. Grimacing, Tyler decided to go get another coffee. Now that she had more time on her hands, she could go back to Starbucks instead of settling for the office's coffee. Tyler messaged Cerene to see if she wanted to join. Surprisingly, Cerene had time and did want to join. When Tyler met Cerene in the lobby, she was surprised by Cerene's relatively disheveled appearance. Cerene still looked immaculate by an average person's standards, but Tyler counted at least five golden retriever hairs on Cerene's dark wash jeans, and her blue and white striped shirt, normally mysteriously unwrinkled (Cerene had told Tyler shortly after they met that she managed this through "good posture") sat strangely on Cerene's trim frame. Tyler realized part of the collar was flipped up and instinctively reached over to fix it. Cerene flinched.

"Are you okay?"

"Of course!" Cerene tried at her usual bright smile, but it trembled and fell flat. Tyler let it drop and gestured toward the door.

"I'm glad you're okay," Tyler said as they walked the short blocks to Starbucks, "but if you weren't that would be okay, too."

Cerene glared at Tyler with undisguised hostility for a split second, before reverting back to a neutral expression. Tyler noticed that there was concealer caked beneath Cerene's eyes. Tyler felt bad for Cerene, but if she was honest, a part of her was glad that for once Cerene was the one having a harder time. The rest of the trip continued in silence. As the women boarded the elevator back up to their respective offices, Cerene nervously rattled the ice around in her venti cold brew, which she had already drank half of, and without making eye contact, said quietly, "Tyler, do you have a second to talk actually?"

"Of course," Tyler pleasantly thought of the document review she could continue ignoring, although her suspicions about Cerene trying to replace Tyler on her nose hair wax cases remained, and she wondered whether Cerene was about to confess. Tyler hoped not, that would be awkward and friendship ending. But then again maybe Cerene looked like shit because she was feeling guilty. "Do you want to come by my office?"

"Actually, if you could come to mine, that would be better."

"Sure."

When they got to Cerene's office Tyler took hold of the door "I assume this is a closed-door conversation..." Cerene nodded. Cerene looked exhausted despite having drank almost the entire venti coffee in under ten minutes. Tyler felt bad for her, then worried again that the exhaustion resulted from trying to add NSK cases to her already-full caseload. Tyler sat down and waited for Cerene to begin. Cerene laid her hands flat on the desk as if to ground herself. It was a gesture Tyler had not seen before and it made Tyler sit back in her chair in anticipation and maybe a little dread. She noticed Cerene's eyes looked glassy and wondered if she had been staring at a screen too long or if Cerene had been crying.

"Have you ever done something that was just really stupid?" Cerene fixed her gaze a couple feet to the left of Tyler. Tyler leaned forward. This did not sound like the beginning of a work-stealing confession, although "something really stupid" was admittedly quite a broad catch-all.

"Like, at work or in my personal life? I guess it would be a yes either way." Tyler tried to catch Cerene's eye for a chuckle, but Cerene's gaze remained fixed to Tyler's left.

"I think this stupid thing encompasses both." Tyler shifted, not sure what was coming next and feeling uncomfortable about Cerene's change from her normal, confident polished self. At least now Tyler felt relatively sure Cerene was not going to announce she was stealing Tyler's work.

"So, do you remember when I came by Brendan's office the other day?"

"I do." Tyler's guard was back up. A tear rolled down Cerene's cheek.

"Cerene, what's going on? Whatever it is, I'm sure you can fix it."

Cerene angrily shook her head, trying to collect herself.

"I wasn't there to chat about work." So, it was a social visit. Tyler immediately relaxed, but she was having a tough time seeing how having a social conversation with someone was such a dramatic event. Another tear leaked down Cerene's cheek. "He *dumped* me!" she said, spitting out "dumped" like it was a curse word. "Me!" Cerene leaned forward and pinched her nose in between the fingers of her right hand.

"What could he be dumping you from, you don't work with him and you're married to Matt," Tyler asked, realizing her stupidity as the words were coming out. "I'm sorry," she put one hand over her mouth, not sure how to react. "Can I ask questions or do you just want me to listen?"

Cerene just shook her head, properly crying now. Tyler looked around for a tissue box. All she saw were framed portraits of Cerene, Matt, and their golden retrievers. Tyler blushed. "I'll be right back." She left and returned with toilet paper. "Sorry, this is all I could find." Cerene took it and loudly blew her nose. Tyler flinched. It really was disturbing to see Cerene so disheveled.

"So, is this something Matt knows about?" Tyler tried to keep an open mind. She did not see the appeal of open relationships, but obviously there was plenty she did not know about Cerene. Maybe she and Matt were comfortable seeing other people. Cerene shook her head and Tyler felt slightly relieved that her perception of Cerene and Matt had not been completely wrong.

"He would have to talk to me to know that. As it is I see him maybe thirty minutes a day, maybe two hours on Saturdays and Sundays. Even if he knew though, it would be unlikely he'd care, so long as I look good and show up to his firm events with a smile." Cerene gave a bitter smile before pinching her nose again.

"That's tough. So how long have you and Brendan been..." Tyler did not know how to categorize in non-offensive terms what seemed to clearly be an affair. Was dating the right word? And why Brendan? Sure, he was nice enough, but he had never struck Tyler as notably attractive, either physically or in his personality. Certainly not enough to risk a marriage over. Hypothetically for Tyler, of course, as she had never actually been married.

"A couple years."

Tyler tried to conceal her shock unsuccessfully.

"Well, don't look at me like that, you know things have not been good between Matt and I basically since we both started practicing." Tyler did not know that. She had always seen Matt and Cerene as a perfect lawyer power-couple. Two sleek halves making up a rich, bourgeois whole. Tyler thought back to their lunch when Cerene had alluded to things being difficult. If that was Cerene's way of telling Tyler that her marriage had deteriorated to the point where Cerene had started a long-term affair with one of the blandest people around, it had obviously gone over Tyler's head. She could not wrap her mind around the idea that perfect, shiny, polished Cerene had been what, dating? Fucking? Brendan. Of all people.

"I don't think I realized the extent," Tyler said carefully. She was trying to avoid sounding judgmental, but truth be told, Tyler was feeling more than a little bit judgmental about the disconnect between the face Cerene showed the world versus what was apparently actually happening in private. And, if Tyler was honest with herself, she was also a little jealous of Cerene's ability to keep all of these issues under wraps. While Cerene could keep churning out billable hours while juggling two men and pretending to be in a happy committed marriage,

Tyler could not even pretend to take in the news of this situation calmly.

"I mean, we should probably just get divorced at this point. We're roommates! But anytime I suggest things aren't going well Matt is so quick to tell me everything is actually fine and that we'll both have more time soon. He's been telling me we'll have more time soon so long I know it isn't true and it will never happen, but I just don't have the energy to do anything about it. I don't work quite as much as Matt, but I'm no slouch, and to be honest I can't see where I would find the time to even begin to seriously consider a divorce." Tyler understood that sentiment perfectly and nodded. Cerene's tears had slowed. Tyler awkwardly reached out to give Cerene's hand a pat, and Cerene hungrily snatched Tyler's hand and squeezed it.

"Thanks so much for listening. This is what best friends are for though, right? I'd do the same for you, of course." Tyler, again, tried to hide her surprise. She did not realize she was Cerene's best friend. She thought they were more like work buddies. Although to be fair, Tyler did talk to Cerene more frequently than anyone else, and she did know more about Cerene's day-to-day life than any of her other friends. So, maybe Cerene was on to something. Luckily, Cerene had started crying again and did not seem to notice Tyler's reaction.

"Oh, Cerene. Gotta say... did not see this coming. So, are you sad about Matt, or Brendan, or both?" Cerene opened her mouth to try to answer but started crying harder. Tyler sat holding Cerene's hand and awkwardly gave it a pat.

Changing strategies, Tyler continued, "Do you want to hear something funny? When you came by Brendan's office I thought he was trying to replace me with you. On the nose hair wax cases."

Cerene rolled her eyes. "That's just like you."

"I won't ask what that means." Tyler thought about being offended, but the insult—or was it just an observation? —felt closer to Cerene's typical style of communication, so she hoped it meant Cerene was feeling a little more like herself.

"I'm serious. Obviously, I'm not getting along with John, and I thought maybe the instruction had gone out to find someone to replace me with. It literally never crossed my mind that you might speaking to Brendan because you had a personal relationship." Tyler's judgmental side prevented her from saying "dating." "Are you going to be okay?" Tyler continued. "Can you take the afternoon?"

Cerene laughed. "God no, to both."

"Can you at least work from home?" Tyler eyed Cerene's puffy eyes and general disheveled state.

"Maybe that's a good idea."

Tyler thought leaving the office was a must for Cerene. "Definitely. You'll be okay." Tyler looked intently at Cerene until she met Tyler's eyes and nodded. "Well, once you get more time, we should do another happy hour." Tyler knew her response was inadequate, but it was the best she could do. And even though Tyler no longer felt quite the burning need to bill her time, it had become habit by this point to cut off personal conversations after about fifteen minutes (0.25 or 0.3, depending on whether the client billed by the quarter hour), which it felt like they had hit. Tyler gave Cerene an awkward hug—Cerene remained sitting in her chair and Tyler bent down, hair swinging forward to hit Cerene in the face—then left. As she gently closed Cerene's door, Tyler heard her loudly blowing her nose on the remaining soggy, mascara-stained toilet paper. Tyler shook her head. Cerene really needed to go home.

Back on her floor, Tyler walked the long way to her office to avoid walking by Brendan's and shut her door. The last two days had really turned her perceptions on their head. John was potentially, well, definitely, a serial sexual harasser, Tyler was no longer worried about John cutting off her work, and Cerene and Brendan were not perfect robot associates like Tyler had always assumed.

Tyler wanted to talk to someone about all these revelations, but who? She talked to her family so rarely she would have to explain who Cerene, Brendan, and John were before explaining the last few days' revelations. Having to explain the entire backstory and identity would take too long. Harry would probably be interested. Tyler typed out a text message to him, then deleted it, remembering the awkward end to their last date. She still associated Harry with that awful night and felt increasingly confident she did not want to see him again. Struck with inspiration, Tyler realized she knew someone who was just as vested in her office's interpersonal dynamics as she was.

Detective Armstrong—I have some interesting information to share with you.

The response came almost immediately: *Don't text me.*

No seriously, you'll be interested! This info might be helpful to your case!

Detective Armstrong's phone showed the "... " bubble as he typed, then it disappeared. Tyler called Detective Armstrong's number and was diverted to voice mail. "Detective. Tyler McCarther here. I have some interesting information to share with you. Please give me a call."

Annoyed, Tyler silenced her phone and slid it into a desk drawer. She did not want to see if Detective Armstrong responded— let him wait for her. An unproductive afternoon followed. Tyler reviewed documents half-heartedly and checked for the court's disposition on the motion to compel for which she had drafted the reply brief. Nothing. She remembered she had another deposition outline to make for John, this time for a named plaintiff who had allegedly developed a persistent itchy rash after waxing his nose ahead of his wedding. The deposition was not scheduled for another week and a half, so Tyler did little but make the skeleton of the outline based on John's comments on the last witness. She sarcastically wondered whether she should throw in some documents regarding NSK's tax returns in case this guy was cousins with someone on the NSK audit team. Tyler could not resist checking her phone periodically to see if Detective Armstrong had returned her call or text. She limited herself to checking once every half hour and grew more annoyed each time her phone showed zero notifications. Fed up and restless, Tyler decided to take a Pilates class at 4:30.

Tyler could not remember the last time she left the office so early (other than on a Friday) and felt uneasy. She gave herself a mental pep talk about how crazy the last few weeks had been, and how she was on track to bill plenty of time for the year, but somewhere in the back of her mind she wondered what would happen if she made a habit of leaving early. She should ask for more work. In the Pilates parking lot Tyler made eye contact with herself in the rearview mirror. "You're driving yourself crazy. Stop it." Tyler was entitled to leave early every now and again, and besides, all that mess with John had to mean she had the right to fall a little behind on document review and catch a few early Pilates classes without negative consequences.

Tyler went straight from Pilates to Whole Foods to pick up groceries and re-stock her wine. After loading up her car, she checked her emails and was surprised to have nothing but a few newsletters. It was almost seven. Tyler felt untethered with an entire evening stretching ahead of her without any pressing work to do. She wondered again if she should reach out to Brendan or John to ask for more work. Tyler had heard to "enjoy the slow times" at work but had never succeeded in taking that advice. The problem with being slow was that you never knew whether you were slow for a day, a week, a month, or forever. And obviously Tyler did not want to be slow forever. The only way to make sure a slow day was not the start of an extended period was to ask for more work. But, on the other hand, asking for more work would mean interacting with Brendan or John, both of whom she felt awkward speaking to at the moment. On top of that, if Tyler asked for more work and this turned out to be just a short slow period, she would have too much to get done. And on top of *that*, Tyler was not even slow, she had tens of thousands of documents to review. Tyler sighed and drove home.

Tyler unloaded her groceries and took out the box she had carried the wine bottles in. As she popped a bottle of white into her freezer to chill, Tyler noticed that her back door was unlocked. That was strange. Tyler used the back door solely for taking out the trash, which she knew she had not done for several days. Had the door been unlocked the entire time? How irresponsible.

Immediately feeling impatient, Tyler pulled the bottle of wine out of the freezer and poured herself a generous glass. Since no one was around to see her being tacky, she put three ice cubes in. They dropped in with a satisfying plop, and the smell of the wine wafted up tantalizingly. Sipping thoughtfully, Tyler considered whether to eat her meal from the hot bar at Whole Foods off a plate like an adult or straight out of the box like she wanted to. Disliking the thought of dishes, Tyler brought the box to her kitchen table. As she sat down, she realized she had not seen Lucy yet, which seemed out of character. Tyler walked up her stairs to see if Lucy was sitting at the foot of her bed—a favorite spot—and stopped, shocked. Her dresser drawers were open and her clothes were halfway pulled out. Her closet door was closed. Not fully processing that someone had been in her house and might still be there, Tyler slowly walked to the closet door and opened it. A frightened Lucy ran out, and Tyler screamed, the gravity of the situation hitting her. The musty smell of cat pee wafted out of the closet and Tyler saw that her clothes and hangers were pooled on the ground.

"Hello?" Tyler called. Her voice shook. She felt around her pockets for her phone, but realized it was downstairs on her kitchen table. *Stupid,* she thought. *And as if a burglar would answer you.* Trying to think logically, Tyler determined that it was unlikely that the intruder was still in her house. After all, they had broken in when she was gone, and she had come home at a fairly reasonable time, meaning the intruder must have arrived during normal working hours. Even so, confronting an intruder without a phone, or at all, was pretty foolish.

Tyler slowly backed out of the room and ran down to her kitchen when she reached the stairs. Snatching the phone up, Tyler redialed Detective Armstrong. She was breathing heavily. Luckily, he picked up this time.

"I'm not interested," came the brusque response.

"No—please—I need help. Someone was in my house."

"What?" Detective Armstrong sounded confused but still annoyed.

"Someone... was... in... my... house!" Tyler shrieked, "And I think they're gone but they might not be!"

"This isn't about your text?"

"No! It's about a robbery... a burglary? Can you help?"

Detective Armstrong sighed. "I'll be over. I'll have a squad car swing by as well."

"Should I go outside in case the person is still here?"

"You could, but I think you would know by now if someone was still there. And burglaries in your neighborhood are pretty routine. No one ever gets hurt, these people really want to get in and out while the resident is gone. They're after stuff, trying to make a quick buck. These people don't want to see you any more than you want to see them. You should be okay to wait, just stay where you are." Before Tyler could respond, Detective Armstrong hung up.

Tyler stood clutching her phone. "In case you're still here there are cops on the way and they'll be here very soon," she yelled. After a few minutes, Tyler went and sat on her couch, where she could see into the kitchen and to the front door. Lucy jumped up on the couch and joined her.

About fifteen minutes later a marked cop car showed up, and two solid older cops, one sporting a thick gray mustache, came in. Non-mustache carried a large black case. They introduced themselves and Tyler forgot their names as soon as she heard them. The one without a mustache said gruffly, "Heard there was a break-in." Tyler briefly explained. The cops seemed unfazed and nodded. Tyler nervously told them that because she had not looked in every room the intruder might still be there. "Doubt it," said mustache, but they dutifully went upstairs, came back down, and opened all her closets.

Tyler offered the cops water, which they declined. They invited her to sit down at her kitchen table because they had a few routine questions. Tyler felt a strange sense of déjà vu. Two cops, but this time in uniform. Again, she was being asked questions, but this time she was the victim. And to be fair she was *kind of* a victim the other time, too, because someone had put a corpse in her trunk for several hours for reasons that remained unclear to Tyler, but at the time Detectives Armstrong and Myer had not known that. These cops asked very different questions. Who had a spare key to Tyler's house (no one but her landlord), whether she kept spare keys hidden anywhere (no, but it was probably a good idea), and whether she was sure she had locked the back door (pretty sure, but hard to say for a fact), and whether anything was missing (no idea).

"Okay," said mustache, slapping his knees, "that's it on the questions front. Last thing is, we'd like you to take a look around and let us know what's missing." They wanted to start downstairs, but Tyler assured them everything looked the same. They noted that Tyler's TV had not been taken and regarded it skeptically.

"It's not new or anything," Tyler observed.

"Looks nice enough to me. TVs are *always* taken," no-mustached responded, shaking his head.

The group walked upstairs, and Tyler explained how her bedroom typically looked, versus how it looked now. She did not see anything missing. The cops pointed out her jewelry box, which was lying upside down on the floor. After receiving permission, Tyler picked it up, and saw that her jewelry was lying on the floor—none of it had been taken as far as she could tell. The bathroom appeared to not have been touched. The second bedroom, which Tyler had set up as an office, was in similar disarray to Tyler's bedroom. Tyler looked around for her iPad and noted to the officers that it was missing. Her monitor and keyboard had been knocked to the floor but were intact as far as she could tell. No-mustache pointed out that these items would typically be removed in a burglary. Mustache shrugged. Tyler luckily had her firm laptop with her, and she only ever brought paper documents home in her laptop bag, so at least she had no concerns about client information getting out. At mustache's suggestion, Tyler tried to locate her iPad on her "find my phone" app, but the iPad had been wiped.

"Typical. It was worth a try," said mustache. "Well, we'll try to get a few prints, but no promises." Tyler hovered in the doorway of her bedroom while the detectives unpacked the case and spread a thick black powder over her dresser. Feeling a little superfluous, she hugged her arms around her waist and leaned against her door frame. After the detectives had moved to the office, noting that it looked like the intruder had worn gloves, Tyler's doorbell rang.

"Prob'ly the boss," said mustache. "Detective Armstrong," he added. Tyler knew that it was most likely Detective Armstrong at the door, but felt anxious nonetheless that whoever had broken into her house had returned. She stood looking at the two cops hoping one would get the door, or at least accompany her, but they continued to leisurely coat her desk in the same black substance. *Obviously, the burglar wouldn't ring your doorbell. Get it together*, she thought.

Tyler slowly walked to her stairs. As she descended, Detective Armstrong's now familiar frame became clear through the wavy glass at the top of her door. Tyler opened the door and surprised herself by bursting into tears.

"Come in," she said, "Please ignore... this," gesturing to her face. Tyler was too embarrassed to look at Detective Armstrong and see his reaction. Instead, she motioned him in while looking firmly up and to the right. She saw him walk in through the corner of her eye, and as he passed he gave her arm a little pat. Still looking away, Tyler wondered if the pat was meant to be reassuring or if it was Detective Armstrong's uncomfortable reaction to her outburst. Tyler locked the door behind Detective Armstrong then walked to the kitchen and ripped a paper towel off a roll on her counter to wipe her face.

"They're upstairs," she said into the paper towel. She did not look up until she heard the stairs creaking. Tyler splashed some cold water on her face to try and collect herself. She tried to wipe the mascara from under her eyes with the paper towel and felt the area redden with irritation. She sat back down at her kitchen table and looked blankly at the Whole Foods dinner. Her stomach started to churn, so she threw the box in the trash untouched. She gazed longingly at the glass of wine, which was undoubtedly room temperature now and slightly watered down, but was not sure what the cops would think about her drinking while they investigated her apartment. Tyler thought she should probably go upstairs to see if Detective Armstrong and the cops needed help but felt completely drained of energy. Instead, she leaned forward and laid her cheek on her table and stared at her kitchen cabinets, trying to distract herself from the situation by mentally listing her outstanding assignments at work.

CHAPTER TEN

Some time later—Tyler had dissociated from the situation so it could have been anywhere from five to fifty minutes—Tyler heard the stairs creak under several pairs of feet and sat up. Embarrassingly, she had drooled onto the table and hurriedly covered the spot with her hand. Detective Armstrong and the officers (Tyler still could not remember their names and their nameplates were too small for her to make out from across the room) came in. Detective Armstrong briefly explained that this appeared to be a fairly routine burglary. Her back door showed no signs of tampering, so they guessed she had left it unlocked. The burglar had worn gloves, so the officers had not been able to capture any prints, but Tyler was very lucky because only her iPad had been stolen. Unfortunately, the iPad was unlikely to be recovered, but no-mustache handed Tyler a card with a number to call where she could register the ID number of the iPad to be flagged if it were to ever be recovered or found among other stolen goods. Tyler thanked no-mustache. She had no idea what the license number on the iPad was, and knew she was not going to go through the effort of figuring it out. The officers shook Tyler's hand and left. Tyler remained sitting in a daze.

Detective Armstrong glanced at her, then went to lock her front door and came back to sit across from her at the table. "You okay?"

"I'm fine." She stared down at the crumpled, mascara-stained paper towel sitting on the table and tried not to cry.

"You look a little... not fine."

"It's creepier than I expected." Tyler looked up at Detective Armstrong and was surprised to see him looking back at her with concern instead of his usual cold gaze. "Thanks for coming." She tried to smile but almost started crying again.

"Maybe you should have some of that." Detective Armstrong nodded at the wine. "And do you have any sugar? That seems to help too."

Tyler found an old bag of chocolate chips at the back of her cabinet and ripped them open. She ate a few, then drank a small sip of wine.

"You must have somewhere else to be, Detective, I'm okay."

"Actually, I was off duty when you called." Tyler noticed then that the detective was wearing a T-shirt and jeans, as opposed to the more business casual button-ups she had seen him wearing each time she had encountered him before.

"Oh... well, then, I'm sure you'd like to get back to your time off." Tyler felt awkward that Detective Armstrong had come personally during his time off. "I guess I should have just called 911. Or the police station."

"I'm never really off, so it's okay."

Tyler nodded and drank more wine. "Those officers seemed to think it was unusual what was taken, or not taken." She watched Detective Armstrong for his reaction.

He shrugged, "I wouldn't think much of it. All-in-all, this was a routine burglary, like I said, very common for the area."

"Lafayette Square?" Tyler thought she lived in a pretty nice neighborhood.

"Yeah, sure," Detective Armstrong rubbed two fingers together in a "money" gesture, "Good stuff to take." Tyler nodded.

She hoped Detective Armstrong was right but felt paranoid nonetheless—this was now two criminal occurrences happening around her in a month. She was not sure whether either occurrence had happened *to* her, strictly speaking, but Kevin's body in her trunk certainly felt personal. Detective Armstrong seemed to think this burglary was routine, which would make it not personal, but it was hard for Tyler to see her clothes ripped out of her dresser and strewn on the floor and not feel a personal element. She wanted to ask Detective Armstrong what he thought but remained wary that making any suggestions might lead him to rethink her current status of not being a person of interest. And, because Detective Armstrong had refused to tell her anything about what was found in the trunk of her car, she was not sure whether he and Detective Meyer believed her about finding Kevin's body and it subsequently being removed. Tyler looked more intently at Detective Armstrong. He had been so nice this evening, again, and she wondered if there was a catch or an ulterior motive she was missing.

"I guess I just can't help but wonder if this had anything to do with, you know, finding Kevin's body in my trunk..."

"Highly, highly doubtful."

As always, Tyler could not resist one last push. "It just seems like it might have been weird that only my iPad was taken. Especially because of how messed up my stuff got. Like maybe the burglar was searching for something else, something specific?"

"Not so weird. If this was one person burglarizing your house, the iPad was the easiest thing to pick up and carry. Not to mention, no one would notice someone carrying an iPad out of a house, not like carrying large electronics. I'd guess your clothes and office were tossed because the burglar was looking for cash, too. Plenty of people keep cash in their house, for the most part in their private spaces."

Tyler looked down into her wine glass, almost half empty now. She was not completely convinced, but what Detective Armstrong said made a lot of sense. She was probably just reacting like anyone else would to having a stranger come into her house while she was gone and touch her things, feeling paranoid was probably normal.

Detective Armstrong started looking around her kitchen restlessly. Tyler guessed he was planning on leaving soon, and although it embarrassed her, she was afraid to be left alone in the house and felt comforted by his presence.

"A little different than last time, right?"

"Hmm?"

"I mean, it's a little different than the last time you were here. I was a suspected criminal, now I'm the victim." Detective Armstrong nodded vaguely. "I'm not a suspected criminal now, am I?"

"Well, if you want to get technical, you're an admitted criminal. You hindered the progress of our murder investigation, and you also found a dead body and failed to report it to the police."

"So, the evidence *did* show that Kevin was in my trunk?"

Detective Armstrong laughed for what Tyler thought might be the first time since she met him. "You are relentless."

"Thank you."

"It wasn't a compliment."

"It is to a litigator." Tyler smiled sweetly. "So that's what the evidence showed? That Kevin was in my trunk?"

Detective Armstrong held his hands up in defeat.

"I'm taking that as a 'yes.'" Tyler was still trying to delay Detective Armstrong leaving. And she was surprised to realize she was actually enjoying his company. "Hey, so you're off work," she stood up, picking up her empty glass, "I'm having another, do you want to join me?" Detective Armstrong seemed to hesitate. It was probably not professional to have a glass of wine with someone involved in his investigation. The nice thing to do would be to back off and let Detective Armstrong leave, but Tyler thought if she could get Detective Armstrong to have a glass of wine he would stay longer. Additionally, she thought if he blurred the professional and personal boundary between them, it might bond them over a secret of sorts and he might tell her more about the investigation.

"Here's what I'll do. I'll pour you a glass and put it in front of you, and then you can do whatever you want with it. It'll be yours to drink or not drink. You can pour it down the sink if it's too much temptation!" Detective Armstrong sat more stiffly in his chair but smiled. Tyler smiled to herself as she got another glass down from her cabinet and poured almost the entire remaining bottle between the two glasses. She sat back down at the table, swirled the wine—less than she might have been able to otherwise because the glass was extremely full—and took an exaggerated sip. "Pretty tasty. It really hits the spot. Just saying!"

Detective Armstrong did not reach for his glass. Tyler looked pointedly at it but knew if she pushed too hard he might get uncomfortable and leave. The more she thought about Detective Armstrong leaving and sitting alone in her ransacked house the more she wanted the detective to stay.

"Oh! Should I give you a snack?" Tyler had just gotten groceries but did not have anything that was presentable while entertaining. "I have... baby carrots? Apples? I had an entire meal from the Whole Foods hot bar but I threw it in the trash because I was upset." Tyler cut up two apples and poured some baby carrots on the cutting board as well. She also found some hummus that she had opened the week before. She surreptitiously sniffed it. It smelled fine, so she put that out too. Detective Armstrong looked at the cutting board and plastic container of hummus doubtfully. Tyler did not blame him. It was far from her best offering. Detective Armstrong took one baby carrot. His crunching sounded loud in the kitchen as Tyler sat staring at him. Then he took a small sip of the wine. Tyler beamed. She looked down to see that a third of her glass was gone already, and on her empty stomach she was feeling a little tipsy already. Her body buzzed pleasantly and made it easier to ignore that she had been burglarized. And now she could postpone being alone in her house a little longer.

Tyler leaned her chin forward in her hand, "So, now that we're drinking buddies, can I call you Tommy?"

Detective Armstrong shook his head in confusion, clearly not sure where Tyler had gotten this nickname.

"That's what your pal Jeannie calls you."

"Right. Well, she's really the only one other than my mom who calls me that. You can call me Tom though."

"Okay, Tom." They sat in silence a few minutes, sipping their wine. Detective Armstrong ate a few slices of apple but did not touch the hummus and carrots. Tyler finished the container and threw it away. While she was up she split the remains of the wine bottle between their glasses. It was barely an ounce or two each. Detective Armstrong, or Tom now, tried to pull his glass away but Tyler laughed and put her hand down on the base of the glass, touching his hand, which felt warm and larger than she expected. He twitched a little but did not pull away.

"I'd really like to show you something," Tyler said, "but if you still don't want to talk about it, I won't." She hesitated, then decided to be honest, "I really don't want to be here alone right now, so if it makes you want to leave, just let me know and I promise I'll drop it."

"Okay," Tom said.

Tyler pulled out her work laptop and opened up her murder outline. "I kind of told you about this when you took me to get my car. It's a sort of outline of the questions I've been asking."

Tom seemed like he was trying not to laugh.

"What? It's good to organize your thoughts, and I told you I'd been doing some investigating!"

"Well, first, I will say—again—that you should leave police work to the police. But I have to say, you're bringing a few firsts to this case. I'd never seen an alibi presented in Excel format, and I've never seen an outline like this into a murder investigation."

"So, this isn't how you do it?"

"No." He seemed amused that Tyler thought he would be making outlines.

"Really? I thought this made so much sense."

"I'd say that you're going about it backwards—we look at what the evidence says and follow that, then try to figure out a motive once the evidence identifies a person of interest. The motive is always helpful, but the goal is to find a perpetrator and build a case the prosecutor will take. And for that what you really need is evidence."

"I see." Tyler felt a little disappointed. She knew her information was limited but she thought she had come up with at least some good ideas.

Tom seemed to take pity on her. "But this makes sense for you. Obviously, you have no evidence." Tom angled the computer toward himself a little more and began to read through the notes. As Tom read, Tyler thought about how she might be able to incorporate the police's evidence-based inquiry into her investigation. She suddenly remembered the pictures she had taken at the police station. She should have looked at those immediately and put them into the outline. Tyler did have some evidence, whether she was supposed to or not, and maybe it could help her figure out what happened to Kevin.

Tyler watched Tom as he read. His lips moved slightly as he scrolled, slower than Tyler would have expected. His face was slightly flushed and shiny, which was explained by the almost-empty wine glass sitting beside him. He was larger than Tyler remembered. Tall, but as she now remembered noticing when she first met him, solidly built and not seeming to be in particularly good shape. Tyler wondered if she should open another bottle of wine. She herself was just tipsy enough to think more was a good idea. She decided to get glasses of water instead. Tyler set Tom's water in front of him as he finished reading the outline.

"Thanks. So, this is what you were calling me about today?"

"Yeah... specifically the John stuff." Tom looked a little confused. "John Delaware. I take it you aren't investigating him."

Tom started to shake his head, then thought better of it. "For the last time, I'm not discussing an open investigation with you."

"What do you think, though, that timing doesn't seem a little weird to you?" Tom shrugged. "It is weird. It should seem weird to you," Tyler said insistently. She tried to explain the conflicts check process and how long that might take, but due to the wine her explanation was long and rambling, with too many tangents, and she could tell Tom was not following. Eventually he cut her off.

"Sounds like you know more than me on whether this timing is suspect, but more than that, it sounds like you just don't like John."

"Well, no, of course not. Have you met him?" Tom shook his head. "You'd get it if you met him. Trust me. So, if you haven't met John then I guess you aren't considering Kevin's work to have anything to do with what happened."

Tom looked like he was about to say something, then stopped. "If you don't stop asking me questions about this investigation I'm going to have to leave." He looked a little disappointed about that.

"It's okay." Tyler sighed. "I have trouble hearing 'no.' I'll drop it."

"Its an interesting idea," Tom said in an appeasing tone, "but for what it's worth it seems more like that information points to Peter Parisi than to John Delaware."

"Unless Kevin really *was* planning on leaving the firm. Then it points nowhere."

Tom paused, then said, "Let's just say, hypothetically, that it didn't seem like Kevin planned on leaving." Tom looked meaningfully at Tyler, and she nodded, appreciative that he was sharing even a tidbit of information.

"Well, I guess that's the end of the road for me then. It's not like I'm going to be asking the managing partner of my office anything about murders."

"Good. So, you'll do that I've been telling you to—knock this off." Tyler felt a twinge of annoyance—she still thought it was foolish to overlook Kevin's work as a potential motive—but she was starting to feel a deep exhaustion settling into her body, undoubtedly the aftermath of her adrenaline running so high added to the wine.

"Can I ask you for a weird favor?" Tyler looked hopefully at Tom, who grimaced. "It's not related to your investigation whatsoever, don't worry. It's just that I have to clean everything up, upstairs. I don't think I'll be able to sleep if I don't. Would you sit with me while I do that? If it's not too much trouble. I can open another bottle. Or you can have some bourbon or a cocktail." Tyler looked down, afraid Tom would leave and not sure what she would do then.

Tom seemed to be hesitating, but he nodded. "One more glass, and I'll order a pizza."

"Thank you." Tyler gripped Tom's arm briefly, and this time he did not flinch. Then she stood to open a second bottle of wine and poured each of them another glass. She still felt pleasantly buzzed and stopped short of the oversized glasses she had poured before, but not by much. Tom got out his phone to order the pizza. They walked upstairs.

"Let's start in the office." She pulled out the office chair for Tom and set her monitor and keyboard back on her desk. She could not remember exactly how the contents of the desk drawers had looked, but she knew they had not been particularly organized, so Tyler scooped up the miscellaneous pens and Post-its from the ground and threw them back into the drawers haphazardly. Detective Armstrong had sat down in the chair as directed by Tyler, but stood after only a few seconds. As Tyler tidied up, he walked over to a window and looked out.

"One second." Tyler returned downstairs to her kitchen for a roll of papers towels and some all-purpose cleaning spray. As she wiped down everywhere the uniformed officers had spread the thick black powder, Detective Armstrong returned to the chair and sipped his wine.

"How long have you lived in St. Louis?"

"Not long," Tyler answered. "Moved here for law school, then stayed for the Cloose & Elkman offer."

"And you've been there three years?"

"Yeah." Tyler scrubbed at a particularly stubborn spot on the doorframe of the office.

"So, six years in St. Louis. Because law school is three years?"

Tyler nodded. "When you say it like that, it seems a little longer." Spot removed, Tyler walked to the desk to wipe the remaining powder away. Thinking, she walked to the bathroom to wet the paper towel—she was not sure whether the cleaner was safe for the wood desk. Tom scooted the chair further away to give her space.

"I'd say six years is a pretty good amount of time."

"Why do you ask?" Tyler spotted some more powder which had blended into the black plastic of her computer monitor.

"You've been here six years, but it doesn't seem like you have many friends in town."

Tyler jerked. "Of course, I do."

"And that's why none of them are here."

Tyler looked at Tom, confused and stung. She thought they were getting along. "Not every friend is someone you want to call in a crisis. If you wanted to go, you should have just left."

"Sorry," Tom looked down at his feet. "I didn't mean to offend you."

"How do people typically react when you call them friendless? And I notice you came over here on your night off—a Friday. Where are your friends?"

"I'm sorry," Tom said again. Tyler gathered the used paper towels together and clutched them tightly in her hands. Visually, the office looked the same as it had before the burglary, but Tyler still had a creepy feeling from the knowledge that a stranger had rummaged through her life uninvited, touching her Post-its and pens and the desk where she worked every night... Tyler shook her head briskly to shake herself out of that particular spiral of thoughts. The room spun slightly. Tyler looked from left to right more deliberately and noticed the room took a minute to come back into focus each time she moved her gaze. She had drunk too much.

"My best friend, I'll have you know, is going through a crisis of her own. She doesn't need to be bothered with my problems," Tyler said formally, carefully enunciating each word. She fully realized the hypocrisy of referring to Cerene as her best friend given her reaction to Cerene saying the same thing earlier that day.

"Seriously. I'm sorry. I don't know why I do that sometimes— I don't have to say everything I think out loud. And you're right, I wasn't doing anything on my night off. My friends are married with kids, and I canceled the last date I had scheduled to attend an after-hours autopsy."

Tyler was not sure how to react and was having trouble keeping up with Tom's abrupt changes in tone, so she threw the used paper towels in her wastebasket without making eye contact, then gathered the spray and the paper towels and walked to her bedroom. She tossed the cleaning supplies on her bed and grabbed her laundry basket from a corner. It was filled with unfolded clean laundry, but Tyler wanted to wash everything that the burglar might have touched, so she planned to throw the clean clothes straight back into the washing machine. Tyler put her hands on her hips and stared at her ransacked dresser, trying to figure out where to start. The clothes felt contaminated, and she did not even want to touch them. Gingerly, Tyler started picking up each item of clothing that was dangling outside of a drawer, using her thumb and forefinger.

Tom walked into the room and cleared his throat. Tyler ignored him and kept throwing clothes into the basket. Stupidly, she felt tears prick her eyes.

"So, um, should I go then?" Tyler saw out of the corner of her eye that Tom had already walked over to the top of the steps.

Tyler sighed but kept looking at her laundry basket to hide her glassy eyes. Purposefully keeping her voice even, she said, "No. It's okay. For future reference though, most people are not going to react well to being called friendless." She picked up a few more workout tops and threw them on the basket, where they slithered down onto the floor. The basket was overflowing and there was still half the room and the closet to cover. "Plus, I guess you already told me what you thought of me the first time we met—selfish." Tom shifted foot to foot. He was cradling the wine glass in between his hands. He looked chagrined but did not disagree with her.

The doorbell rang and Tyler jumped, spilling some clothes off the top of the heaped laundry basket. "It's the pizza," Tom said.

"Oh, duh," Tyler smiled with relief. As she walked by Tom, he reached out and pulled her into a hug, the back of one of his hands cradling her head. The other hand held his glass of wine which sloshed onto her shirt a little. Tyler wondered if Tom was also a little drunk, but relaxed into his chest, noticing a slight paunch. It felt cozy. The doorbell rang again and Tom dropped his arms.

Back in the kitchen, Tyler grabbed two plates. The pizza smelled amazing and was a size larger than she had expected. Lucy jumped onto the table and Tyler threw her back on the ground.

"Glad somebody is feeling like themself again."

"You will too."

Tyler smiled, "Is that a professional assessment?"

Tom nodded as he ate half of a slice of pizza in one bite. Lucy jumped on the table again and Tyler walked her out of the room and put her on her couch. When she came back Tom was eating his second slice of pizza. She noticed he had finished his wine. Tyler was surprised to find she was starving, and they quickly finished the pizza. Tyler wondered how the calories compared in half of a large, fresh pizza to an entire frozen pizza. Neither option was Tyler's best dietary decision, but she was due a little leeway after being burglarized so she decided not to worry about it. Tyler loaded the plates into her dishwasher.

"Back to it?" said Tom. His hair was sticking up on one side, but he had lost his flush and unfocused look from before. Tyler, too, had subsided from drunk back into a pleasant buzzing tipsiness, and nodded.

Quickly, Tyler dumped the entire basked of clothes into her washing machine and started it, then continued collecting the clothes into the basket. When the clothes filled the bin so much that they began sliding off the mound on top, she gave up and sat the basket in the corner of her bedroom. There were still more clothes that had been knocked off hangers in her closet, but things were contained enough to at least close the closet door. She had forgotten that Lucy peed on her closet floor, so Tyler sprayed Nature's Miracle on the spot, then carefully blotted it with paper towels. Tom had briefly sat down at the edge of Tyler's bed, but quickly moved to the floor and was sitting leaning against the foot of her bed. He made small talk with her, asking about her family and how she had decided to become a lawyer.

Finished, Tyler shut the closet door and moved the laundry basket in front of her washing machine, then sat down next to Tom heavily.

"Thanks again, for coming on your night off and staying."

Tom shrugged. They sat next to each other, staring at Tyler's dresser against the wall.

"Do you really think I'm selfish and a bad person? I mean, do you still think that?" Tyler could not put her finger on why she wanted Tom's approval so badly, but she very much wanted Tom to tell her he had changed his mind.

"Oh, you're no worse than anyone else. Probably more selfish though."

"Why? Because I care about my career? Because I'm busy?" She turned to face him.

Tom pushed up the other side of his hair, clearly thinking. "No. It's because you think your time and your goals are more important than everyone else's. You told me you didn't report criminal activity relating to a murder because it would have been inconvenient for you. And you also haven't asked me a single question about myself tonight. You just assume that you're more important, or more interesting, I guess."

Shit, Tyler thought, *he has a point.* Tom turned to look at her and Tyler was surprised to see he looked worried he had offended her again. "But you like me anyway," she said it between a question and a statement. Tom nodded. Nervous that she was misreading the situation, but tipsy enough to do it anyway, Tyler leaned forward and kissed Tom. After a brief hesitation, he kissed her back with an intensity that surprised her. He grabbed the back of her head with the hand farthest from her. Tyler ran her hand up Tom's chest, then got to her knees and swung her leg over to straddle him. He ran his hands up and down her waist and started to lift her shirt. His hands moved up the side of her rib cage and to the back where her bra would have clasped, if she had not been wearing a sports bra from her Pilates class earlier in the day. Tyler kissed his neck and reached down to remove her shirt. As she was lifting it over her head, Tom suddenly reached out and pulled the hem back down, then firmly grasped Tyler by the hips and moved her off him. Tyler blinked rapidly, in a daze.

"This is totally inappropriate," he said, rubbing his hand across his eyes and forehead.

"I don't care."

Tom laughed. "Of course, you don't." He sighed. "I have to go." Tyler thought about asking whether he could drive safely—she herself felt well beyond the legal limit—but figured as a police officer he would know better than anyone whether he should drive or not. Still, she wanted him to stay.

"Are you sure?" Tyler reached forward and ran a finger down the inside of Tom's arm. Tom hesitated, but then stood up, and held a hand out to Tyler to pull her up. They both stumbled slightly. Tyler ran a hand through her hair, her mind still trying to keep up with the events of the night. She followed Tom down the stairs and to her front door. Tyler desperately wanted Tom to stay, but her brain was moving too slowly to think of how she could convince him.

Tom unlocked Tyler's front door and took his car keys out of his pocket. "Well..." he trailed off. Tyler stood on her tiptoes and hugged him, her arms around his neck and her face pointed slightly upward, hoping he might kiss her again. He looked straight ahead, but held her tightly against him for a minute, then resolutely separated her body from his and walked out. As he walked to his car Tyler called after him, "I'll ask you some questions about yourself next time." He waved with his back to Tyler but said nothing and did not turn around.

Alone again, Tyler tripled checked the locks on her front and back door, and went around to every window on the first, then the second floor to make sure they were locked. The pleasant buzzing in her head had transformed into more of a fuzzy pain only made worse by her confusion over what had happened between her and Tom and whether she should be embarrassed, so she chugged a glass of water and took two Advil. Tyler turned on the shower, but felt too nervous at the prospect of being naked, wet, and unable to see what was happening in the room or hear whether someone was breaking into the house to actually get in, and turned it off again. Instead, she washed her face and got in bed, making sure her phone was plugged into the charger on her nightstand and easily reachable. Tyler knew logically the burglar would not return but jumped at every creak nonetheless and ended up leaving on most of the lights in the house, sleeping fitfully as a result.

CHAPTER ELEVEN

Tyler woke up slowly the next morning. The events from the day before returned in pieces. First, she felt a pit in her stomach as she remembered the burglary, then confusion and embarrassment over Tom. At the time, she had the impression Tom left because he was afraid of taking things too far, but what if he had left because he felt zero attraction? Tyler thought she remembered Tom kissing her back, but everything from the night before was slightly blurred from her heightened emotions and the wine. She clearly remembered his hands under her shirt, but what if he had more to drink than he realized and that had been the alcohol talking. Although her mouth was dry and she had a minor headache, Tyler was surprised not to feel more hungover based on how drunk she had been the night before. Then she remembered eating half of a giant pizza. That explained how good she felt, but it was not going to do anything to help her toward her fitness goals. Tyler groaned, thinking about the nice healthy meal from the Whole Foods hot bar that she had thrown in the trash.

Tyler checked her phone, squinting her eyes against the screen's glare. More documents had been uploaded to the review site, but John had not sent her any more ominous emails about a month turnaround. Tom had not texted. Tyler scrolled through their text conversation. The last text was Tom telling her not to text him. Tyler thought she must be totally delusional to have thought Tom was attracted to her. And what did she want with him anyway? They probably had nothing in common, and Tom had been consistently, rudely, refusing Tyler's help her own investigation. So why had Tyler put herself out for rejection that way? Why did she still want to feel his hands on her body and his mouth on her mouth? What was wrong with her?

Tyler could feel thoughts start to spiral, so groaning again, she pulled herself out of bed and tried to distract herself. She brewed coffee and preemptively took two more Advil. As the coffee brewed, Tyler restarted the laundry, which had sat wet in the machine all night and smelled musty. It looked like there would be at least three more loads, so that would keep her busy for a while. Tyler's phone pinged with a text and she jumped, hoping despite herself that it was Tom. Her screen instead displayed a text from Harry seeing if they were still on for drinks. Tyler did not remember agreeing to this and thought she would see if Harry could meet up the next weekend, but when she opened up the text chain she saw Harry had invited her out the weekend before and she had pushed it out a weekend already.

Tyler did not particularly feel like drinking on the heels of the night before, and she felt even less like engaging in her recognition that she was far more attracted to and interested in Tom, who clearly did not reciprocate, than Harry, who expressed strong interest and continued to take Tyler on dates despite the fact she had routinely displayed unhinged behavior around him. To avoid going down that rabbit hole, Tyler decided to do what she pictured a fully functional, emotionally mature adult might do and sent an enthusiastic text back to Harry and suggest he meet her at a cocktail bar walking distance from where she lived. To be fair, an emotionally mature adult would probably have dinner with Harry, but Tyler could only go so far and had deliberately chosen a spot that did not serve food. Harry agreed immediately.

In the daylight with the bright summer sun streaming in through all of her windows Tyler felt confident enough to shower, but she left the bathroom door ajar and the shower curtain partially open to allow herself a better chance to hear any unexpected noises. After the shower, she delayed getting dressed and padded around in her robe. Her wet hair soaked her back and she felt almost chilled in the air conditioning.

Tyler went to the last Pilates class of the day in the early afternoon and texted Cerene to see if she wanted to get brunch on Sunday. Tyler had never tried to make plans with Cerene outside of work because she always assumed Cerene was busy with her husband, but apparently that had been wrong. By midafternoon, Tyler had finished her laundry. There had been so much that it was hanging in every room of her house, including the back of her sofa, padded by towels. Having done her grocery shopping the night before, Tyler had nothing to do until she met up with Harry. Reluctantly, she plugged her laptop into the docking station and logged on in her home office. Cerene was online, and messaged Tyler immediately to report that she had discovery responses due on Monday and was working all weekend. No brunch.

Tyler idly put together some skeleton outlines for upcoming depositions. As Tyler started to flag documents as potential exhibits in the document review software, she remembered that plaintiff's counsel had supposedly made a big deal out of the production line issue. Tyler had meant to investigate that issue months ago. She emailed the paralegal that accompanied John to the deposition to see whether the transcript was ready. Tyler should see what plaintiff's counsel had been asking and incorporate preparation for those questions into the outline, as well as conduct an independent review.

She filtered the documents to find ones she had flagged for herself and went through the emails slowly. Going through the documents again, Tyler saw that in the "notes" portion of the software she had actually written "potentially hot; re-review; raise for call with B if appropriate." She cringed at having forgotten and resisted the knee-jerk urge to delete the note and try to cover up her mistake. While Tyler still thought that no matter what the production line issue was, it was not something anyone would anticipate to come up at the deposition of an accountant, her notes reminded her that in the grand scheme of the case these emails could very well point to an issue with some of the nose hair product which, if discovered, would provide strong support for the plaintiff's case.

The email chain did not identify the actual issue with the production line. The issue was referenced obliquely, and from the context, it appeared that the specifics of whatever the issue was had only been discussed over the phone with a select group. As Tyler vaguely remembered, the issue had been flagged by a production line manager to a middle manager, who in turn discussed with a VP. The VP consulted with the company's in-house attorney, but not one Tyler recognized. This suggested two things to Tyler. First, that somewhere along the line an NSK attorney had provided good training to management employees to discuss sensitive issues over the phone rather than describe them in emails. Second, that the issue may have been serious, or at least concerning enough to discuss rather than write down in emails. Tyler downloaded the emails, Bates-stamped, and put together an email to Brendan outlining the emails with the identifying numbers applied for discovery.

Brendan,

John alerted me that a couple of the docs attached above were flagged by P's counsel during Mr. Brown's depo last week. Depo transcript is not yet available, but I will pull out relevant pages and provide a separate summary of this topic for you in addition to the routine summary we put together—likely around the end of next week.

Docs were not marked hot by us prior to the depo (although I have updated that in the system). John was very concerned that we did not have these documents flagged before. I have reviewed them and I think if we want to fully understand the context, we will need to connect with the client. I summarized the documents below, and as mentioned above, they are also attached to this email. If you agree, I thought you might discuss on your weekly discovery call with Bruce.

The docs outline an issue with the nose hair wax production line that occurred sometime around March of 2016, but do not describe the specific issue (so again, if we think we need to know details/the substantive mechanical problem we will need to discuss with the client).

- *The issue was flagged by Bob Bryce (line manager) to Teresa Spinner (facilities manager) verbally on April 3, 2016 [TRU000010798-99].*

- *Teresa Spinner alerted Genevieve Donner (VP, Facilities) on April 3, 2016 [TRU000021001], and sometime between that day and April 10, 2016 Teresa and Genevieve discussed. Teresa identified an issue with part T3002-3 on Production Line 4. [Brendan, I am not familiar with this part's significance, not sure if you are.]*

- *On April 10, 2016 Genevieve emailed Shariff Benson (Assistant General Counsel for NSK) [TRU000010052-53], and on April 20, 2016, Shariff emailed Genevieve and Teresa to alert them that per their discussions he recommended taking no further action. [TRU00000999 — slipsheet, withheld, A/C privilege].*

Note that I have not seen Shariff's name in other A/C privileged emails and based on a LinkedIn search he appears to have left NSK and currently works as counsel for Nair, so he is unlikely to be available to discuss. I did not perform an exhaustive search of all docs for Shariff Benson or for T3002-3 or Production Line 4, but if you would like me to just let me know and I would be happy to do so.

Please let me know what else I can do to help, or if you'd like to discuss!

-Tyler

Less than an hour later, as Tyler was taking a break from document review to eat an apple and peanut butter at her kitchen counter, her computer pinged with a response.

Agree that we need to familiarize ourselves with this issue ASAP if P's counsel is looking into these emails. Also not familiar with that part. Regrettable that these were not flagged originally for John...

I will discuss with Bruce this week.

Tyler felt a twist of shame and annoyance. Brendan, using his typical brand of passive aggression, obviously agreed with John that Tyler should have flagged the documents when she first reviewed them. The passive aggression was tougher to deal with than straightforward criticism because Tyler struggled to know when an issue was large enough that she should apologize and when apologizing would draw more attention to something that Brendan would forget about given time. And here, Tyler had already reluctantly admitted to herself that failing to flag and investigate the documents was an oversight. Apologizing could completely backfire and just draw more attention to her mistake. Tapping her fingers on the kitchen table, Tyler weighed her options.

Brendan,

Any chance I can sit in on the call? I don't need to bill for it, but it would be helpful to stay up to date as I prepare depo outlines. Apologies for not flagging those documents sooner.

By way of answer, Brendan forwarded her the meeting invite for his call with Bruce, NSK's attorney who was assisting with document collection and other document production-related issues.

Tyler noticed she was due to meet Harry in an hour and started getting ready. Her hair had air dried into somewhat of a triangle shape—fuzzy and frizzy at the bottom and smooth at the top. She also observed that the ponytail she had put her wet hair into for Pilates had left an unsightly ripple around the bottom of her head. Tyler heated up a curling iron, then decided she could not be bothered and threw her hair into a bun and secured the flyaways with hairspray instead. Tyler threw on a loose black maxi dress that draped down open to her lower back. She paired the dress with heeled sandals and examined herself in her mirror. She decided she looked a little too nice for someone she was not actually very eager to meet up with and put on flat strappy sandals instead. Now approving of her reflection, Tyler threw her keys, phone, and wallet into a round woven and headed out to meet Harry, double checking that her back door was locked before she left and doubling back to check the lock on the front door after she got a block away.

Tyler arrived at the bar before Harry and texted to let him know she was on the patio. It was still humid, but the temperature was dropping from its peak, and multiple fans strategically positioned at the edges of the patio kept a breeze flowing. Harry arrived fifteen minutes late looking slightly wrinkled, but handsomer than Tyler remembered. When he hugged her hello his hand lingered on the exposed skin of her back. His hand felt pleasantly cool and dry.

"You look great."

"Thanks, you too."

Harry waved the waiter over and ordered his drink and nuts, the only food that was available. Harry turned back to Tyler. "So, what have you been up to today?"

"Oh, the usual, how about you? Did you have to work today?"

"The usual as well. So yes, a little work."

"Anything you can tell me about? Cheating spouses? Fake injuries?"

"A little bit of both. One cheating spouse... but I think he's not cheating." Tyler raised an eyebrow. "Yes—I've been following this guy for more than a month now and he hasn't cheated."

"Are they usually cheaters?"

"Oh yeah." The waiter delivered Harry's drink. He took a long sip and continued. "If I get hired, nine times, no nine point nine times out of ten, the spouse is cheating. The people who hire me usually know something is going on. They're either hoping to be proved wrong, or they're wealthy and they're hoping to be proved right. From what I understand most prenups for the wealthy offer much more favorable terms when there's cheating."

"But this guy isn't a cheater. Do you think he knows you are following him?"

Harry looked offended. "He'd better not! I would not be very good at my job otherwise."

"Sorry, of course." Tyler smiled. An awkward pause followed. "So, a month, huh?"

"On and off," Harry conceded. "It *is* just a cheating spouse, I'm not being paid enough to only tail this one guy for a month, so it's not like this is the only job I'm handling."

Tyler nodded. "Well, you said a little of both. I guess the fake injury is not a nose hair wax one! I hope I'd have known about it if it were."

"No," Harry agreed, "just your garden variety car crash." Tyler waited to see if Harry would elaborate, but he seemed content to sip on his drink. Tyler vainly tried to summon up the attraction she had felt toward Harry when she first met him in the Oak conference room. The waiter returned with the nuts. Tyler watched Harry eat a couple. She felt detached from the situation, almost as if she were observing from another table. Tyler could see that Harry was conventionally attractive—it was what had attracted Tyler to him in the first place, and she had slept with him more than once—but now she felt completely uninterested, even awkward when he expressed interest in her. Some of her thoughts must have shown in her face because Harry uncertainly wiped his mouth with his napkin. "Is something on my face?"

Thinking quickly, Tyler lied, "Yes, just a little salt I think, but you got it." She smiled brightly, internally trying to guess how long they had been sitting having drinks and when it would be acceptable to wrap things up.

"So, anyway, you worked today too, how are those old nose hair wax cases coming? I haven't heard anything about them for a while."

"Slowly!" Tyler laughed. "Thanks to you, as you know, we proved that one guy was faking his injuries. He represented the class for one of the actions, but plaintiff's lawyers came up with another representative, so the case is still active."

"Can I expect more business?" Harry winked.

"Sadly, this representative seems a lot more legit. He came with multiple doctors' records."

"I guess they can't all create jobs for me, although I wish they would!" Tyler smiled with Harry. "If I'm remembering right," he continued, "you were doing some investigations of your own, too. Asking some questions about that guy who was found in the garage." Tyler wondered if Harry was purposefully not mentioning Kevin's name or if he had forgotten.

"Sure, sure," Tyler agreed. "But like you said, what do I know about that type of investigation?" She had meant to say it lightly, but it came out more than a little bitter.

"Aw, you know I didn't mean to offend you."

"No worries. I talked to everyone I could think of as much as I could, but other than that..." Tyler shrugged. She found her heart still started to pound when Harry brought the topic up, as if she were back in that hot night air looking down at Kevin's lifeless body while Harry stood less than a block away. Maybe this link between Harry and finding Kevin, and not Harry's availability, was what had killed Tyler's attraction to him. Tyler certainly liked that idea better than thinking she was only attracted to people who had no interest in her. She realized Harry was in the middle of telling her a story and tried to pay attention. She had no idea what he was talking about, but the story was clearly intended to be funny, so she laughed at the end. They had another cocktail each, but when Harry suggested going down the street for dinner, Tyler demurred.

As they walked out of the restaurant, Harry offered to walk Tyler home. Tyler tried to dissuade him, but he insisted. The humidity from the day remained, but in the dark, the air felt pleasantly cool. Harry took her hand as they walked, and Tyler felt her body stiffen and the drink sour in her stomach. All of her prior attraction to Harry had evaporated, and now any expression of interest on his side repelled her. She knew she should say something to him—it was not like they would be breaking up since they had not dated long enough to be in a relationship, but obviously they were not on the same page.

"Got your car back," he pointed at her Subaru as they approached her house.

"Oh, yes." Another topic she wanted to avoid.

"How long did you have that rental for again?" He stopped by her car.

"Just a week or so." Tyler dropped his hand and continued walking ahead. She turned around in front of her house and looked at

Harry expectantly. He was still standing by her car and almost seemed to be looking inside of it. When he noticed Tyler watching him, he smiled and walked over, encircling her in his arms. Tyler knew now was the moment to say something and she paused looking into Harry's chest as she tried to collect her thoughts. As she looked up to tell Harry she thought they were not compatible after all, her face connected with his as he leaned down to kiss her. She briefly kissed him back, but the attraction was gone. Tyler felt Harry's mouth on hers, but no butterflies.

"Harry—" she started. He mistook this for an invitation, and took her by the waist, moving her toward her front door.

"Harry," she said more firmly. "I'm so sorry. Can we just sit here a second?" She sat down on her front steps. Harry remained standing on the sidewalk and crossed his arms.

"I'm sorry, I just don't think I'm in the right head space to be dating right now."

Harry rolled his eyes.

Tyler slouched forward, putting her head in her hands. She stared down at the painted wood under her feet. "I just have a lot going on. The timing's not right."

"Fine." Tyler was surprised to hear venom in Harry's voice. She kept looking down, not wanting to engage further. After a pause long enough for Tyler to realize she was overdue for a pedicure, she heard Harry's footsteps moving away down the sidewalk. Tyler sat a few minutes longer, watching Harry's disappearing figure. Searching for any regret, Tyler was pleased to find she felt only relief.

CHAPTER TWELVE

On Monday morning, Tyler was surprisingly looking forward to going back to the office. Without pressing work or errands, she had watched six hours of reality television on Sunday which had been enjoyable at the time but left her feeling unproductive and craving stimulation. Tyler logged onto her computer and saw that Debbie the paralegal had responded to her email letting her know the accountant's deposition transcript would be available that afternoon. Tyler's call with Brendan and Bruce, NSK's in-house counsel, was on Wednesday morning, so that would give her plenty of time to review in case the transcript provided additional details.

Midmorning, an email came in from John.

Team,

Please give a warm welcome to Ty Collins. Ty will be joining our team later this week. Ty has experience with complex products liability cases concerning tire malfunctions and will be a great asset to this team.

- JD

Tyler quickly googled Ty—she was confident John had done auto litigation work at his prior firm, and sure enough, Ty's LinkedIn ("Tyler Francisco Collins") showed that he was working at the same firm. "Mother fucker," Tyler said quietly. Ty and Tyler were both fourth-year associates. When she started, Brendan had been a fourth-year associate, and although several other new associates had initially helped on the nose hair wax cases, after a year or so only Tyler regularly worked for NSK. And this was generally true for most of the clients— Cerene was the only fourth-year associate working on the car seat cases. Generally, clients would not pay for two associates of the same level because it was perceived as inefficient.

Just as Tyler felt like she had gained traction with John and found a little job security, it was ripped away. Although Tyler had told John she would report his behavior to HR, she really did not want to go that route. Tyler had a feeling that even if she was believed, she would struggle to find work going forward. After all, most of the partners were men of John's age or older and, being lawyers, were risk averse. Surely, working with a young woman who had accused a peer of sexual harassment would feel quite risky to them. And that was assuming the lawyers at the firm generally believed her, which was a bigger "if" than Tyler thought in the moment. Especially given that the alternate story John would tell—that Tyler was making things up to cover up for her shoddy work product—would be more consistent with what the partners would expect from associates.

She forwarded John's email to Cerene, then messaged her.

Fuck!

Good morning to you too :)

Look at my most recent email. Fucking John...

Ouch. What are you going to do though, new partner comes in and wants to work with his own people... understandable.

I'm not feeling so understanding. What am I supposed to do?? Freaking out here. And what are the chances he has my same name?

Just try to keep your hours up. And maybe keep an ear out for new cases? I guess if he replaces you no one will have to learn a new name lol! Sorry... couldn't resist.

Ugh. Lunch?

Sure... meet in the lobby at 12:30?

Yep. See you there.

Tyler nervously started reviewing documents. *Ty probably doesn't review documents anymore*, Tyler thought angstily, *he probably supervises document review and writes motions. Cerene will probably like him better too; they'll be birds of a feather.* The tight squeeze of anxiety that Tyler had felt free of for several days quickly returned. Her email pinged, and she jumped, but it was just John's paralegal forwarding her the deposition transcript. Tyler eagerly opened it up. Her email pinged again—an invite from Gina for a lunch to welcome Ty on Friday. Tyler rolled her eyes. She would go of course, but she did not welcome Ty's presence whatsoever. At least being invited to the lunch meant that at a minimum Tyler had not been totally frozen out. Yet. Maybe she was invited just so that she could train her own replacement. Like Cerene said, nobody would even have to learn a new name. Tyler shook her head briskly, she no longer had time to spiral into these thoughts. "Welcome, Ty," she said sarcastically to herself as she clicked "accept".

Turning back to the deposition transcript, Tyler located the section discussing the production line. As she expected, the accountant had no idea what production line information the emails referred to and had no experience with the production line generally. Tyler called up Debbie, the paralegal who had attended the deposition, to see if she remembered anything else. Debbie remembered the interaction because John had seemed upset and had called a break immediately after the emails were discussed during which he made several comments about being poorly prepared, but in Debbie's opinion it was a minor point.

"I thought he seemed pleased with the depo overall," she observed. "Was he upset?"

Tyler laughed, with a bitter edge. "You could say that."

Debbie laughed too, but without an edge. Debbie had been a paralegal for at least twenty years and had seen and survived much worse. "That might put you in a tough spot, but it seemed like there was no harm done to the case."

"Okay, thanks so much, Debbie. Anything else that stood out to you?"

"No, that was the only surprise."

"Got it. Well thanks for forwarding that transcript, we're going to check out what this issue might be so it's good to hear what happened during the depo to have all the background."

"No problem."

"Okay, have a good day." Tyler hung up the phone and typed up an email to Brendan responding to the earlier chain about the emails.

Brendan,

See attached above the depo transcript discussing the production line emails on pages 155-160. I also pulled the pages out in an excerpt, which is also attached above. The witness had not seen the emails before and did not provide any information. I also spoke with Debbie, who confirmed that no other relevant information came up during the break immediately following the introduction of these emails.

Please let me know if there is anything else I can do to help ahead of the call with Bruce.

Although I had planned to summarize this portion of the depo separately from my usual summary, after reviewing the transcript I concluded that a separate summary would not be necessary. Plaintiff's counsel simply identified and introduced each document, and the witness was not familiar with any of them and did not know anything about the production line operations. John registered a number of objections. I will be sure to send my usual summary over ASAP.

Thanks!

Tyler turned back to reviewing documents. She remembered she had told John to either allow her to staff two first-year associates to do the review for her or to let her review the documents in her own time. He was to tell her on Monday—today. With Ty coming and all of her leverage gone, Tyler wondered whether John would say anything to her either way. Maybe Tyler could follow up with John about whether she should be finding first-year associates and try to feel him out that way. She grabbed a notebook and tried to casually take a lap around the floor. John's door was closed. Light was coming out from underneath his office door, but Tyler could not tell whether the light was coming from a lightbulb or if it was the bright summer sun streaming into the floor-to-ceiling windows that made up one wall of every partner's office. She deliberately walked by slowly a second time, straining to hear a phone call, but heard nothing. Frustrated, she walked back to her office and resisted the urge to close her door. She saw she had one new email, but it was from Brendan and read only, "Thx." Tyler turned back to the document review and worked as quickly as she could.

Tyler had been hoping Cerene would give her a pep talk at lunch. Instead, Cerene, restored to her perfect self once again with a fresh blowout and a crisp, dog-hair-free black sheath dress, held Tyler at arm's length. In response to Tyler's questions about Brendan and whether Cerene and him remained broken up, Cerene only gave Tyler a small smile and tilted her head as if she was confused, before discussing the discovery responses that she had worked on all weekend and how boring that had been for her golden retrievers. According to Cerene, she barely had time to take the dogs to the park, but the partner's effusive thanks that morning in response to the quality of the responses made it all worth it. Tyler suppressed an eye roll. If that was true, Tyler was jealous, but it sounded unlike any interaction Tyler had with a partner. Given Cerene was pretending like she had never said anything about Brendan, Tyler was now skeptical of anything that came out of Cerene's mouth.

When Tyler tried to draw Cerene into a conversation about Tyler's own problems (historically a comfortable topic for Cerene), Cerene just nodded and repeated what she had said on the chat—it made sense that John might want his own associates on cases and that Tyler should work to keep her hours up. In fact, maybe Tyler should think about what other cases she might be interested in. Had she considered any of the construction litigation? (Tyler had not, because the partners in charge of those cases were well-known for treating the associates horrifically, and that Cerene would even suggest Tyler try to do that work felt like a slap in the face.) Worse, when Tyler mentioned the rumors of how associates were treated, Cerene just lifted one perfectly shaped eyebrow, leaving Tyler to wonder if Cerene thought that was all Tyler deserved. Tyler became more and more irritated as the lunch went on. By the time they parted ways at the elevators Tyler was gritting her teeth but managed to force out a fake "Have a great day!" as they parted ways. *What a fucking fake*, she thought to herself.

Still, Cerene's unwillingness to see Tyler's worries from Tyler's perspective or say anything supportive whatsoever left Tyler feeling increasingly anxious. Cerene could be a total fake and also be completely right in her prediction that Tyler would be pushed out of the NSK cases. As a result of Tyler's ensuing anxiety, for the rest of the day she was more focused on work than she had been since the Kevin incident. Tyler periodically walked by John's office, but the door remained closed.

The next day was nearly the same. Tyler finished a few deposition outlines and emailed them to John. After that, every time her email pinged she jumped, anticipating and dreading his response but getting none. Additional discovery requests were served in one of the cases. The requests were forwarded to Tyler by Gina. Tyler immediately began to draft responses. She took a break to go to Pilates and to watch one episode of the *Real Housewives*, but worked steadily otherwise. Although it might be too little too late, Tyler's hours were back up, so at least she was doing what she could before Ty arrived.

On Wednesday, Tyler messaged Brendan ahead of the call with Bruce, NSK counsel.

Would you like me to dial in and take notes for you during the call with Bruce today, or would you prefer that I come by your office?
Swing by, thanks.
Got it. See you soon.

Tyler printed out copies of her email summaries, the NSK emails, and the relevant portion of the deposition transcript. As she walked to the printer, Tyler took a detour past John's office again—the door was open now and the light was on, although John himself was not there. With five minutes to go to the call, Tyler walked over to Brendan's office. His door was open and he was engrossed in a Word document pulled up on his monitor.

Tyler cleared her throat. "Hi, Brendan."

"Hey, Tyler." He didn't look away from the screen.

"Still want me to sit in here with you? I can call in from my office if you prefer." Tyler actually would have preferred to call in from her office, where she could take notes from the call on her computer instead of in a notebook.

"No, no, just hang on a second." Tyler sat down across from Brendan in the chair closer to his phone and crossed her legs. Brendan's desk was covered with stacks of documents, so she balanced her own notebook and printouts on her knee. Brendan's mouth hung slightly open as he read whatever document was on his screen. As always, he had deep circles under his eyes and looked like he might fall asleep at any second. Tyler reshuffled her papers, and added the date, time, and call attendees to the top of her sheet of notebook paper. She discreetly checked the time on her phone—two more minutes until the call started. The five minutes were passing incredibly slowly. Tyler wondered whether Cerene had sat in the same chair as Tyler was now, back when she was a junior associate starting her... affair? Relationship? Tyler still did not know how to categorize the information Cerene had shared. Had anything physical happened in *this office?* She felt herself blushing. One minute until the call. Tyler cleared her throat, but Brendan remained engrossed in his document. She noticed he had missed shaving a patch of hair under his jaw.

Tyler glanced down at the stacks of documents on Brendan's desk again and noticed a letter that looked like it was addressed to Kevin from the Missouri Bar Association sitting haphazardly on a stack of accordion folders. Before she could stop herself, Tyler reached out and grabbed the letter to confirm it was indeed addressed to Kevin.

The notification sounded for the call, and Brendan turned to the phone and quickly dialed into the conference line. Tyler jumped and slid the letter into the middle of her notebook among unused sheets of paper. Brendan hit mute and finally turned to Tyler.

"Bruce is always late."

Tyler nodded and smiled. Brendan turned back to his computer. Tyler started counting the seconds in her head to see how long before his mouth fell open again. At two hundred and seventeen a deep man's voice announced "Bruce" followed by the conference call's female robot voice "is entering the conference line." Kudos to Brendan, his mouth had remained closed. Brendan quickly pressed "unmute" on his phone.

"Bruce! How's it going?" Brendan's voice exuded more energy than Tyler had ever experienced from him before, although his face kept its usual haggard expression.

"Brendan," the deep male voice answered. "All's well here. How about for you?" Bruce had a slight southern accent and a lovely, relaxing speaking voice.

"Oh, great! Keeping busy." Brendan's expression belied the heartiness in his voice. Tyler wondered if somewhere in Tennessee at NSK's headquarters Bruce was also putting on a brave face for the phone line, or whether he was actually relaxed and happy like he sounded. "Listen," Brendan continued, "I know normally its just you and me on these calls, but I wanted to let you know that I'm joined by my colleague Tyler McCarther today."

"Hi, there," Tyler said, "pleasure to meet you."

"Likewise," Bruce said. "Not every day you meet a Tyler who's a girl."

"That's what they tell me! It's a family name though and I'm an only child," Tyler answered.

"Now, I'm not sure whether you had a chance to see the email I sent this morning," Brendan cut in, shooting Tyler a disapproving look for speaking without permission, "but I invited Tyler because she's the one who flagged this potential issue, and she's the one in the weeds with the documents and best-placed to answer any preliminary questions from you."

"Busy morning, Brendan, unfortunately I did not have a chance to review your email."

"Of course, it's no problem. Let me just pull it up here." Tyler was surprised that Brendan did not have the email ready. It was the type of thing Brendan would have criticized Tyler for failing to do. He looked at Tyler and she realized Brendan expected Tyler to have the email. She silently handed Brendan the packet of documents she had printed for herself. He nodded at her and looked down at Tyler's summary.

"Okay... so..." Brendan proceeded to read Tyler's timeline almost word for word, referencing the documents by their Bates labels. He looked a little surprised as he finished reading, and Tyler wondered if Brendan had read anything she sent before the call. "So, it sounds like we're not able to get Shariff. I had Tyler do a little due diligence, looks like he is no longer at NSK?" As Brendan spoke, he flipped through the copies of documents stapled to Tyler's email.

"No," Bruce agreed, "Shariff went over to Nair. Great guy."

Brendan paused, perhaps waiting for Bruce to offer an alternative employee to talk to or any other insight about the incident on the production line, but Bruce remained quiet. "Alrighty..." Brendan flipped to the very back of Tyler's packet, to the printout of her email regarding the deposition, "it looks like this is a big area of interest for plaintiff's counsel. Last Thursday your accountant was asked about it during his depo. Obviously, he knew nothing about it, being an accountant, so no harm done." Tyler stifled a snort and Brendan glared at her. "That being said," he continued, "John is wondering why plaintiff's counsel is zeroing in on this issue. He also figures that it will keep coming up at the depos, so he'd like to get ahead of things and get the full background and come up with a strategy for handling."

"He really thinks this is going to keep coming up? I'll be honest with you, Brendan, this seems like a big to-do about a little thing. I don't know if I want y'all spinning your wheels over some potential production line issue. I mean, is it even in scope?"

Brendan looked a little annoyed but kept his voice even. "Certainly, if its out of scope that would be ideal, we could let plaintiff's counsel waste his time at the depositions asking about it. But without knowing anything else we really can't say if it's in scope or not. We're dealing with a ten-year statute of limitations for injuries, and 2016 is well within that window. If the production line issue has anything to do with product quality, it could theoretically be linked to customers' injuries, especially if they can prove they used that batch of product. On the other hand, if that product was pulled and never went out to consumers, we are not necessarily out of scope, but we're unconcerned because it would have no effect on the cases. Does that help, Bruce?"

Bruce sighed. "All right, gimme those dates and the personnel involved."

"Excellent, so for personnel, we've got Bob Bryce—Bryce with a Y, a line manager; Teresa Spinner, that's a T E Teresa not a T H E Theresa. We've got a facilities manager; Genevieve Donner, vice president of facilities, and then Shariff who we've already discussed. As far as dates the emails are showing... issue discovered April 3, 2016 and wrapped up with no further action recommended on April 20, 2016. And this is all in my email to you just in case you need it in writing. That give you what you need?"

Tyler heard a keyboard tapping through the phone. "Sure does. Let's discuss again next week, I'll see what I can find out. And don't bother spending any more time on this before then, remember that we're trying to keep those bills down!" Bruce chuckled heartily.

Brendan and Bruce moved on to discussing search terms for the newest class action, and Tyler zoned out and stared at a photo she had not noticed before on Brendan's shelf of him looking slightly younger and more well-rested with a blonde woman. Not Cerene, but the woman was similarly pretty and neat-looking. Brendan and the woman stood side by side somewhere outdoors, shoulders touching, and smiled happily for the camera. The body language was ambiguous; Tyler could not tell whether the woman was a sister or a girlfriend.

"Okay, well looks like we're just about out of time," Brendan said. "Let's plan to finalize those search terms next week. I'll touch base with our tech team and let you know about threading, and you let me know if the terms and phrases we discussed are acceptable for NSK. And let's plan on discussing that production line issue too. If you think it makes sense to discuss with any of the employees, we can set up a separate call, just let me know."

"Great. Thanks, Brendan."

"Thanks, Bruce, nice to meet you!" Tyler said, speaking without permission for a second time. Brendan sent her a sharp look.

"Well have a great week, Bruce. Talk to you soon."

"Uh-huh." Bruce hung up.

Brendan started to turn back to his computer. Tyler recrossed her legs and gripped her notepad. "Brendan," she said before he could completely zone her out, "can I come next week? To the call?"

"Sure," he said, disinterested, "but just try to keep your commentary to a minimum."

Tyler ignored the reprimand. "I know we didn't find out much today. Do you think I should send John an update or..."

"Oh, I send him weekly updates, why don't you just send me a summary of the call. I'll tweak it for my weekly update."

"Of course. I'll get that to you ASAP. Thanks again for letting me   sit   in."

"No skin off my back since you're not billing for it. You heard the man—keeping costs down!"

Tyler nodded. She had been hoping her presence might have been deemed helpful enough, especially now that she was keeping notes, that she could bill her time for the call. "Okay, well, I'll send you the summary in the next hour or so. Thanks, Brendan."

"Yep." He turned back to his computer and Tyler walked back to her desk.

She started typing up the summary, but when she got to the portion of her notes following the discussion of the production line issue they became illegible, which made sense since Tyler had stopped paying attention. "Fuck," she said softly. She should have at least jotted down the big topics. Now she would have to spend additional time trying to figure out what Brendan had been talking about with the search terms. She looked up the discovery responses he referenced on the firm's document management system and made up notes as best she could. Grimacing, she sent her summary to Brendan. Three minutes later he copied her in on the summary being sent to John. Brendan had changed her narrative summary to bullet points but had made no other changes. Tyler wondered if he had even read it. Hopefully the part she fudged had been accurate. She nervously rubbed her hands on her skirt.

Tyler remembered the letter shoved into her notebook and pulled it out. Sure enough, the addressee was Kevin, not Brendan. Perhaps Brendan was getting Kevin's mail forwarded to him, but Tyler was not sure why Brendan would save a letter from the Missouri Bar Association, which probably contained an updated bar card or an advertisement for life insurance. Tyler knew she should bring the letter back, but curiosity had gotten the better of her. She flipped the envelope over and noticed it had already been neatly opened. Tyler pulled out the letter inside and was surprised to see a personalized letter to Kevin. The letter was dated the day before he died, so it had probably arrived at the firm just a few days after his body was found. Tyler frowned as she read. Contrary to her expectations, the letter provided Kevin with official notice that a hearing date had been set before the ethics board. Under the subject of the hearing, "Trust Accounts and Property of Others, Mo. R. Gov. Bar Jud. Rule 4-1.145" was written.

Grasping the letter between both hands, Tyler stood up and started pacing her office. The Missouri Bar Association was the governing body in charge of enforcing the ethical rules for attorney conduct. Mostly the association was only notified of potential misconduct due to complaints made by other attorneys, or very rarely clients. Attorneys were loath to tattle on each other, and most clients simply lacked the education to know that was an option. Essentially, complaints were rare, and investigations were even rarer. Getting to the stage where the ethics committee held a hearing was extremely difficult and looked terrible for Kevin. It was something that would have been a part of Kevin's record, and something he would have to disclose in a variety of circumstances.

Tyler leaned over her desk, still standing, and quickly googled the rule. It sounded like Kevin was being investigated for potentially misappropriating client funds, but surely that had to be wrong. She began reading: "(a) A lawyer shall hold property of clients or third persons that is in a lawyer's possession in connection with a representation separate from the lawyer's own property. Client or third-party funds shall be kept in a separate account designated as a 'Client Trust Account' or words of similar import maintained in the state where the lawyer's office is situated or elsewhere if the client or third person consents." *Shit*, she thought. There were various other details contained in the rule, but her initial take had been correct.

Well, she rationalized, *the hearing never happened, so maybe it was just a misunderstanding.* She knew, though, that a hearing before the Missouri Bar Association's ethics committee was unlikely to be a misunderstanding. Quickly, Tyler opened up her murder outline and copied the contents of the letter underneath Section (I)(e)➔ Secret (self). Quickly scrolling through the outline again, she highlighted her notes about the timing of John's move over to Cloose & Elkman. Reading between the lines, Tyler wondered whether John had been contacted because the firm had been notified about the complaint and investigation into Kevin by the ethics committee. It was possible that the complaint was baseless, but because it had become an investigation the firm wanted Kevin to leave because of reputational concerns. Or it was true. Either way the firm would want him to leave. And according to John, Kevin was indeed leaving before the end of the fiscal year. But Tyler had never heard anything about that. Kevin must have been quietly being forced out of the firm, or perhaps he agreed to leave. The fact that the Missouri Bar Association had reached the hearing stage of an ethics investigation, and the fact that Kevin was leaving strongly indicated that he had actually engaged in unethical behavior.

Taking it a step further and pleased to be following the police-approved, evidence-first investigation strategy, Tyler wondered whether this new information gave anyone a motive to murder Kevin. John seemed unlikely, he was going to benefit from Kevin leaving, and according to John he never wondered what was behind the move. Even if Tyler still doubted that, John seemed unlikely to kill someone when he was already in line to get that person's book of business. Tyler did not know Kevin's family, but she could see a spouse being furious that the breadwinner had fucked up so magnificently, and disgraced law firm partners certainly could not support Kevin's family's lifestyle. She made a note to that effect in the outline.

Thinking back to the firm, Tyler considered Brendan, who she had discounted earlier because she knew he would never kill off the person who was going to usher him through the partnership process. If Kevin was going to leave the firm in disgrace, he would not be able to help Brendan. Would that push Brendan to kill Kevin, though? Tyler still could not picture it. Brendan was more likely to kill Kevin by annoying him with passive aggression, although on the other hand Tyler did think Brendan was organized enough to murder someone without leaving evidence. And he was duplicitous enough to hide an affair with a subordinate for years. Tyler almost wrote his name down, but decided it was too ridiculous—she knew Brendan, he was not a murderer. Plus, Tyler had no reason to think Brendan had heard anything about Kevin's impending departure prior to seeing this letter.

That left, as far as Tyler knew, Peter. Tyler wished she knew more about Kevin's reaction to the ethics investigation. If Kevin was quietly leaving as Peter wanted him to, it would not make sense for Peter to kill him. But if Kevin was fighting the decision... Tyler sighed and threw herself back down in her chair. Tyler wanted the pieces to fall into place, but she felt like she only had half of them. It was useless, she lacked access to enough information to make any conclusions, and as she already knew, she could hardly march herself up to Peter's office and question him.

Tyler put the letter away in a drawer, thinking she would drop it off at Brendan's office after he left, and decided to try to refocus on work. It was useless though, after reading the same document (relevant, boring) three times, Tyler flipped to her calendar and remembered that she had only two days before Ty's welcome lunch. Steeling herself internally, she grabbed her notebook and pen and walked over to John's office. She finally had gotten the right timing— John's office door was open and he was inside facing his computer. Soft classical music played. Tyler knocked on his door frame and John swiveled his chair around.

"What," he said flatly.

"Hey, John!" Tyler realized she had not come up with a strategy for how exactly she would try to figure out what was going on in John's head, but decided she would try a friendly approach, "just wanted to follow up on a few things."

John crossed his arms and said nothing.

"So, I guess first of all, I just wanted to make sure you got those depo outlines. Did you have any comments? Did they look okay?"

"I haven't read them." John blinked impassively. He was obviously not going to play along with Tyler's friendly approach. This did not bode well for Tyler's continued presence on the NSK cases. If she still had leverage over him, Tyler figured he would have played along.

"No problem! Hopefully these are more in-line with what you're looking for than the last one. But if not, of course, just let me know and I'll make any changes that are needed. And I made sure those new emails are included. By the way, did you see Brendan's email on that?"

"Yes. We have answers from Bruce?"

"Well, no."

"Then I'm not sure why you would bring that up. It isn't productive for me to hear about how you are trying to take care of something. Take care of it, then give me answers. As you still seem to struggle to understand, I'm incredibly busy, I can't be bothered to track the progress on things you should take care of on your own." John started to turn back toward his computer. Tyler worked to keep her face and body language neutral as her heart started to thud in her chest. While neither of them had mentioned Ty and what that meant for Tyler, Tyler could take a hint: she was back on John's shit list and he no longer thought he had to pretend otherwise.

Still, Tyler knew she needed to bring up the document review, which was not going to meet John's turnaround standards. Maybe she could gently remind John about their agreement and bring up Ty directly to see his reaction.

"Thank you so much for that feedback," Tyler began, "It's so helpful to have insight into how I can help you best." She could tell she was laying it on too thick and sounded sarcastic to her own ears, but John turned back to her slightly and looked pleased, so maybe this was the reaction he expected. "And just before I go, I wanted to circle back on that document review issue." Tyler put a special emphasis on the phrase "document review" to make sure John understood. "I saw that, um, Ty, is starting on Friday and he's my same year. So, are we going to work together on those documents? Or did you think any more about giving some flexibility on the timeline or bringing a first-year on board?" Tyler smiled at John intently.

"Subtle."

Tyler did not think she had been so obvious, but clearly John disagreed. She let the ensuing pause in the conversation grow.

"Let's decide once Ty is on board. He might have some helpful thoughts. He's really fantastic, I think you'll learn a lot from him."

Tyler did not miss John's insult—that she would learn from someone who had been practicing the same amount of time as her. Not wanting to make the situation worse—at least John had not told her she would not have a place on the team once Ty arrived—Tyler decided to ignore the insult and smiled brightly. "I just can't wait to meet him. Of course, I'll be happy to show him the ropes on all of our C and E systems. Well, I'll let you go, as you said you are very busy and I don't want to waste your time. Brendan and I will be back in touch once we hear back from Bruce and have a plan for moving forward."

Tyler tried to focus on reviewing documents for the rest of the day but fell down a rabbit hole stalking Ty instead. He was chubby with round, dark-framed glasses and bright orange hair. Tyler had pictured a protégé of John's being more of a bro type, especially as a lawyer going by the casual nickname of "Ty," and while looks could be deceiving, Ty had apparently written a law review article that was published about contradictions in federal and local wildlife protection laws in Wyoming. And his Instagram had only three posts—his family, a craft beer, and a dog. Tyler reported her findings to Cerene.

So, do you think I can bill that time, lol? Prepare for onboarding of T. Collins?

Ummmmm. No.

Tyler clicked out of the chat. She thought about Kevin telling her that the definition of insanity was doing the same thing and expecting different results. He had really been onto something there. A new chat popped up from Brendan.

What the fuck did you say to John?

A pit opened up in Tyler's stomach. She had never heard Brendan swear. Taking a deep calming breath Tyler typed out three different responses and deleted them. Finally, she sent: *I'm so sorry... but what do you mean?*

You said something to John about our conversation with Bruce, which I had already summarized in an email.

I just brought it up while I was talking to him about various open items in the case! I'm so sorry, I didn't realize that was the wrong thing to do!

Tyler's phone rang.

"Hi, Brendan," she said hesitantly.

"Now John is on *my* case about mis-managing the junior associates."

"I'm so sorry. I was asking John about the depo outlines and I just wanted to see if he had any thoughts about our conversation with Bruce. He was so upset about those emails before, I thought he would be happy we were on it!"

"Tyler, we were working on that issue together. And just in case you forgot, you're the junior," *midlevel,* Tyler thought, "and I'm the senior. So don't jump me and talk to the partner unless you get my approval." For the second time in as many hours, Tyler prepared herself to eat shit.

"Thank you so much for that feedback, Brendan. I'm still learning how John likes to be helped best, and all insight is extremely helpful." Tyler's delivery had improved; she thought she sounded quite sincere this time. And she really did feel bad if John had chewed out Brendan.

"Don't try to get cute with me, Tyler. If you and I are working on something together, you don't go to John, you come to me. Got it?"

Tyler bit her tongue. That was literally what she had just said, but Brendan evidently had not finished giving her a piece of his mind. "Understood. Thanks again for that feedback."

"Don't thank me for the feedback, stop... fucking up." That was the second f-bomb from Brendan. John must have really gone after him. Tyler was at a loss for words. "I'm sure you saw we're getting a new associate... Ty?" Brendan continued.

Tyler nodded.

"Hello?"

"Yes, I saw. Sorry, I was nodding my head."

"I can't see a head nod, Tyler. Sheesh, just get it together. Okay?"

"Okay. Brendan, I'm so sorry."

"Again, the goal is for you to avoid having to apologize. You have to stop making mistakes. Especially basic ones like that. Okay?"

"Okay, I'll stop making mistakes. Got it."

"Good." Brendan hung up.

Thirty seconds later Tyler's phone rang again.

"Hi, again, Brendan!" she tried for a cheery tone.

"Don't bill for this." He hung up again.

Tyler had never heard Brendan so angry. Maybe she did not know him as well as she thought. Shaken, she was about to close her door so she could have a quick cry in privacy, but remembering the open-door issue, she pinched herself on the inside of the arm until the urge passed.

CHAPTER THIRTEEN

On Thursday night, Tyler was sitting at her kitchen table organizing deposition exhibits to send out to the printer—she had been working more or less nonstop since her call with Brendan and had not even stopped for dinner—when she heard a loud knock on the door. She jumped. Ever since the burglary Tyler had not felt comfortable in her house at night. She slowly walked toward the front door. Without undoing the chain, she opened the door a crack and peered out, feeling the damp, warm air seeping in immediately. Tom and Detective Meyer stood on her front porch wearing almost identical dark slacks and white shirts. Tyler undid the chain and opened the door.

"Detectives." She looked up at Tom to try to get some sort of clue about the purpose of their visit, but his expression gave nothing away.

"Can we come in?" asked Detective Meyer.

"Of course." Tyler let them in. Detective Meyer's shirtsleeves were rolled up, and he wiped sweat off his face as he walked in and removed the aviator sunglasses he had been wearing even though the sun had started to set. As Tom closed Tyler's door she saw a sweat stain on his back. "What's going on?" She nervously crossed her arms.

"I'll cut right to the chase," Detective Meyer said. "We've received an anonymous tip that there's evidence related to Kevin's murder here."

Tyler balked. "What? Absolutely not."

"So, you don't mind if we take a look around?" Detective Meyer cocked an eyebrow.

Tyler knew what she should say: not without a warrant. But Tom had told her she was no longer a person of interest, and Tyler knew there was no evidence in her house since she had nothing to do with Kevin's murder. She looked at Tom again for some assistance, but he remained silent.

"Well?" said Detective Meyer.

"Ummm. Okay?" Tyler said. "But there's nothing here... I had nothing to do with his murder. I told you everything I know."

The detectives started to walk up Tyler's stairs and to her spare office. Tyler felt uneasy—Detective Meyer had not been upstairs in her townhouse before, but he was confidently headed toward her home office. Had Tom told Detective Meyer about the layout of her house? What else had he said? She stopped two steps from the top to do some circular breathing. When she reached the doorway to her home office she saw Detective Meyer leaning over her open office drawer. He had put on one rubber glove, and he rummaged around the drawer with that hand briefly before pulling out what appeared to be a large watch. He dangled it for a second as he and Tom looked at the watch, then dropped it into an evidence bag Tom held open.

"What is that?" Tyler asked, walking over to the detectives.

"It's a watch," said Detective Meyer.

"No, I can see that. But it's not mine. It's huge."

"It's a man's watch," Detective Meyer said, as if that addressed Tyler's confusion. Tyler looked closer at the watch, which sat winking in the light at the bottom of the evidence bag. Funny, only part of the watch face was catching the light. With a shock, Tyler saw that the rest of the face was caked with a red substance.

"Is that blood?"

"Could be." Tyler sat down in her office chair. Tom manipulated the watch through the bag to look at the back of the face.

"See those dates?" he pointed down, addressing Detective Meyer.

Detective Meyer nodded. "This is it all right." Detective Meyer reached back into the drawer and pulled out Tyler's missing security badge. He dropped it into a second bag. Tyler's eyes widened.

"Okay. One of you tell me what's going on," Tyler said faintly. "That's not my watch, and I didn't put it in there. And that's the first I've seen that badge in weeks."

"Let's go sit downstairs and chat," said Detective Meyer. Numbly, Tyler walked back down to her kitchen table and sat down, flipping her laptop closed and moving it to the side. Detective Meyer set the bags containing the watch and the badge down in the middle of the table.

Looking at Tom, she said, "We gotta stop meeting like this." Detective Meyer looked over at Tom expectantly.

"I told you," Tom said, "she was burglarized the other week." Detective Meyer frowned slightly. He seemed to be about to say something to Tom but held it back.

"So, here's the deal," Detective Meyer said. "We received an anonymous tip that there was a piece of evidence tied to Kevin's murder in the top drawer of the desk in your office bedroom. And this watch," Detective Meyer gestured toward it, "is definitely Kevin's. It's got his kids' birthdates inscribed on the back, and according to Mrs. Stevens he never took it off." Detective Meyer paused, perhaps to allow Tyler to explain the watch, but she was at a loss for words. She wondered why she was not being put under arrest. To the contrary, Detective Meyer was looking at her with an almost pitying expression. "Now, I understand that you were burglarized last week, and that the burglar tossed the place pretty well. Is that right?"

Tyler nodded.

"And I understand your iPad was taken. Where was the iPad?"

"It was up in my office, I think."

"And I'm assuming your office was tossed?"

"I mean, yeah, my stuff was everywhere, all over the floor." Tyler shuddered at the memory. "It was horrible."

Detective Meyer nodded. "That's what I thought. So, what I'm wondering is, why would a burglar take an iPad but not a Rolex?" Tyler looked down at the watch. Sure enough, the watch was a Rolex.

"Because it wasn't there?" Tyler guessed. "If I had seen it when I was cleaning up, I would have said something. Tom, Detective Armstrong, that is, was right there." Detective Meyer pressed his lips together and looked over at Tom.

"She was feeling pretty jumpy after the burglary," he said. Both detectives had excellent poker faces, and she could not tell whether

Tom's presence after the burglary was a surprise to Detective Meyer or whether she had merely confirmed something Detective Meyer already knew.

"I mean, you didn't see a watch, right?" she confirmed with Tom. She felt embarrassed to bring it up at all given the night ended with rejection, but she wanted to make sure the detectives knew she had nothing to do with the watch. Tyler remembered Tom saying it was totally unprofessional to kiss her, but if she had to guess, she thought Tom had cleaned up the story of what happened for Detective Meyer.

"No," he said. He looked calm.

"But I mean, I just dumped everything back in my drawers, it's not like I had it organized before, so maybe it was there? But I swear, I didn't notice it."

"I didn't pay attention to how she put her things back into the drawer, but I definitely didn't see a watch," confirmed Tom.

Detective Meyer nodded again. "This watch was located in the very back of your top drawer. You had to pull the drawer out of the desk to see it." He looked at Tyler gravely. "Tyler, I'm sorry to say I don't think you experienced a random burglary. While its possible the burglar missed this watch, given the rest of your possessions were removed, I think that is highly unlikely. I'll be straight with you, I think someone planted that watch and took your iPad."

"Oh, my god," Tyler said. "The uniformed cops said it was weird that nothing else was taken!"

"Well, I don't know about that, but it *is* unusual for a burglar taking small goods to leave a valuable watch behind."

"So... what does this mean?" Tyler asked. She felt relieved on one hand—she had a sense finding Kevin and the burglary were linked, and now that seemed to be confirmed. On the other hand, what did it mean that someone was out there trying to implicate her in Kevin's murder?

"Nothing for you," Detective Meyer said. "I'm not arresting you, but I am going to take your desk drawer away for prints. Although I would guess there are none if none were found after your burglary."

"Do I get, like, protective custody now? Isn't someone targeting me?"

Detective Meyer nodded thoughtfully. "No. There is obviously a link between you, Kevin, and Kevin's murderer, but the murderer hasn't done anything to suggest that you are in physical danger."

"Seriously? I think putting a corpse in my trunk and a bloody watch in my desk, and then calling the police on me certainly suggests bad intentions."

Detective Meyer shrugged. "You haven't been physically harmed."

"So, you're going to catch this guy, right?" Tyler rubbed her upper arms, feeling a chill.

"Of course," Detective Meyer said. Tyler wondered if it was a coincidence that Tom had remained silent this whole time.

"Are you close? I mean, this is pretty scary."

"We can't comment on an ongoing investigation, Tyler," said Detective Meyer, echoing a line that Tyler was becoming more and more familiar with. "Now, if you don't mind, I'll get a larger bag and take your top desk drawer."

"Umm, okay. So that's it? Someone planted evidence in my house presumably to try to frame me for a murder, and you're just taking it and leaving?"

Detective Meyer looked puzzled. "Yes, we're doing our jobs investigating a murder."

Tyler could feel her face heating up. "So, you have to be assaulted or dead to get help. Cool. Amazing."

"There's no need for that, Tyler," Detective Meyer frowned.

"Well, I hope you feel really wonderful about yourselves when you investigate my murder. Or would an assault be enough? Attempted assault? Probably not, since I wouldn't be harmed then, huh? Maybe you'd feel a little bit bad, but still wouldn't do anything."

"I see that you're upset," Detective Meyer said, as if talking to a small child. "But our responsibility is to investigate this murder. And because I have no reason to believe you are in danger, and in fact, I still have no proof that you were not involved in the murder, there's nothing else for me to do here." He stood up. "Tom?"

Tom stood and briskly walked out to the car, came back with a large evidence bag, and took the top drawer from Tyler's desk. Tyler, fuming, walked to her entryway and stood silently in disbelief. Tom avoided making eye contact with her. Barefoot on her front porch, Tyler watched the detectives drive away. Then she walked inside, slamming the door behind her, turned on every light, and checked every door and window twice.

As Tyler's anger subsided, fear took over. It was around ten, but she felt wide awake. She bribed Lucy to sit on the couch with her by giving her copious treats. Tyler opened her computer to keep working—she might as well bill some hours if she was going to be awake, but struck by a thought, opened up the murder outline. Under motives, she added:

II. Murderer Characteristics
  A. Had my security badge
  B. Strong enough to move Kevin's body out of my trunk (man?)
  C. Familiar with C & E garage
  D. Knows where I live
  E. Knows I had a connection to Kevin (work)

With a shiver, Tyler realized the murderer most likely knew her personally. That meant it was someone who Tyler interacted with regularly. And given that the people Tyler knew were overwhelmingly C and E employees, it was most likely that the murderer was someone at the firm. Thinking more, Tyler realized her address was probably listed in the firm's internal directory. She quickly confirmed that was the case. Therefore, the murderer could be almost anyone at the firm, not necessarily someone she knew well. Tyler could not tell whether that made her feel better or worse. How was she supposed to go to work when someone, maybe someone who she spoke with every day, was trying to frame her for murder? She hoped the detectives would find the culprit quickly.

Although she knew the murderer might be someone she did not know well, Tyler started to mentally run through the employees she saw every day, to see which seemed strong enough to move a body. With a start, she remembered she had taken pictures of forms and reports at the police station and had never looked at the photos. Maybe the forms would help her narrow down her list. Tyler opened up her phone with trembling fingers and started to scroll through the pictures of the pages.

There were seven photos total, and Tyler remembered she had not photographed two or three pages. Out of those seven photos, five were clear and contained the entire page. She quickly flipped through those five and saw she had managed to snap a list of everything found in the trunk of her car, a written description of the condition of the trunk, and a technical chemical report. The list noted that a number of short brown hairs had been found in the trunk that were being sent for DNA testing. Kevin's hair was brown, and Tyler wondered whether something about the hairs appeared different from Kevin's, or whether sending the hairs off was simply standard police practice. Unfortunately, there was no DNA report, or if there was, it was on a blurry page or one Tyler had not managed to photograph. The written description of the trunk noted that Kevin was most likely moved into the drunk after he was deceased—he had died due to blood loss, and there were only a few spots of blood on the trunk. The blood had also been sent off for testing, but was presumed to be Kevin's. The report also noted that another substance was smeared on a small area next to where Kevin's head was believed to have laid. That substance had been sent off for testing as well.

Tyler added "F. Short brown hair?" to her outline. If the hairs were not Kevin's, Tyler's guess that the murderer was a man was correct. Then again, a woman could have short brown hair as well. Tyler exhaled in frustration. The pictures had not helped at all. Taking one more pass through them, something caught her eye in the chemical report. She zoomed in and saw the report was a list of chemicals making up the smeared substance. Several of the names appeared familiar, even though they were multisyllabic technical words. Tyler started to type a couple of them into google. As she typed out the words she gasped. The chemicals were the active ingredients in NSK's nose hair wax. They were familiar to Tyler because she had read and written about them for several years.

But why would nose hair wax be in the trunk with Kevin? Tyler had seen a sample on one occasion after Kevin flew down to visit the NSK warehouse and familiarized himself with the production line, but Tyler had never purchased it herself. The product had certainly never been in her trunk. Tyler briefly wondered whether Kevin perhaps used the nose hair wax, but quickly dispelled that idea. No one who exclusively dealt with the negative side effects of a product would actually use it. Tyler now felt certain the murderer was someone at the firm. The whole thing must be tied to Kevin's work. The murderer was trying to frame Tyler, one of Kevin's team members, and the body was found with the product that Kevin made his career defending. She added "G. C and E employee familiar with NSK cases" to the outline.

Tyler hoped the detectives had made the connection that the smear was NSK nose hair wax, but when she painstakingly reviewed the chemical report, she did not see anywhere where the product was identified. Just as she was wondering whether she should text Tom and tell him, even though she technically should not have seen the report, her phone pinged with a text notification from him. Tyler twitched so violently that her laptop fell off her lap onto the ground. Thankfully, it was not damaged. The text was from Tom.

Hey, are you ok?

No.

I'm off. Do you want company?

So now you're offering...

I'll keep my phone on. Let me know.

Tyler wondered whether Tom was trying to be nice or trying to get laid. Or both. Either way, if he came over she could tell him about what she had seen in the chemical report without creating a written record revealing that she had seen confidential police documents, so she responded, *Come over.*

Fifteen minutes later, she opened the door to Tom, now dressed in jeans and a T-shirt again. Seeing him dressed the same as the burglary night, Tyler felt embarrassed at his rejection all over again. She felt even more embarrassed that she was still attracted to him.

"I don't know why I invited you," she said peevishly.

"What a way to greet a guest! I don't know why I offered to come over. Except your place is much nicer than mine, so maybe I just like it here better."

"Yeah, I thought it was so unprofessional to be involved with me," she said accusingly. "Seems like you didn't tell Detective Meyer exactly what happened the other night."

Tom shrugged cheerfully. "It is. And I didn't."

Tyler stood glaring at Tom for a moment longer, but mostly she was annoyed at herself for being so desperate. There was no point in punishing Tom for that. She sighed. "Well, since you're here, do you want wine?"

"Yes, thanks. And I think you promised to ask me some questions about myself."

Warming, Tyler smiled. "I did, didn't I."

Tyler poured them both a glass of Sauvignon Blanc and sat down at her kitchen table.

"So," said Tom. Tyler waited, but he seemed to be unsure of how to continue.

"So," said Tyler, "I did something I wasn't supposed to, and I need to tell you about it, but not if I'm going to get in trouble."

"That's so vague I'm really not sure how to answer."

Tyler took a big sip of wine, and then a deep breath. "When I went to pick up my car, Jeannie had me sign a form that was on top of a stack of other papers. And she was chatting with another officer," Tyler paused, then continued slowly, "and I took some pictures of the other papers." Tyler paused again to see Tom's reaction. It was not immediately clear—Tom had the same poker face on that she had seen earlier with Detective Meyer—but he gestured for her to continue. "One of the pictures that I took was of the chemical report from the smear in my trunk." She paused again, but there was no change to Tom's expression. "The smear was NSK nose hair wax. Did you guys know that? I know you can't comment on an ongoing investigation, so maybe blink twice if you knew. Wait, pull your left earlobe."

Tom chuckled and pulled his left earlobe.

"Oh, my god, and you guys still don't think I'm in any danger?" Tyler slapped her hands on the table and stood up. "The guy is obviously one of my coworkers! He's going to realize when I go in tomorrow that framing me didn't work. What's going to happen then?" Tyler's voice rose as she got worked up all over again and paced back and forth around her kitchen.

Tom reached out and grabbed her wrist, stopping her from pacing. "It's going to be fine. We're going to solve it, and I have to agree with Detective Meyer here—nothing has happened that suggests you are in any physical danger."

"Except, um, the murder? And the corpse in my trunk?"

Tom shrugged. "We've seen a lot. You've got to trust us. And look, I'm here now. Sure, I'm not here in my professional capacity, but you're not alone." He smiled reassuringly at Tyler, who remained skeptical. "How about another glass of wine, which by the way is much nicer than I ever have at home, and I'll order a pizza."

Tyler got up to refill the glasses, and became distracted wondering whether Tom was purposefully creating a parallel to the last time he was there, meaning something might happen between the two of them, or whether he just really liked pizza. "It's almost midnight, no pizza for me."

"All right, probably for the best," Tom patted his stomach. "I can't resist."

"Well, I guess I promised to ask you some questions about yourself," Tyler said. "So, let's go. How old are you?"

"Thirty-three."

"Where are you from?"

"Suburbs outside of Chicago."

"How long have you been in St. Louis?"

"Ten years."

"What brought you here?"

"A woman."

Tyler raised an eyebrow. "Girlfriend?"

"Fiancée."

She raised both eyebrows. "What happened there?"

"None of your business."

"Any siblings?"

"No."

Tyler opened her mouth to ask another question, but before she could Tom came around the table and kissed her. After a few minutes they moved to her couch, then up to her bed. As she was falling asleep next to Tom, she blearily calculated that she would get three hours of sleep if she fell asleep immediately, which, for once, she did.

CHAPTER FOURTEEN

Tyler woke up to her alarm blaring at seven in the morning. Her blanket felt like it weighed about a thousand pounds, and the light from her window burned her eyes. She groaned and rolled over, wondering whether Tom had left while she slept, but he was lying on the other side of the bed with his mouth open. A thin trickle of drool ran out of the right side of his mouth onto the pillow. Tyler smiled, amused and happy that Tom had stayed. She was about to turn her alarm off and go back to sleep when dread cut through her exhaustion. The alarm was on because Tyler had to go to work, where a murderer would also probably be, that is, unless the murderer was working from home. And the icing on the cake: Tyler had to attend a welcome lunch for her replacement who, adding insult to injury, was also named Tyler.

Tyler rolled onto her back, then whispered herself a quick pep talk. "Don't be a fucking quitter." She had to repeat it three times before it did the trick and she found the will to roll out of bed. Tom did not move throughout the entire process.

Tyler did not want to look in the mirror and see what she looked like after an extremely stressful day, followed by three hours of sleep. Maybe the sex would have counteracted things slightly for the better. *Nope*, she thought as she looked at herself in the mirror. At least her hair was clean. That was the only good point she could come up with. It was already seven fifteen, and Tyler rushed to try to salvage the situation with the help of a lot of concealer. At least it was Friday, a.k.a. Jeans Friday—she threw on her stretchiest pair of skinny dark wash jeans, a light silky shirt, and after a minute of consideration, some new, lower block heels (purchased after Tyler had seen Cerene wearing a similar pair) rather than her typical four-inch pumps. She had planned to wear a more formal outfit to appear more intimidating to Ty, but given her lack of sleep she had to go for comfort and worry about intimidating him later. Somehow Tyler managed to get out the door by eight. She briefly considered waking Tom up but decided to leave him. Instead, Tyler put her spare key on the nightstand, and texted Tom to let him know where the coffee was and to ask him to lock up.

Trying to increase her energy for the day, Tyler blasted rap music in her car on the way to the office. As she drove into the garage the attendant gave her a surprised look, and Tyler turned the music down, realizing it was probably audible outside of the car. As she listened to the muted beats, her body was flooded with stress and dread. Tyler had felt a similar cold sensation trickle out from her stomach toward her extremities plenty of other times when she drove into the C and E garage—the time she filed an exhibit as a separate motion at five minutes to midnight the night it was due and she had to call the clerk the next morning to get the docket corrected and embarrassed Kevin, and the time she forgot about a deadline to answer a complaint until the day it was due and she had to hire local counsel and get an extension in six hours, and even most recently the time she had stayed home to review documents and Brendan messaged her to let her know John was looking for her. But none of that held a candle to what she felt driving in wondering whether she would see Kevin's murderer, and what he or she might do when they realized Tyler had not been arrested. After she parked her car, she lifted her left hand off the steering wheel and saw it was shaking. Glancing around the parking lot, she wondered whether there were any cameras. The detectives had never answered her when she asked that first night around her kitchen table, but she assumed there were none, otherwise they would have seen who was using her badge and caught the murderer by now.

Normally, Tyler took the stairs from the garage to the lobby, but this morning she walked to the elevator as quickly as she could in her heels and mashed the button to go up until the doors opened. Tyler managed to get in the elevator and press the door close button before anyone else could join her, but then the elevator stopped on the partner floor one above and a nearly-retired partner who Tyler had met a handful of times—he was either in the real estate or bankruptcy group and did not sit on her floor—slowly walked on, toting a bulging, brown old-fashioned leather briefcase. Tyler considered bolting out of the elevator. She looked suspiciously at the partner's hair. It was silver, although that hardly proved anything, since the short brown hairs could have been Kevin's. Tyler noticed the partner's shoulders were stooped, and his suit looked a little loose on him, as if he were shrinking with age. He was probably not strong enough to drag a corpse around. She stayed on the elevator.

"Morning," the partner said.

Tyler thought she had met him before but could not remember his name. "Morning," she said suspiciously.

Tyler and the partner, Ernst, that was his name, walked across the lobby to the office elevator bank. As the doors were closing to take them up to their respective floors, a pale hand reached in, and Brendan stepped on, slightly breathless.

"Morning, Tyler," he said, "Happy Friday." He appeared to have moved on from his annoyance with her the day before.

"Morning, Brendan," Tyler said, maneuvering herself to the back corner of the elevator where no one could stand behind her. She clocked Brendan's hair: blonde. But again, it could have been Kevin's. Tyler could not help but think back to Brendan's rage earlier in the week, his ability to lie by omission about his affair with Cerene, and how his mentor, who Brendan likely thought would help him become partner, was actually about to be disciplined by the Missouri Bar Association. Tyler carefully watched Brendan, but he had no outward reaction to her presence. If he was surprised that Tyler had not been arrested, he was not showing it. To be safe, Tyler let Brendan leave the elevator before her and dawdled so that they were not walking down the hallway together.

"Happy Friday!" Gina sang to Tyler, as she walked to her office.

"Happy Friday, Gina!" said Tyler. Several steps away from Gina, Tyler stopped in her tracks. Gina had a light brown bob with bangs. The bangs were composed of short brown hair. A senior associate walked by and gave Tyler a curious look. He also had short brown hair. Tyler continued with a start and closed the door to her office, memo be damned. Could Gina really have killed Kevin? Gina was nearing sixty, but she was tall and sturdy. Anything was possible, Tyler thought doubtfully, but Gina seemed extremely unlikely to murder anyone. And for some reason Tyler thought Gina seemed more like the poisoning type, if she was going to kill anyone. Tyler pulled up the firm's website online and started reviewing headshots to see which attorneys had short brown hair. She made a list under section F ("Short brown hair?"). By lunchtime there were thirty people on the list, and that only included attorneys: no staff. And the list was hardly reliable. Most attorneys' headshots were five to ten years out of date; they all looked strong and healthy enough to move a body in the picture when any number of them could be much weaker now, not to mention have gray hair. And Tyler had not even considered the possibility that a woman could have changed her hairstyle. There was no way Tyler would be able to narrow down suspects that way. Groaning, she pushed away from the desk and rested her forehead down in front of her keyboard. She counted to sixty silently in her head, then gathered herself as best she could for Ty's welcome lunch.

Tyler stopped by the bathroom on her way up to the Willow conference room where the welcome lunch would be held. Looking in the mirror, she nervously re-arranged her hair to move the part further to the side. Her face was shiny, and somehow the outer parts seemed swollen while dark bags sagged underneath her eyes. She also had a red spot on her forehead where it had been leaning down on her desk. Tyler ran back to her office for her tube of concealer and added some more to the offending regions. She was now going to be late for the lunch, and she took the stairs two at a time.

Slightly out of breath, and as always during the summer, sweating, Tyler shoved open the door to the Willow room three minutes after the hour. The door was lighter than she remembered and it flew open, almost hitting Brendan, who had just walked in. Tyler cringed backward. A couple other associates who Tyler guessed were working on John's other sets of cases were already seated and chatting with each other about an upcoming motion to dismiss hearing. Tyler made an apologetic face and mouthed, "Sorry!" to Brendan, who frowned at her. She anxiously looked around but saw that luckily neither John nor Ty had arrived yet.

Brendan was the only person in the room Tyler worked with regularly, so even though he was on the suspect list, Tyler followed him to the table and sat down in the chair he had left between himself and the other associates. She tried to catch his eye, but he was furiously typing an email on his phone. Tyler craned her neck to nosily try to read the email but saw that it was actually an extremely long text to Cerene that included several all-capital phrases. She made out *WHAT DO YOU NOT UNDERSTAND*, then blushed and looked away. Tyler turned to the associate sitting on her other side, but he had completely rotated his chair to face his team member, leaving his back squarely to Tyler. Tyler clocked the associate's short brown hair. She had maybe met him once before. Could he be the murderer? Tyler surreptitiously pinched her thigh under the table to avoid spiraling into panic. She looked back at Brendan's screen. He glared at her and turned the brightness on his phone down low enough so Tyler could no longer make out anything but the shape of a text bubble that extended the length of his entire screen.

She looked over at the counter at the back of the room and was annoyed to see that lunch was a build-your-own gyro buffet from a restaurant a few blocks away rather than the condiment-heavy sandwiches made by the firm's cafeteria. Ty sure must be special to get a true catered lunch. As if on cue, the door to the conference room flung open again and John walked in, followed closely by Ty. Tyler would classify John's hair as black, turning to a distinguished salt and pepper, but now she wondered whether it was technically a very dark brown. Although based on John's report that he was set to move to Cloose & Elkman before Kevin's death and Tyler's discovery of the ethics committee investigation into Kevin, it seemed highly unlikely that he was the murderer, but it was theoretically possible John had some other motive to kill Kevin. Ty had put on weight since his headshot was taken and had gone from chubby to fat. His hair was shockingly bright orange in person. He might be here to steal Tyler's job, but at least there was no way he was the murderer. Tyler tried to refocus on her goal of keeping her spot on the cases at least for the next hour.

John and Ty entered the room on a wave of confidence—John was laughing heartily, and Ty was smiling right along with him. Tyler could see already she stood no chance against Ty—not only did John like Ty's work, he seemed to even like Ty personally. Tyler forced a smile onto her face and promised herself a generous .5 to cry alone in her office later. Ty took the seat across the table from Tyler and John strode to the front of the conference room.

"Everyone, thanks for making the time to join us. I'm very excited for us to welcome Ty to the team." He smiled benevolently down at Ty. Tyler fixed her eyes on a point beyond John's right shoulder and blinked rapidly. She had to keep her shit together for at least one more hour. Out of the corner of her eye she saw Ty shift in his chair. "I've been working with Ty since he first started practicing several years ago, and I'm so pleased I was able to bring him with me here to C and E. Ty is going to be primarily working on the NSK cases and the auto cases that I hope to be bringing over in the next month or so, but he'll help out here and there as needed on all of my cases. Ty, want to say a few words?"

Tyler forced herself to look at her replacement. Ty's hands were pressed flat onto the table, and he intentionally clasped them in front of his body before speaking, as if he were nervous and trying to avoid fidgeting. Tyler saw spots of condensation under where his palms had laid on the table seconds before. Even knowing Ty was not going to be the bro type she had expected based on her online stalking, she was still surprised that this fat nervous man was John's beloved protégé.

"Hey, everybody," Ty began in a nasally voice. He paused and looked down at his handprints on the table. He briefly made eye contact with Tyler and she lifted the corner of her mouth into a quarter of a smile to let him know she had noticed. "I guess, like John said, I've been working closely with him since I started practicing, so almost four years now. I'm really looking forward to working and getting to know all of you, and I'm sure I'll have lots of questions about the C and E way of doing things, so thanks in advance for your patience on those." It was a surprisingly friendly and humble speech.

John pointed to everyone in the room, named them, and shared which cases they worked on. As he was pointing out Brendan, the door to the conference room swung open and Peter Parisi, managing partner, walked in. The room immediately fell silent.

Peter smiled at John. "John, I hear I have a wonderful new associate to welcome to the team, and I have you to thank for bringing him to us!"

Tyler did not remember getting a special, individualized, managing partner welcome when she started. She glanced around at the other non-Ty associates. They all wore variations of the same jealous look Tyler was sure was on her face.

"We surely do," said John, "Ty, meet our managing partner, leader extraordinaire, Peter Parisi."

Ty tripped over the leg of his chair as he rushed to stand up and shake Peter's hand.

Peter asked Ty a few questions about how his first day was going and welcomed him again. Ty practically vibrated with enthusiasm. Tyler took in Peter's tall, lanky frame and dark brown, elegantly styled hair. Strength to move a body: check. Short brown hair: check. Peter had been the first person Tyler added to her list this morning based on his physical characteristics, however Tyler had some doubts that Peter would kill someone who was already leaving. That is, if Tyler was not missing some other information. Although she knew she had to focus on getting through this lunch without a meltdown, Tyler wondered whether she might be able to ask Peter a couple questions during lunch.

John joined Peter and Ty and clapped Peter on the shoulder, "Petey, are you joining us for lunch?" Of course, John was on nickname terms with Peter Parisi. Tyler, and everyone else in the room, hung on Peter's response.

"Oh, prior engagement unfortunately," Peter pulled up the cuff of his navy jacket to look down at an expensive-looking watch, "to which I'm actually running late." Tyler could feel the disappointment from every associate thicken the air in the room. "Ty, wonderful to meet you, I look forward to seeing what you accomplish here at Cloose & Elkman."

Ty stammered a thanks and collapsed into his chair. Sweat beaded his forehead.

"Okay," John clapped his hands together once, "Let's eat!"

Tyler found herself behind Ty in the line to make gyro plates. Everyone else was chatting, and she felt awkward and alone. With satisfaction, Tyler noted that no one was talking to Ty either. She kept her eyes fixed on the food, but out of her peripheral vision she could see Ty kept turning toward her. When Tyler brought her food back to the table she angled herself toward Brendan, only to see that he was still fixated on his phone. She took a deep breath, sighed loudly without trying to hide it, and turned the other direction toward Ty.

"Hi, Ty. Welcome. I'm actually also a Tyler, too!" She tried to project a confidence she did not feel.

"Oh, great, nice to meet you. Not many girl Tylers out there."

Tyler forced out a fake laugh. "I guess it's a good thing one of us has a nickname, huh?"

"Umm, yeah, sure. I go by Tyler outside of work though, too."

"Oh? So, what made you choose Ty for work?" Tyler tried for a light tone, but the question came out aggressively.

Ty glanced down the table to John. "John just started calling me that when I started working, and I guess it stuck."

Tyler was surprised. "You never told him you went by Tyler?"

Ty shook his head. He looked confused. Obviously, the thought of correcting John, even on his own name, had never crossed Ty's mind. Tyler was starting to see what John liked about Ty.

"Well, I guess I won't take it personally that I never got a nickname." She forced out another fake laugh. "So, what have you been up to the past couple weeks? That must have been interesting to have John leave your old place." Tyler's phone chimed, and she looked down to see a text from Tom.

Just got up. Your cat was sitting on my face, I think it tried to kill me.
Tyler smiled involuntarily.

Lucy is a girl, not an it! In a meeting, help yourself to coffee or whatever else you can find.

As she was texting, Ty answered nonchalantly, "Oh, you know, just worrying about getting fired, then shitting myself over passing conflicts to come to C and E after John got me the offer." Ty's honesty surprised Tyler into an authentic laugh.

John's voice cut through the conversation, "Ty, Tyler," he emphasized the "ler" in Tyler's name, "so glad you two are getting to know each other. Ty, I was just telling Tyler how much she's going to learn from you." Tyler's face flushed a deep pink with embarrassment. Undoubtedly the under-eye concealer she had generously applied was giving her an extremely flattering reverse-raccoon look. She flushed deeper.

"Aren't you also a third-year associate?" Ty asked. Tyler glared at him and nodded. "I'm sure we have a lot to learn from each other," he told John, "After all, I don't know anything about nose hair wax."

John looked like he was about to say more, but the associate next to Tyler, whose back was still facing her, cut in with a fawning question to John about how he came up with such brilliant legal arguments.

"We should get coffee and talk about those NSK cases," Ty said, "I bet we can bill for it, we'll work out our time descriptions together to sound legit."

Tyler could think of few things she wanted to do less but did not want to be accused of not being a team player on top of her other faults, and said, "I'd love that!" It came out sarcastically.

"No, seriously," Ty continued seriously. "He wants me to jump right into these cases and I've got no idea what's going on with them outside of what I could see from the motion practice on PACER."

Tyler glanced down the table to make sure John was not paying attention. "No offense, but I want to stay on these cases, and I'm not going to lay out the red carpet so my replacement can push me out even faster."

Ty looked surprised. "I'm not here to replace you."

"Come on," Tyler said, "we're not going to have two fourth-years on the cases."

"John told me we were."

"And you believed him?"

Ty nervously glanced down the table again. "Look, I know there's a learning curve with him. He's just like..." Ty seemed to be struggling for a positive spin on what John was like. Tyler waited patiently. "Well, anyway, he'll come around. I don't want him to myself though. I mean, you don't either... right? Look, if we get coffee and you try to get me up to speed on the cases, I'll tell you everything I know about getting on John's good side, deal?"

Tyler squinted at Ty suspiciously, but eventually replied with, "Deal." She was still extremely suspicious of Ty and did not believe for a second that John planned to continue to staff them both on the NSK cases, but obviously she could learn a thing or two about working with John from Ty. Maybe she would be able to focus the conversation on that topic and avoid giving too much away about the cases. Grinning, Ty stuck his hand out to shake with Tyler. As their equally clammy hands met, Tyler wondered for a split second whether they might get along after all.

Putting his phone down face down on the table, with slightly more force than necessary so that it let out a crack, Brendan leaned in and said quietly, "Don't want him to yourself, huh?"

Ty and Tyler looked at each other with twin looks of horror. "Relax," Brendan continued, while looking anxiously down the table at John, "I just want an invite to the coffee."

"I'd love to grab coffee with you, too, Brendan, so that I can learn how best to help you," Ty said smoothly. Tyler had to admit he had a nice style. Subservient, maybe, but effective.

Brendan drew his eyebrows together. "No, I want to go to the coffee where we talk about how to work with John."

"I'll add that to our agenda, sure!"

Brendan looked perturbed but nodded. "I keep my calendar up to date, just throw something on there."

"Looking forward to it."

Brendan abruptly picked up his phone again, drew his eyebrows even closer together, then used his free hand to try to drag them apart. It was a losing battle. Tyler craned her neck to try to see whether texts or emails had him so worked up, but the brightness was still low. Ty shot her a questioning look and she shrugged.

"So, what are you up to today?" Tyler asked Ty. "Tons of training?"

Ty rolled his eyes, "So far, I've learned how to use a phone and how to log onto a computer. Although to be fair, with all the security login procedures I needed that computer training."

"Did you use the same billing software?"

"Haven't got that far. What do you use here?"

Tyler started to explain, when at the other end of the table, John got up and threw his empty plate away. He grabbed a Diet Coke from the fridge and walked over to the door. Tyler noticed it was twelve fifty-eight.

"Ty?" John smiled again. It was unnerving to see John be so nice.

Ty had thrown his plate away too and was hurriedly brushing pita chip crumbs off his pants. "I'll send you that invite!" he said to Tyler. "And you," he added, belatedly, to Brendan.

With the guests of honor gone, the lunch broke up quickly. Tyler waited for Brendan to finish typing something out on his phone so she could try to walk out with him. If Ty was John's favorite, Tyler could try to be Brendan's. As the senior associate he would control the workflow at least as much as John. And she was pretty sure Brendan was not a murderer, so how dangerous could it be? Brendan walked back over to the buffet instead of the door and made himself a second plate.

"Hungry?" Tyler asked, raising her eyebrows.

"Dinner," he said shortly.

"Oh, smart." Tyler would have been embarrassed to take a second plate, but she had to admit it was a pretty good idea. "So, are you working late then?"

Brendan nodded.

"So," she said, drawing out the "o," "what did you think of Ty?"

Brendan shrugged. It was like talking to a brick wall. *Maybe,* Tyler thought, *I should have exhibited a little self-control and kept my eyes to myself at the start of the meeting.*

"He was a lot nicer than I expected," Tyler said, trying to draw Brendan out. "John really likes him."

Brendan frowned, "I know."

Brendan was still giving her nothing, but at least he had verbally responded. Pursuing the angle, Tyler said, "Think he's really going to tell us how to get on John's good side?"

"I think he's going to do the same thing you are—try to get as much information out of you as he can without sharing anything himself."

Now she was getting somewhere. Tyler gave Brendan a half smile. "Am I that predictable?"

Brendan laughed, "To be fair, it's what I would do, too. Oh, by the way, Bruce emailed me this morning. He wants to discuss that production line issue this afternoon."

"Really? I thought we were going to discuss it on the call next week." Tyler included herself in the "we" although she had not been formally invited to the weekly discovery call. She had heard once that one should dress for the position they wanted, not their current position, and she tried to apply the same philosophy to being included in meetings. "I thought Bruce was trying to keep the bill down."

"I know," Brendan said darkly, "if he wants a call, and sooner rather than later, I'm guessing we're about to get some bad news."

Tyler frowned. She hoped whatever the bad news was, it would not be made worse by the fact that she had not identified the issue in a timely manner. "I'm flexible this afternoon. Do you think I could sit in?"

"Sure, I'll forward you the invite once I get it."

"Thanks!"

Tyler walked back to her office and closed the door. She had promised herself.5 to cry, and even though relatively speaking the lunch had gone well, she was still anxious about Ty's arrival. Only having gotten a couple hours of sleep exacerbated her anxiety. However, now Tyler might be called into a meeting at any time, and she hardly wanted to go with puffy, red eyes. She already had enough issues with her appearance for one day. Tyler tried to focus on document review but ended up drinking three cups of coffee, obsessively googling Ty on her phone instead, and jumping every time someone walked past her door. Tom sent her a picture of Lucy sitting on her kitchen table.

She's never done that before! Tyler lied. *Put her on the floor!*

I'm out of here anyway. Give me a text when you're off work, maybe we can grab dinner.

Around four, Tyler started to pack up. It was a Friday in the height of summer, and the office was silent. Her nerves were frayed, and despite all the coffee, she was exhausted. Brendan must have changed his mind about the meeting and not invited her. Normally, Tyler would push the issue and message Brendan to follow up, but given her lack of sleep and the potential murderer on the loose, Tyler opted to log out instead. She could catch up with Brendan on Monday. As Tyler was finishing logging off, her phone chimed with, of course, a meeting invite forwarded from Brendan for five o'clock.

Sighing, Tyler plugged everything back in and went to get one last cup of coffee even though she knew it would probably keep her awake later. She did not see a single other person as she walked to the coffee machine and back to her office. Although, in theory this was good news because the murderer was likely to be out of the office, Tyler felt more jumpy. After all, what if Brendan was the murderer? Was she walking into a dangerous situation? The empty halls made her feel exposed and vulnerable. Back at her office, Tyler did not even bother to open up the document review software, instead she idly scrolled through the Beyond Yoga website looking for new Pilates outfits that she did not need. The minutes ticked by seemingly slower and slower. Finally, it was 4:50. Too early to go to Brendan's office, but Tyler was so desperate for company that she would even prefer to tick Brendan off and watch him read his emails than sit for a second longer in her office alone. Plus, if she got there early she could surprise him just in case he was up to no good.

Tyler gathered a notepad, pen, her cold cup of coffee, and her phone, then doubled back to shove the letter to Kevin from the Missouri Bar Association back in the middle of her notebook and walked to Brendan's office. This time, she noticed that a couple partners' office doors were closed. She could not tell whether the lights were on, and the thick doors prevented her from hearing whether anyone was speaking unless she basically pressed her ear against the door. One of the partners was a newly promoted, model-skinny woman with long glamorous red hair (not on the list) and the other she vaguely knew from large group meetings and was on the list of short-brown-haired employees. She picked up her pace as she passed that door.

Brendan's door was also closed. Tyler knocked.

"Hello?" said Brendan, sounding annoyed.

Tyler cracked the door open and stuck her head in. "I'm here for the call! I assumed I would join you from here?" She furtively looked around Brendan's office and was pleased to see it looked the same—there was no indication he was up to anything but billing his time. Tyler's instincts had been correct about him.

"Oh, right, wow it's almost five."

"Well, I'm a little early, so sorry about that, but I wasn't getting anything done anymore. Feel free to continue if you want, I can just sit here quietly."

"No, it's okay, it's the least productive time of the week, huh?"

Tyler nodded. "I get more done on Sundays than Friday afternoons!"

Brendan smiled, but in a way that suggested he was laughing at Tyler and not with her. As always, she felt chafed by the "my shit doesn't stink attitude." A quip about screwing your subordinates not being billable work was on the tip of her tongue, but she held it in. She could hardly afford to alienate Brendan.

"So, did you hear anything else about this call?" she said instead, changing the subject. "It's six on the East Coast, this is a late Friday for Bruce."

Brendan shook his head. "I heard nothing. Honestly, I wondered if I should bring John into the meeting—I can't imagine what would be so bad that Bruce would call a last-minute Friday afternoon meeting when we're not on deadline, but I guess we need to see what Bruce says first."

Tyler twisted her mouth and looked down at her notepad. "I can't believe I didn't flag the documents earlier. I'm so sorry about that."

Brendan shrugged. "You should have, yes, but you'll get them next time. In my experience, when you make any serious mistake once the memory of it will always haunt you and you'll never do it again. We'll figure this out whatever the issue ends up being. When I was in your shoes, my senior associate told me there were only two unfixable mistakes: lying, and blowing an appeals deadline. You didn't do either of those."

"I think if we're comparing my mistake to either of those two, I'm in pretty bad shape."

Brendan looked at her sympathetically but did not disagree.

"So," Tyler said, changing the subject, "are you having issues with John, too? I thought it was just me."

Brendan hesitated. "You know I'm in the partner look-back period, right?"

Brendan was referring to the three-year period leading up to when an associate was considered for partner. The associate's billable hours and work product would be under extra scrutiny as the partners determined whether he or she was fit to join them as an "owner." Owner in quotes. Twenty years ago if an associate made partner it meant they were a part owner in the firm. In current times associates got promoted to salaried-partner first, which some might say was simply a glorified senior associate.

"Right. It's your second year, right? You'll be up at the end of next   year?"

"I *should* be up at the end of next year," Brendan said, "but having the person you do ninety percent of your work from... leave... presents certain difficulties."

Tyler frowned. "So are you saying you don't think John will support you like Kevin would have?"

Brendan grimaced. "No I'm not saying anything of the sort."

Tyler waited for Brendan to clarify. The silence stretched on. Tyler suspected that was exactly what Brendan was suggesting, but he did not want to say it directly for whatever reason: either he felt it was an inappropriate message to give to a subordinate or he did not want to give the idea too much life.

"Ooo-kay," Tyler said, "It's 4:59, should we call in?"

"He's usually late, but yeah." Brendan nodded and punched in the conference number on his phone. As Brendan punched in the number, Tyler quickly pulled out the letter from the Missouri Bar Association and slid it back among Brendan's papers. Even though it was not in the same place as she had found it, Brendan's desk was disorganized enough that Tyler doubted he would notice. As the phone rang into the conference line, Brendan pointed at her. "Don't say anything this time unless I prompt you." Tyler nodded. To both their surprise, they were notified that Bruce was joining the call almost immediately.

"Bruce!" Brendan said in the same faux-enthusiastic voice Tyler remembered from the last call.

"Brendan," Bruce answered. In just that one word Bruce sounded worse for the wear. Brendan and Tyler exchanged glances.

"Bruce, I let you know over email that Tyler would be joining us, but I just wanted to remind you that she's on the line."

"Hi, Bruce," Tyler said. Brendan rolled his eyes and raised his hands in a "what are you doing" gesture. Surely, she was allowed to at least greet the client without asking permission.

"Bruce, we're on pins and needles." Brendan was maintaining his cheerful voice, but Tyler could see the worry on his face. "What's keeping you in the office late on this Friday afternoon?"

Bruce sighed heavily. Tyler clenched her pen and her notepad. "Brendan, Tyler, it's not good news." While Bruce paused, Brendan tried to pull his eyebrows apart again. Tyler held herself perfectly still and felt every muscle in her body slowly tense up. She felt her left eye start to twitch.

"I spoke with Gennie—that's Genevieve Donner with our facilities—about the emails. Thought I'd have to refresh her recollection, but she remembered immediately, which I already knew was bad news. Long story short, we had a very small amount of product go out that wasn't up to code."

Brendan had pulled out the email packet. "I see a reference to part T3002-3."

"Yep. I wasn't familiar with that part, but essentially, it's where the active ingredients are added to the wax. Instead of sitting for fifteen minutes, during a twenty-four-hour period from two p.m. April one through two p.m. April second, the wax sat for three hours at a time."

"Okay, so how much product are we talking about here?"

"Very, very little, probably ten thousand units."

Tyler raised her hand, and Brendan reluctantly nodded at her. "Usually there's more like sixty thousand units produced in a twenty-four-hour period, right? Did the line run twenty-four hours as it normally does?" Six months ago, Tyler had reviewed the operating procedures for the production line, and she wanted to get some brownie points in exchange for the hours of her life spent reading the procedures that she would never get back.

"Yes, it did run the full twenty-four hours. And that's correct on the units, but because of that longer time sitting in the vats we only got a fraction of the units."

"So, that's good!" Brendan jumped in. "Do we have the tracking codes for that product? Did it possibly go abroad? Or to Alaska? I'm assuming you didn't pull the product because, if so, we wouldn't be having this conversation." Tyler crossed her fingers. If the product went abroad or to Alaska or Hawaii, and they could prove it, the issue would be outside of the scope of the litigation, since the cases only covered injuries to citizens of the continental United States.

Bruce paused. "We do have the tracking codes," he rattled off some SKU codes, "we did not pull it, and I've just made a note to check where that product went."

Tyler raised her hand again, and Brendan rolled his eyes, but gave her another "go-ahead" signal. "Bruce, do we know what the impact to the product was from sitting in the vat for extra time?"

Bruce sighed heavily. "Here's the potentially worst part. It's not just that the product sat for extra time. The active ingredients continued to be added as normal, so these units have twelve times the active ingredients as they should. Obviously, some of the ingredients sat for the standard fifteen minutes, but some for up to three hours."

Tyler grimaced.

"I suspect I can guess the answer to this question," Brendan said, "but is there any chance that adding extra active ingredients had no impact on the end product?"

"We don't know the answer to that question," Bruce responded. "We've never done that before, we hope to never do that again, and to that end, we enacted some extra checks on the machinery to try to avoid this situation occurring again. That being said, the decision was made between Teresa our facilities manager, Gennie, and Shariff, that given the small number of units that were produced, to investigate the impact of those extra active ingredients just didn't make financial sense."

Brendan looked a little pale. "Understood." His nostrils flared as he visibly collected himself. If plaintiff's counsel was aware of the production line issue, and if some of the class members could prove they had obtained the tainted wax, it was terrible news for the case. "Well, obviously this is tough news, but I think we still don't know the full impact to our cases. Let's see what comes of the tracking numbers. We're keeping our fingers crossed over here that the product went abroad. I know that we're trying to keep costs down, but given the potential severity of this situation, I do think it makes sense to loop in John. We're talking a potential application of a strict liability standard for any injuries if we knew about the defect and did not do anything about it. It's in the window, so we'll need to prepare a strategy for disclosing this on our end. Additional document searches will likely be necessary, but we will need to take a careful look at those discovery requests before we come to any conclusions. We have our regular discovery call scheduled for next Wednesday—let's plan on touching base then, although if you have anything you would like to discuss before then, by all means please reach out. Sound okay?"

"Sounds great, Brendan, thank you," said Bruce.

"Enjoy the weekend," Brendan said.

"You too, Brendan. And Tyler."

Brendan pressed the "end call" button on the phone, then picked up the receiver and hung it up for good measure.

"Fuck," Tyler said.

"Fuck," Brendan agreed. The word sounded unnatural in his mouth.

"So. how can I help? Do we want to prepare a summary for John or is this better as a conversation?"

"Definitely a conversation," Brendan started to massage his temples, "or it would have been with Kevin."

"I definitely get the sense that John wants us to handle things on our own," Tyler added. "But that being said..."

"And, of course, it's the end of the day on a Friday. Of course." Tyler could see the gears turning in Brendan's head, weighing out bothering John on the weekend versus losing precious time to strategize on next steps. After a couple seconds he continued, "We can't sit on this for two days. We can't. Okay, here's the plan: you send

John an email and say very generally that we have received further information on the production line malfunction referenced in the email, and that we told the client that while they finish tracking down the facts, we would socialize the issue with John to discuss preliminary discovery strategy. Then offer a call this weekend, and whatever you do don't leave your computer and phone."

Tyler nodded and twirled her hair nervously. She thought it was a toss-up on how John would take this news. "I don't suppose you would want to send this email, would you?"

"Okay, fine, I'll send it. Please write up the draft right now."

"Got it. Thanks, Brendan."

Back at her office, Tyler typed up the email and hit send. She waited ten minutes to see whether Brendan would have comments but got no response. Her stomach was growling, and she thought regretfully about the leftovers from the gyro buffet lunch that had probably been thrown in the trash. She sent Brendan a quick follow-up email letting him know she was leaving the office but to call, text, or email with questions. Then she logged out, but pulled up her application on her phone to make sure she would not miss any incoming emails.

Being the height of summer, the sun was still shining brightly although it was almost six thirty. Tyler slid her laptop into her tote bag and dug out her car keys. Just in case, she held the keys interlaced through her fingers as she had been shown in a self defense class she had taken with girlfriends during her undergraduate years, back when she had girlfriends and time for hobbies. The upside to leaving the office so late was that with almost everyone gone, statistically the murderer was likely to have already left. But the downside was that no one was around. *No one around to hear me scream*, Tyler thought darkly then shook her head. The sleep deprivation must really be getting to her, that was a bit melodramatic. Still, Tyler shivered and gripped her keys more authoritatively.

Walking briskly, Tyler passed by Brendan's office—maybe he would also be leaving and they could walk together. Instead, his door was closed, and Brendan was arguing with someone—a woman—inside. Tyler could hear the muffled conversation, and with doors as thick as these, that meant raised voices. *Cerene?* she wondered. Anyway, not her business. She continued to the elevator for the lobby.

Although no one on the Cloose & Elkman floors in the office got on, several floors down, where Tyler thought the office housed a high-end plaintiff's firm, a middle-aged woman with bad roots and a thick midsection hopped on. She wore a stretchy synthetic top with a floral print that would not have been out of place on a couch in a senior's home, and she was harried and arguing on the phone with who had to be her husband. Tyler wrinkled her nose; no one at Cloose & Elkman would be caught dead in that top, not to mention publicly arguing with family. At least, Tyler realized, there was absolutely no way this woman was the murderer—wrong hair, wrong body, wrong firm. She lowered her shoulders which had unconsciously crept up several inches, but kept her keys in her hand.

In the lobby, the woman shot off to the elevators to the garage. She was wearing flats (of course, another thing no self-respecting C&E woman would do) but in the deserted lobby the shoes shushed loudly across the floor. Tyler used her knuckle to refresh her emails while keeping her keys interlaced and at the ready. Nothing new in her inbox. She tilted her head from the left to the right thinking about whether to take the stairs or the elevator. She felt a bit ridiculous but settled on the stairs. She could run there at least, and she was wearing sensible-ish shoes. On an elevator she could be trapped by the murderer. Glancing around but seeing no one, Tyler strode toward the door to the garage stairs and yanked the door open with her key-holding hand, digging the keys painfully into her fingers. Wincing, she started walking down the stairs as quickly as she could. Her block heels clomped loudly with every step.

One floor down, Tyler's phone pinged. She took a couple more steps—she could check her emails from her locked car—but then the phone pinged three more times. Tyler looked down at it. Of course, the face unlock feature was not working, it had been on the fritz since she cracked the screen throwing the phone across her living room couch. The garage stairway was not air conditioned, and her fingers were sweating and sliding around on the keys. As she tried to unlock the phone with her knuckle the keys slipped out of her fingers and onto the floor.

"Fuck!" As Tyler bent down to get the keys she felt two hands shove into her back and she tumbled down the last six stairs to the landing.

CHAPTER FIFTEEN

Tyler lay in a crumpled daze, clutching her tote bag on top of her body. She had been reaching down for her keys with her right hand, and her right shoulder had taken the brunt of her fall. As Tyler processed what had happened, her anxiety and adrenaline kicked into high gear—someone had *pushed her down the stairs*. Not someone—the murderer. It had to be him. Tyler tried to scream but only a wheeze came out, the tumble had knocked the wind out of her. As she attempted to roll to her side and pick herself up, a face loomed over her. A blue man—what? No, a person wearing a blue ski mask and sunglasses loomed over her. Tyler's right hand scrabbled around for the keys, but they must still be several stairs above her where she dropped them. Tyler took another breath to scream as large hands—a man's hands—closed around her throat. Tyler managed to bend her left leg and grab her shoe from her foot. Hefting the chunky heel, she swung it into the man's head as hard as she could, feeling a satisfying "clunk" as it hit where the man's ear must be under the ski mask. Thinking strangely clearly, Tyler wished she had worn her typical heels—she could have punctured this asshole's eardrum.

The hit stunned the man and he let go of Tyler's neck. She quickly rolled to the side, onto her tote bag. Thinking quickly, she yanked out the laptop. Its corners caught on the handles of the tote and various receipts, pens, and other detritus rained out of the bag. Screaming now—her breath had come back, Tyler wildly shook the laptop free and whirled to hit the man again, this time along the left side of his head. He had been getting to his feet and stumbled briefly, throwing his hands in front of him. Pressing her advantage, Tyler stood up, wound up and hit him again on the left. The laptop made a soft "whump" against the ski mask, and the man was thrown to the right, down onto one knee but not all the way to the ground. This time, Tyler held the laptop by its edges and drove the narrow edge into the man's throat. He made a choking sound but reached out to try to grab the laptop or Tyler's wrist. Still screaming, she slammed the laptop into his throat again, again, then into his forehead. She heard the sunglasses crack, and he fell onto the ground.

Not waiting to see if he got up, Tyler grabbed her phone, ran up the stairs to grab where she saw her keys had fallen, and kicked off her right shoe. She ran to her car, started it, locked the doors, and breathed a sigh of relief. Then she drove as quickly as she could diagonally across the floor—there was only one other car on her level. At the first security checkpoint she swore, her wallet, including her security badge, was still in the stairwell. She pushed the call button on the scanning box. When no one answered she pressed again and again. Finally, a bored voice said, "Hi, how can I help you?"

"Don't have my security badge, let me out. Please!"

Tyler heard a buzz and the gate lifted. Barely waiting for it to clear her car, she charged through. The garage worker must have seen her car, because the second gate lifted as she drove up. *Thank god.* Tyler sped away from the building, heart pounding in her chest. She did not see any cars emerge after her from the garage, but who was to say whether the ski-mask-wearing man had parked on the street. Breathing shallowly, she nearly drove the car into a light pole as she opened up her phone to dial 911.

"911, what's your emergency?" a crisp male voice said.

"I was attacked, on the stairs!" Tyler's breath was starting to come in wheezes. Was it being choked or a panic attack? A car honked as it drove past her. Undoubtedly, she was weaving all over the road.

"Ma'am, where are you right now?"

"In the car!"

"Can I have a cross street?"

"Uhh, uhh," Tyler looked around and almost sideswiped the car next to her, the car honked and its driver flipped her off.

"Tucker and Cole!"

"Thank you. And are you in immediate danger right now?"

"No. He's on the stairs. He's knocked out."

"Is there a safe place for you to pull your car over?"

Tyler pulled into a McDonald's parking lot. "Okay, I'm sitting in a McDonald's parking lot."

"Thank you. Are you hurt?"

Tyler paused. Her adrenaline had been running so high, she had no idea. Her right shoulder ached where it had hit the stairs, and she flashed back to the man's hands closing around her throat. "I don't know—I fell down the stairs and my shoulder hurts, and my throat hurts where he choked me."

"Are you bleeding anywhere, or do you think you need an ambulance for any reason?"

"No, no."

"Okay, thank you. Now where did this incident occur?"

"In the stairwell to the Cloose and Elkman garage."

"And you left the assailant there?"

"Yes."

"And, to your knowledge, was he armed?"

"I don't know... I didn't see anything but it all happened so fast..."

"That's fine, thank you. I'm going to send officers to the scene of the accident. I'm going to send them to meet you, too. Can you stay where you are?"

Tyler glanced around. She wasn't in the best neighborhood, but it could be worse. She checked that her car doors were locked, "Yes, I can stay right here."

"Okay, thank you, and that's the McDonald's on Tucker?"

"Yes."

"Name?"

"Tyler McCarther."

"Okay, thank you, officers will be with you shortly."

The operator hung up. Tyler tried to slow her breathing. She hoped the police officers would arrive soon. Remembering the events immediately leading up to the assault, Tyler returned to her email application. As she was refreshing the inbox a notification of a text from Brendan dropped down from the top of her screen.

I told you not to leave your phone or computer!!!!

The emails contained Brendan's email to John. *Fine*, Tyler thought, it looked like what she had sent Brendan so obviously he had not needed to make too many changes; a response from John asking for a call the next morning, *also fine*, although Tyler could see why Brendan was texting her because she should have created the call invite immediately upon receipt. Sure enough, the next notification was a call invite for nine a.m. on Saturday from Brendan. The invite was time-stamped a minute before Brendan's text came in. Tyler sheepishly accepted it. Finally, plaintiff's counsel had filed a deposition notice for Genevieve Donner. *Not fine*. As a rule of thumb, plaintiffs were always in the driver's seat in litigation simply because they started the lawsuit and were the ones seeking relief. But, as Cloose & Elkman was a much larger law firm, with resources to match, the playing field typically felt more level, or if anything like an uphill battle for plaintiffs. This case was starting to feel the opposite—out of control and worse and worse for the client. Tyler sent a quick response to Brendan:

So sorry on the delay... attacked in the stairway. Waiting to speak w cops now.

Brendan's text bubbles appeared, then disappeared, then appeared again.

You'll be on the call tomorrow am—right?

Seriously? Tyler thought. It had been a stupid move for Tyler to apologize for being attacked, but it seemed pretty cold for Brendan to not even ask how she was doing. She responded with the thumbs-up emoji, although the thumb was not exactly the finger she had in mind.

Catching a glimpse of a figure walking toward her car, Tyler jumped and let out a yelp, but it was a cop with a flashlight. The cop looked questioningly at Tyler's car and Tyler realized she was probably trying to figure out whether she had been sent to talk to Tyler—she had not described her car to the 911 operator. Tyler gave the cop a wave and rolled down her window.

This cop—Officer Watson, Tyler read from her name badge—was young and blonde. Between the detectives and the post-burglary mustache/no mustache duo Tyler was on track to meet the entire force. Officer Watson's uniform was starched and wrinkle-free, and her hair was styled in a ponytail and curled. She looked like an actress playing a cop, not the real thing. And, weirdly, she reminded Tyler of Cerene.

"Tyler?" Officer Watson asked.

"Yes," Tyler responded.

"Why don't we go sit down and you can tell me about what happened," Officer Watson suggested. Although Officer Watson appeared to be younger than Tyler, the police officer had a calm, confident energy that put Tyler at ease. Tyler grabbed her laptop and phone and got out of her car. She realized she was not wearing any shoes.

"I've got a pair of socks," Officer Watson offered. Tyler sat in the driver's seat of her car with the door open and her legs dangling outside. The sun was finally starting to set, but it was still humid enough for Tyler to feel sweat forming on the back of her knees. Officer Watson returned with a thick pair of white athletic socks. They looked clean enough, and beggars could not be choosers. Tyler put the socks on and followed the officer into the McDonald's, where they slid into a booth in the back corner.

"Okay, so you were assaulted in the stairway of the Cloose & Elkman building. Can you tell me step by step what happened?" said Officer Watson, pulling out a notepad and pen.

Tyler breathlessly recounted the events, beginning with finding Kevin's body in her trunk and finishing with pulling into the McDonald's parking lot.

"I'm going to ask you some follow-up questions now," said Officer Watson. She opened her mouth to continue when the radio attached to her belt crackled to life and requested that she call in. Officer Watson held up one finger while tapping at her phone.

"Officer Watson here." She paused for several minutes to listen to the other end of the call. "Uh-huh. Yeah, I got it." She paused again. "Roger that." She ended the call and set her cell phone back down on the table. "I have a number of follow-up questions, as I mentioned. First, I'm going to share some information with you, and then we'll proceed with the questions. As you can guess, there are officers at the Cloose & Elkman building right now. They've recovered one Tory Burch tote bag, a pair of brown leather shoes, size seven and a half, and a variety of items that appear to have spilled out of the tote bag—pens, Post-its, et cetera."

Tyler nodded along, but realized something big was missing from that list. "And the guy? The ski mask guy? The murderer?"

Officer Watson made a sympathetic face. "Gone. And that's the information I wanted to share with you. Let's move on to my questions for you. You said your assailant wore a ski mask and sunglasses?"

"Yes."

"And did the sunglasses fall off at any point? Could you see eye color or skin color?"

"Ummm," Tyler struggled to remember, "I don't think so. I just can't remember, it's all a blur."

"I understand. What else can you tell me about the assailant? You said 'the guy.' Was the person who attacked you a man?"

"I think so," said Tyler hesitantly.

"And what made you think that? You can take your time."

Tyler took the officer's advice and thought for a few minutes. "The hands," she said finally. "He had man's hands—big, hairy."

"Great, you saw his hands. Can you remember what color they were?"

"White!" Tyler said triumphantly, "with some dark hair on them."

"Great work, Tyler. Can you remember anything else? He was wearing a ski mask and sunglasses, what else?"

"Dark clothes," Tyler tried to concentrate, "A suit maybe? I'm sorry I can't remember that well."

"So maybe a dark suit. What else, was he tall? Short?"

"Honestly, I have no idea. He was strong," Tyler involuntarily brought her hands up to her neck and shuddered.

"You're doing great," Officer Watson assured her. "I have to ask some tough questions now, okay?"

Tyler nodded.

"You've mentioned being shoved to the ground and being choked. Was there *anything else* that happened."

"Uh, no?" Tyler could tell Officer Watson was getting at something, but Tyler was not sure what it was.

"Honey, were you sexually assaulted?" Officer Watson stared straight at Tyler sympathetically.

"Oh," Tyler blushed, "no, no nothing like that. I mean, I fought him off pretty quickly."

Officer Watson nodded. "Okay. I see a little bruising around your neck." Tyler's eyes widened. "Nothing crazy," Officer Watson assured her, "but I'm going to ask you to come down to the station to have it photographed. I'm also going to ask for your laptop. You never know what evidence we'll be able to grab from it."

"My laptop?" Tyler flashed back to Brendan's text. "I don't know if I can spare it."

"It's not optional, so you're going to have to," said Officer Watson matter-of-factly. She pulled a large evidence bag out from next to her and picked up the laptop dog-poop style to avoid touching it. *Where did the bag even come from*, wondered Tyler. She was reminded again of Cerene. If Cerene was a cop, she would definitely always have a variety of evidence bags at the ready. "Now, if you'll kindly follow me, I'll give you a ride to the station for photos, then back to your car."

On the way to the station, Officer Watson made several more calls. First to the officers on the garage staircase, convincing them to meet her at the station with Tyler's bag—the shoes were also staying as evidence due to one having come into contact with the murderer. Her next call was to the officers who handled the burglary at Tyler's house. Finally, to some kind of coordinator to report that Kevin's murder, Tyler's burglary, and now Tyler's assault might be related. Tyler sat in a daze. At the station, Tyler mutely followed Officer Watson to a room where a kindly, overweight, older female officer helped Tyler strip off her shirt. The officer photographed Tyler's neck and examined her hands and torso to confirm there were no other injuries. Afterward, Tyler waited for Officer Watson on the bench she had seen the homeless men sitting on when she picked up the paperwork for her car. She picked up one foot and looked at the bottom of the athletic sock she was still wearing. It was black and disgusting. Noticing the socks set something off, and Tyler's ankles started to itch uncontrollably. She wanted to take the socks off, but had nothing else to put on. Luckily, Officer Watson showed up after only a minute or two of waiting. A short car ride later, Officer Watson was handing Tyler her business card and shutting Tyler's car door after her.

Officer Watson motioned for Tyler to roll her window down. It was déjà vu from several hours earlier, but the sun had set now, and Officer Watson was backlit by the neon signs in the McDonald's window.

"I'll follow you to your house and make sure you get in okay," Officer Watson said, "And I've notified the unit on duty around your house of what happened, they're going to do a couple extra drive-bys tonight."

"Thank you... do you really think it's safe for me to go home? The murderer knows where I live, obviously, and he might have a key. When I was burglarized there weren't any broken windows or anything."

Officer Watson pursed her lips. "I asked about that while you were being photographed, and the answer was to send you home. So, there's nowhere else that I personally can offer for you to stay. But if it was me..." she trailed off, "if it was me, I'd stay in a hotel. If you can afford to."

Tyler nodded nervously. "I'll do that."

"All right," Officer Watson tapped the top of Tyler's car, "so, I'll follow you back home and I'll make sure you get in okay. If I don't get any other calls, I'll stick around out front until you head out to the hotel, but," she shrugged, "it's a Friday night so people tend to get into trouble."

"Thank you," Tyler said. She hastily pulled out of the parking lot and drove the short distance back to her house. Luckily, a spot was available right outside her door. Officer Watson had her flashers on and was illegally double-parked across the street. She waved encouragingly at Tyler and gave her a thumbs-up. Tyler grabbed her keys, her phone, and her tote, which felt unnaturally light without her laptop, and walked up the stairs to her house. She unlocked the door and turned back around to wave at Officer Watson, who was speaking into her radio and gave Tyler a quick nod. Shivering, Tyler closed the door behind her, locked it, and engaged the security chain. Then she walked to the back door—it was also locked, and as an extra security measure Tyler wedged a chair from her kitchen table under the door for good measure. Lucy meowed behind her and Tyler jumped.

"You scared the shit out of me!"

Lucy looked up at Tyler innocently and meowed again.

"Okay, okay." Tyler put some wet food that she kept for special occasions out in Lucy's bowl. They had both been through a lot this week, and on top of it all, Tyler was going to leave Lucy for the night. "Look, I'm sorry that I'm leaving you tonight, but I don't think you want someone breaking in here and murdering me any more than I do. That could be extremely traumatic for you, and you already got locked in a closet this week which was bad enough. Plus, if I die, who feeds you? You'd end up eating me, and let's be honest, that would really be a low point for both of us."

Lucy ignored Tyler and dug into her food.

Tyler checked to make sure each of her windows was locked and turned on all of the lights on the first floor. She looked for Officer Watson out her front window, cupping her hands against the glass, but the police cruiser was gone. Officer Watson must have been called to another scene. Tyler was too creeped out to venture upstairs away from a door she could run out of easily, but she knew she had to pack an overnight bag so she could spend the night at a hotel. To stall, Tyler googled hotels and made a reservation at a Hyatt in a nice suburb about twenty minutes away. Out of her neighborhood, in a busy area, Tyler figured that was as safe as she was going to get.

As Tyler was punching in her credit card information to complete the reservation, several emails from Brendan came in with requests to put together information to share with John if he asked on the call the next morning. Without her laptop, Tyler was not sure how she could get Brendan's request done. Tyler could bring her iPad with her to the hotel and try to log on remotely that way. Wait, the iPad was stolen. She was losing electronic devices at a truly alarming rate. Tyler typed a quick message out to tech services requesting a backup laptop be made available, if possible, tomorrow morning. She would have to go to the office early in the morning and use a computer in a guest office to complete Brendan's requests before the call with John. Tyler was already panicking thinking of going back to the deserted office. The murderer probably had a badge to access the Cloose & Elkman offices, just like Tyler. Hopefully he would not know she was there on a Saturday. Or maybe she would get lucky and John would be in the office in person, too. Tyler shook her head thinking that being alone with John in an office would ever have been a good thing. But if you had to choose between some quid pro quo sexual harassment or murder, Tyler would pick sexual harassment every day.

Working backward, Tyler figured she would have to be at the office at seven to have enough time to put together the materials Brendan wanted. It would just be a matter of combining things she had already identified and summarized in a new format. It could be a long day, though, depending on if she got the loaner laptop, so she would need to stop at her house on the way to the office to feed Lucy, meaning she would have to be leaving the hotel around six fifteen.

Hopefully the hotel served breakfast early. Tyler typed out a quick email to Brendan.

Brendan,

Got your emails on materials for the call tomorrow a.m. As I mentioned over text message, I was assaulted in the garage stairwell tonight (I'm fine), so I've been away from the computer.

Unfortunately, because I used the computer to fight off the attacker, the cops took it as evidence. I will put together the materials you requested first thing tomorrow morning, and if there is time for you to review, I will send them to you. Otherwise, I will be sure to have them available and ready to share on the call. FYI, I will have to go to a guest office to get this done. I have a request out to tech to get a loaner laptop, so hopefully I'll be fully up and running again tomorrow afternoon.

I'm available by email the rest of tonight, but won't be able to log on.

Sorry about that!

After she sent the email, Tyler rolled her eyes and wondered why she had apologized again for being assaulted. It was already nine thirty, and Tyler was running on three hours of sleep. She had to get her fear under control, pack her bag, and head to the hotel. Tyler walked over to the stairs and looked up. She flicked on the light. She put one foot on the staircase. It was too creepy, the burglary, the assault, it was all too much. Her email chimed, Brendan, responding with "Thx." What an asshole. To think she had considered Brendan to be one of the nicer associates. Tyler put her other foot one step above. *This will take ten minutes, come on, Tyler.* But she remained frozen.

"Ugh!" Tyler let out a frustrated exclamation. She wanted to sleep so badly, and she wanted to get out of her house so badly. Tyler just had to climb these stairs. She pinched the inside of her arm hard to try to snap herself out of her paralysis. The pain helped her stop the swirl of thoughts, and she ran up the stairs before she could second guess herself again.

Focusing on action items, Tyler snatched a duffle bag and threw clean underwear and socks, jeans, some Golden Goose tennis shoes, and a short-sleeved button up linen shirt. It would do for a Saturday in the office. Tyler grabbed a small, quilted bag and walked into her bathroom. She started shoving in her toiletries. She tried to hurriedly zip up the bag, but items kept falling out. Tyler bent down to grab a tube of mascara rolling toward her toilet, and when she stood up, she saw motion behind her. She opened her mouth to scream as she saw the same man in a blue ski mask—no sunglasses this time—moving toward her. Her scream was cut short as the man clapped a cloth that smelled vaguely like nail polish remover over her mouth, and her vision went dark.

CHAPTER SIXTEEN

Tyler slowly blinked. She was sitting upright, and her head was dangling forward on her chest. She jerked it upright quickly and felt a dull ache across the back of her neck—how long had she been sitting unconscious? Her head was pounding—the sleep deprivation, Tyler thought, until remembering that the last time she had been awake she had been home in her own bathroom. Tyler opened her mouth to scream and realized it was duct-taped closed. Panicking, Tyler tried to kick her arms and legs, only to realize they were zip-tied to a chair that looked suspiciously like a guest chair in a Cloose & Elkman office. All Tyler succeeded in doing was rocking the chair back and forth violently. She stopped, she did not want the chair to tip over while she was stuck to it.

Tyler had obviously been kidnapped and tied to a chair. As preposterous as this would have seemed even one month ago, it now seemed to be a natural escalation of recent events. Did she have her phone? Tyler wiggled around to try to feel it in a jeans pocket. No phone. Her mind flashed back to setting her phone on her bathroom counter to pack up her toiletries. Well, it was not as if she could reach it to call for help even if she had it. Tyler flexed her hands and feet a few times. She still had circulation, but the zip ties were cutting painfully into her wrists. Tyler noticed she was still wearing those dirty white athletic socks Officer Watson had given her, without any shoes. The socks lessened the pressure from the zip ties on her ankles. Tyler experimentally wiggled her feet to see if she might slide them out of the socks and get her legs free. No dice.

Tyler tried to take a deep breath and assess the situation. *Okay, where am I, and how did I get here? And how long have I been here?* Number one: where was she? Tyler looked around. She was sitting in a dark room, but her eyes had adjusted to the low lighting, so she could easily see the things around her. Her eyes were darting around too fast to process anything, and she took another deep breath through her nose and focused on taking in one thing at a time. As she had noted before, her chair was a Cloose & Elkman guest chair. Tyler squinted, trying to see more details. On her left was a wall made up entirely of windows through which she could see office buildings. She could not possibly be in a Cloose & Elkman partner office—could she? Tyler kept looking—directly in front of her was a large hardwood desk, and behind that was a smaller desk with dual monitors and a phone. Tyler looked down—beneath her socked feet was a rich Persian carpet. Craning her head three-quarters of the way around she spotted some extremely healthy houseplants. She was in John Delaware's office. Was John the murderer? Immediately Tyler doubted that train of thought. John might be an asshole, but he was a smart person—he would not kidnap someone and bring them to his place of work. *Although,* Tyler thought, *he did try to sexually harass me in a law office just down the hall from some employment attorneys.* Maybe he was not so smart. Not to mention she had known the man only a couple weeks. He might be completely unhinged, in which case trying to apply logic to the situation would be a useless exercise.

Tyler was getting off track. *Okay, number two, how did I get here?* Tyler remembered seeing the murderer in her bathroom mirror and the cloth pressed against her mouth, then nothing. She must have been driven into the office and somehow brought in unconscious. This naturally led to her final question—it was dark out the window, so still night. It was the height of summer, and the days were long. The sun was always up by the time Tyler got up, she guessed it probably rose somewhere between five and six in the morning. Officer Watson had left Tyler at her townhouse late in the evening. Tyler did not remember exactly but somewhere between nine and ten. She must have been abducted somewhere around ten thirty, and it was still completely dark outside the floor-to-ceiling windows. Not to mention, Tyler must have been brought into the office very late at night for it to be deserted and have no one notice her unconscious body being carried around by a ski-mask-clad maniac. The murderer must have used a service elevator, if there was one. Tyler had never seen one before or even wondered if one existed. Her mind started to drift again wondering about the location of a service elevator.

Focus. The drive from Tyler's townhouse to the Cloose & Elkman office was short, and obviously the murderer knew his way around the office, but factoring in the time it would take to tote Tyler's unconscious body, she figured she had arrived here at the earliest somewhere around eleven thirty. Meaning it could be anywhere from midnight to almost five a.m. If it was closer to five maybe Tyler would get lucky and someone would wander past the office. Tyler looked out the window again. No sign of sunrise. Not to mention the office door was closed, which Tyler knew muffled most conversation and even some yelling. Plus, anyone organized enough to orchestrate her abduction probably would not have stashed her somewhere she would be immediately discovered.

Okay, if the murderer wanted to kill me, I'd already be dead. Right? The question sent a shiver through her body. No matter what the murderer's intention was, it was not going to be good for Tyler. She tried to free one of her limbs again but only succeeded in cutting her right wrist. She winced at the sting. Trying something new, Tyler leaned her torso towards her right hand and tried to rip the duct tape off her mouth so that she could scream for help. Her hand was secured with her palm facing the ground, tightly enough that she could not rotate it to the side. Tyler had to crane her neck awkwardly to bring the side of the tape to her hand repeatedly. The tape was adhered tightly, and after several attempts she gave up trying to grip the duct tape and used her thumbnail to try to peel it off. Unsuccessful at that attempt too, she craned her neck down to the left side to give the other hand a try. Using her left hand, Tyler was able to loosen up a corner of the duct tape, but her fingers, swollen from lack of movement and the tight zip ties, would not grasp onto the tape tight enough to rip it off. Tyler shrieked in frustration, which came out as a muffled sound not unlike Lucy's meow.

Okay, next plan. Although Tyler had spent the last month in a state of constant panic, she found her mind to be incredibly clear, zeroing in on any chance to escape her current predicament. Tyler realized that although she did not have *her* phone, there was *a* phone in her vicinity—John's landline. It was on the other side of the large desk sitting on a smaller desk against the wall. If Tyler could shuffle herself and her chair over there, around the window side of the desk, then lean toward the desk maybe she could reach far enough to tap out 911.

Tyler took an exploratory shuffle. She winced—the zip ties cut into her even more painfully when she attempted the movement and she felt a trickle of blood run down her right hand. But she thought she had covered a couple inches. She shuffled a couple more times. She was definitely making progress. Tyler tried shuffling faster and the chair careened over to the left. Tyler barely righted herself. As the right two legs of the chair hit the ground, her bottom popped off the seat, and she realized that she could stand up in a fashion if she crouched over. She could still barely lift up her feet, and moving this way caused the zip ties to cut into her wrists so hard both began to slowly drip blood, but she was moving much faster. Gritting her teeth, Tyler shuffled along as quickly as she could. To maintain her crouched position, she had to keep her head pointed down toward the ground, and it was not until she reached the corner of John's desk that she realized she had not allotted enough space for herself; her right arm was stuck on the edge of the desk. Tyler tried to shuffle backward, but it took about twice as long as going forward.

As she made another attempt to round the desk, this time leaving ample space, Tyler heard the door to the office click open. Startled, she jumped mid step. As she craned her head around her right shoulder to see the door behind her the chair toppled toward the window. Her fall was muffled by the thick carpet, but Tyler's head snapped to the left and thudded painfully against the ground. She tried to scream again and again, but was muffled by the duct tape.

Tyler heard a man's soft chuckle, and after a few seconds a pair of black loafers came into view. A pair of hands—Tyler assumed they were the same hands that she had seen in the stairwell, although they were now covered in rubber gloves—grabbed the right arm of the chair and hauled Tyler up into a seated position. The murderer was wearing a well-fitting suit, but one that was made out of cheap material. He was still wearing the blue ski mask, but no sunglasses. Something about his eyes appeared familiar. It was obvious that Tyler's screams were not attracting any attention, and she stopped and looked defeatedly into the murderer's face.

The murderer slowly pulled Tyler's security badge out of his pocket with an almost magician-like flair, then bent it back like a playing card and let it fly at her. The plastic card struck her in the cheek, and although it had not really hurt, in her surprise, Tyler flinched and almost tipped backward. The murderer reached into his pocket again and pulled out Tyler's guest badge and flicked that at her, too. She tried not to flinch but could not stop herself as the plastic card bounced off her cheek. He pulled out one more item from his pockets—Tyler's car keys—dangled them in front of her, then gently placed them in her lap.

Tyler was not sure what the point of this show was, other than to confirm what she already suspected about how she ended up at the office, but she hoped the fact that the murderer kept his ski mask on meant he was not going to kill her. As if reading her mind, the murderer slowly peeled off the mask. It was Harry. Tyler noticed that there were horizontal bruises on the bridge of his nose and neck—that must have been from her laptop earlier in the evening. She still did not understand how, or why, Harry would be the murderer. He did have short brown hair but he was not a Cloose & Elkman attorney, and Tyler shook her head in confusion. Harry smiled at her. His eyes were opened too wide and looked manic, and his mouth was stretched too wide. Tyler started to cry. As she cried, her nose started to run to the point where she was struggling to breathe, and she started to hyperventilate.

"You and the anxiety," Harry said, pulling out John's rolling chair to face her. He spread his legs and leaned forward on his elbows to look into her face.

"You're probably wondering why you're here."

Tyler started to cry harder and shook her head. She wanted to say, *I don't care, just let me go.*

"I'll cut the suspense. I'm going to kill you, the same way I killed Kevin." He held up a small bottle. Tyler squinted, and saw it was the nose hair wax. She shook her head uncomprehendingly. She really was struggling to breathe and she started to see pinprick stars at the edges of her vision.

"Come on, Tyler, you're supposed to be such a smart girl, right? An attorney? Always working so hard?" He said the last part in a faux whiney voice. "Poor you. So much busier than the rest of us." He paused and looked at Tyler to see if she was catching on to whatever he thought she should know about the nose hair wax.

"Maybe this will help." He started to read out the SKU code on the box. It jogged something in Tyler's mind, and her eyes narrowed.

He nodded and smiled again. Tyler wondered if the insane gleam in his eyes that had appeared with the smile had always been there, and she had simply not noticed it, or whether he could successfully hide it on command. She tried to blow her nose to clear it. It kind of worked. Tyler expelled so much snot she could feel it sliding down the duct tape covering her mouth, but her nostrils were still barely taking in enough air to keep her conscious. Slowly and deliberately enunciating, Harry finished reading off the SKU code.

He paused again, but when Tyler showed no more signs of understanding whatever he was getting at he continued, "Let's go back, to fall 2016. My big sister, Diana, was getting ready for her senior year homecoming. Did you know I had a sister?"

Tyler shook her head.

"Well, that's not so surprising. You wouldn't know, because you're only interested in work. Anyway, imagine, my beautiful big sister, my hero, is getting ready for homecoming. She's on the homecoming court, and she knows she'll be presented to the student body, and the presentation is happening on a balcony above everybody else. She's got her nails done, her spray tan, an appointment to get her hair done. There's just one problem, she's self-conscious ever since her first boyfriend pointed out that she's got hair in her nose. Like anybody doesn't," he scoffed. Tyler was trying to pay attention to what he was saying, but she was still stuck on the words "kill you" from a few moments before. There was so much she still wanted to do with her life. And she never even got to make partner.

Harry seemed to sense that he was losing Tyler's focus, and he grabbed her shoulders and violently shook her so hard the car keys flew out of her lap. "Could you try to focus on one person other than yourself for five fucking minutes out of your life? Jesus Christ." His voice started to rise and he jumped out of John's chair and took a lap around the large desk Tyler had been trying to shuffle around. Tyler heard him mutter to himself a little but could not make out any words other than "knocked the fucking keys off." Tyler quickly stood up into the same crab-like position she had held before and started to move toward the door. She was not sure what she would to when she got there, she certainly would not be able to open the heavy door with four limbs tied to a chair, but she was not about to just sit around and wait to die.

Harry rounded the corner of the desk, roughly grabbed the chair, and dragged it back to its original position.

"Where the fuck do you think you're going? Honestly." Tyler started to cry. "Now, focus up," Harry said, the manic gleam in his eyes intensifying. "Okay, so it's fall 2016, my big sister is going to homecoming and she's got a stupid complex about her nose hair. Are you paying attention?" Tyler just stared at him. "I said... are... you... paying... attention?" He snapped his fingers in front of Tyler's face in time with his words. She nodded, frightened.

"Good. So, her best friend goes, well why don't you just trim your nose hairs, or even better, wax them."

Tyler started to have an idea of where this story was going and shook her head.

"Oh yes. So, Diana drives herself down to CVS, picks up some nose hair wax—this nose hair wax in fact," he dangled the bottle again, "locks herself in the bathroom and carefully follows the instructions. And yours truly shares a bathroom with her, so several hours... hours later," Harry's voice broke, "I go to shower, and the door's locked. I bang on the door, 'hey sis!'" He walked over to the window and banged on it theatrically, reenacting the scene. "But Diana doesn't respond. I bang again, and now I'm starting to worry that something is up. So, I go get my mom, and we're both knocking on the door now. Still no response. We're both freaking out. My mom's trying to pretend to be calm, but we call 911 and the fire department shows up. They break down the door and poor Diana is lying in a pool of her own blood. It was horrific. She'd pulled the wax out of one nostril and started on the other. The blood must have just been gushing out. She tried to stop it with a tissue. That tissue was just sitting on the floor next to her hand. Completely soaked, you could barely see it, it was red, the pool of blood on the floor was red. Diana was coated in red, too." Harry shook his head, lost in the memory. "The wax had ripped off the skin inside of her nostrils and she just hemorrhaged out."

Tyler was shocked, but also not sure what about this story necessitated tying her up in John's office, and evidently nose hair waxing her to death. Even in her panicked state, Tyler could connect the dots: Kevin's bloodless body and the traces of nose hair wax in the trunk—Harry had obviously used the product on Kevin. Tyler figured that the product resulting from the production line malfunction was in the bottle, explaining why the SKU number was familiar. Still, why was she the target now? Harry knew as well as anyone that she was nowhere near important enough to advise the company on what to do in response to malfunction, not to mention she had still been in law school when the malfunction happened. It seemed much more logical that if Harry was going on a killing spree that it would have focused on NSK executives and in-house attorneys, but obviously Tyler was not really in a position to offer suggestions on killing spree logic, both literally due to the duct tape and figuratively due to her overall position as an about-to-be-a-victim-of-murder.

Tyler might not be able to give Harry pointers on his revenge strategy, but maybe she could still convince him not to kill her. Tyler tried to adopt a sympathetic expression as best she could without the use of her mouth and with snot running down her face. Harry had turned back to the window, and he was gazing into his reflection pensively. "I knew it was that fucking wax immediately," he said quietly. "But the doctors weren't so convinced. They seemed to think she just had thin skin in her nostrils." He slapped his hand onto the window. "At the time I was too young to do anything about it. I became a PI so I could learn how to investigate and uncover what had really happened to Diana. Little did I know I would be one half step above a pornographer, photographing cheating spouse after cheating spouse... Eventually, though, I did gain what I thought were enough skills, and I returned to Diana's case. I went back to the records, I got my hands on police records, autopsy results, and a couple letters from NSK that don't say anything determinative but weren't intended for my eyes. Oh right, and the original wax container, out of the evidence locker. Don't ask!" He chuckled, the sound was full of bitterness and rage and made Tyler shudder.

"Anyway, I found out enough to prove to myself that the wax had caused Diana's death. But not enough to prove anything to the public. There was one doctor who was consulted who questioned whether the wax had something to do with Diana's death. The doctor was in touch with NSK, and that doctor is now retired, with three homes. And has been since he was forty." *Was Harry suggesting the doctor was paid off?* "You can guess how that happened," he said bitterly. *Evidently, he was.*

Tyler wondered whether Harry was right, that the doctor had been paid off by NSK, or whether the tragedy that struck Harry at a young age had caused him to have a break with reality. She would not have been surprised either way.

"I saved the bottle of wax. Obviously. I wanted to have it tested to see why this particular bottle had killed someone, and that would have given me the proof I needed to go public, but all the labs I contacted told me I would have had to give up the entire bottle, all the product. And what if NSK got to whoever I hired?" Harry was sounding paranoid, and his words had started coming out faster and louder, although his posture had begun to stoop forward.

"After that, I hit a real low point," Harry continued more softly, curling downward even more. "I had lost my beloved sister, but I couldn't figure out how to prove it. I'd been spending every waking hour investigating, poring over the records, and I'd been drinking heavily almost every day. I wondered, maybe one more person had to die, to prove that Diana had been killed. One more person would have to unquestionably be murdered by this product. If it was public enough, and attention was directed toward the product enough, the truth would come out. So, one night, I wrote up a suicide note."

Tyler would have gasped if the tape had not been over her mouth, and she almost tipped over in her chair again. She assumed that Kevin was the person selected to die. Harry glanced over at Tyler and looked pleased she was paying attention.

"I applied the wax inside my nostrils, and I was about to pull it out when I realized, what a waste... why should I be the one to die? Not to mention I was drunk, and I'd lost sight of making the death be public. I was the wrong person to die, I was just some regular PI. No family, not prominent in the community, not to mention I was a borderline alcoholic. You've told me about how much more cache an appealing victim has when you're settling a case, so you get it. I wasn't the most appealing victim. My death? Alone in my sad apartment filled with empty bottles? It just wouldn't do. Thank god, I was able to re-melt the wax and get it out of my nose. I had work to do. I had actually started identifying potential executives at NSK, trying to find the right one, the most sympathetic, when who happened to call me, but Kevin about the nose hair wax cases. Well-regarded in the community, beautiful family, working closely on lawsuits filed by people injured by the NSK wax. Kevin was perfect to draw attention to the issue. Him hiring me to do the PI work on the named plaintiff was fate."

Abruptly, Harry straightened up and turned to face Tyler. "As you've probably guessed, yes, I'm going to apply this wax to your nostrils, then yes, I will pull it out and you'll bleed to death. Or not—maybe Diana's nostril skin really was too thin. And maybe Kevin's was too. You can be another test subject. Now, I had a couple hiccups with Kevin. I put the wax in his nose, but then he couldn't breathe, and if he suffocated to death that would defeat the entire purpose, so I had to un-tape his mouth. Then you could imagine how he screamed, but luckily, I had invited him to my office after everyone had left for the day. He had mentioned my office was on his way home, so I knew he wouldn't mind meeting me there one evening."

Tyler shuddered.

"Then of course you know about the second hiccup."

Tyler stared at him as tears continued to leak out of her eyes. She had deduced by now that Harry was the person who put Kevin's body in her trunk. She still had no idea why he had done it, but she hoped Harry was not about to tell her. The more details he shared with Tyler the more confident she was that he really and truly was going to kill her. Even though she knew it was a futile gesture, she tried to scream again. Harry chuckled.

"You know, I actually thought you would turn to me for help when I put Kevin in your trunk. I'd staged it for maximum dramatic effect. In hindsight I really should have left Kevin bloody, not washed him off and changed his clothes, but I thought adding a little mystery 'how did he die,' you know? I thought that might build public interest in the case. And I'd dropped just a little bit of wax onto him for the police to find after I cleaned him off." He shook his head. "But I way overestimated your character. And police capabilities for that matter. Here I was, thinking that when you found Kevin you would turn to me, we would call the police together, and then I would guide you to putting the pieces together and you might become a whistleblower—I knew you had access to all kinds of documents. And you being an attractive young woman was bound to get plenty of media coverage. But you..." he paused and smiled manically again at Tyler. "You pretended you didn't see the body! And you kicked me out! And I had no fucking clue what you were going to do! So now my work was doubled... I had to move Kevin so he could still be discovered in a public and dramatic way. And on that point, thanks for the badge, saved me a lot of time and effort, being able to drive Kevin right into the garage in his own car was a solid plan B. I even knew the right floor to park on because of you."

Tyler wanted to clap her hands over her ears to avoid hearing more. She could not believe she had dated and slept with this man and had not noticed that he was absolutely insane. Harry had killed someone and was showing absolutely no regret. If anything, he seemed annoyed that she and the police had not reacted the way he had hoped. Tyler really was going to have to start asking people questions about themselves if she survived this ordeal, surely if she had learned more about Harry she would have had some sort of inkling that something was not right about him.

"And then," Harry let out what was supposed to be a laugh but sounded more like a wheeze, "then I thought I'd keep dating you to keep my eyes on you, maybe see how the police investigation was going, and I still had not completely given up on you being a whistleblower, but you wouldn't even fucking go along with that! You wanted that piece of shit cop instead!" The volume of Harry's voice was increasing.

Tyler flashed back to his fury at being dumped. She had thought it was just some run-of-the-mill toxic masculinity at play. Little had she known Harry was actually angry because she was not playing along with his convoluted, insane scheme. "I'd already copied your house key though, so once I got your iPad it was simple enough to track your emails. And your texts, and your Slack messages, and your calendar. Shit, you even had the document review software downloaded on that iPad, so I could see all of the emails and documents from the company. Basically, I knew everything you were up to. But Tyler," that wheezing laugh again, "when you learned about the production line malfunction and you still didn't put two and two together I knew you never would. Again, I thought you were supposed to be so smart. But it's me who has to do everything."

Harry picked up the bottle of nose hair wax again and looked down at it thoughtfully.

"I'll paint you a picture of what's happening now. I've learned my lesson from Kevin—nothing subtle, everybody's too fucking stupid to get it. But I still think I was onto something with a public death. So," he put the nose hair wax down and clapped, "something extremely sad, maybe even tragic, is about to happen here. You," he pointed at Tyler, "are here in your new boss's office. Why? You're about to..." he looked at Tyler as if she could answer even though it was him who had taped her mouth shut. "You are about to commit suicide!" He grinned at Tyler as if she would understand. Tyler started to sob. Her vision blurred with the tears. "Your new boss hates you, I learned that from your Slack, and your job is everything. Everything! You overlooked some key documents, and now you know that certain bottles of nose hair wax are causing death. You feel so guilty, and so sad because your new boss is going to ruin your career which everyone who knows you knows is the only thing you care about. You can't take it anymore and you've decided to end it all. And how are you ending it? NSK nose hair wax!" Harry looked at Tyler expectantly as if she would congratulate him on this fantastic plan. Instead, she kept sobbing.

"No cleaning up this time," he muttered to himself, "We're going to get a nice bloody scene."

Harry reached into his pocket and pulled out a plastic bag holding a cloth.

"Goodbye Tyler," he said, and pushed it over her nose.

CHAPTER SEVENTEEN

Tyler tried to scream again and again as the cloth covered her nose. The last time the cloth had covered her face she had lost consciousness immediately. This time Tyler noticed after a second that although her vision was a bit fuzzy around the edges and she was lightheaded, she did not feel like she was about to pass out. As if watching herself from the outside, Tyler wondered whether this was because her nostrils were smaller than her mouth, so she was getting less of whatever chemical had soaked the cloth. Then, still strangely detached, Tyler noticed that this time she smelled nothing. Her nose must be so stuffed up from crying and having a panic attack that the chemical, she assumed chloroform, could not get through. Thinking quickly, Tyler took as big of a breath in as she could which caused the fuzziness to ooze further into her field of vision, then slowly, slowly, slowly let the breath out while closing her eyes and letting her head drop down limply to her chest.

The strategy worked—Harry pulled the cloth from her nose. Tyler heard some rustling, but she did not dare open her eyes even a little to see what was happening. A couple seconds later Harry roughly shoved her head backwards and ripped the duct tape off her mouth. It felt like the skin on her face was being ripped off, and it was all Tyler could do to hold her head limp and not make a sound. Tyler guessed that the duct tape was coming off to avoid the second hiccup with Kevin—it would not meet Harry's deranged plan specifications to apply the wax to her nose and have her suffocate to death. The relative freedom was better for her, although Tyler was only barely holding her panic in check at the thought that she was momentarily going to bleed out if she did not think of a way out of the situation. Despite her panic and the sting of pain where the duct tape had been, Tyler remained limp and did not open her eyes.

As she heard more rustling, she considered her options. Tyler's mouth was now uncovered, and she could scream for help, but there was likely no one in the office to hear her. She was still secured to the chair, so she could not run. And Harry probably still had that cloth soaked in whatever chemical knocked her out at her townhouse, so he could just knock her out again now that the duct tape was removed and she could actually breathe.

Tyler heard cursing, then the door to John's office clicked open and closed. She counted to sixty, then slitted her eyes open. She could not see Harry. She slowly opened her eyes all the way and looked around the office. Harry was gone and she was alone. He must have forgotten something. Assuming what Harry was looking for was in Tyler's car, Harry would have to take the elevator to the lobby, then either climb stairs or take another elevator down to the garage. She probably had at least ten minutes before he would get back. Wasting no time, Tyler shuffled over to the landline. She could not reach the phone, so she used her head to knock the receiver off the unit, stuck her tongue out, and dialed 911. She hoped. The red light on the phone turned on indicating it was in use, so she had succeeded in calling someone at least. The volume on the phone was low, and Tyler could not hear anything other than an indistinct woman's voice speaking. The button for the speakerphone, which would allow Tyler to actually hear what the woman was saying, was right next to the button to hang up, and Tyler was unwilling to risk hanging up the phone. The voice on the other end of the line paused.

"Hello," Tyler said softly, "I'm trying to call 911. I've been abducted, my name is Tyler McCarther. I'm in the Cloose & Elkman office in downtown St. Louis in John Delaware's office on the forty-fith floor. Send help please. My abductor is gone but I don't know for how long. He told me he's going to kill me. Please help. If this isn't 911, please call 911."

Tyler shuffled back over to where Harry had left her originally, or close enough to where he had left her originally. She glanced over at the phone. The red light was still on, so whoever she had called had remained on the line. She listened carefully but either the woman on the other end had stopped speaking or the volume was low enough not to notice. *Good.* Tyler tried to remember whether Harry had left her head tipped forward or back. She thought forward. She leaned her head forward and slightly leaned to the left so that it was angled toward the door, and closed her eyes. Tyler hoped desperately that help was on the way, and that she was not left waiting to hemorrhage out like poor Diana and Kevin. Tyler could feel her heartrate increasing, and an attempt at circular breathing failed. She started counting to try to remain calm, which worked better. She had reached two hundred fifty when she heard the door click open again. Working to keep every muscle in her face relaxed, Tyler opened up her eyes the slightest amount.

She could see a fuzzy shape, Harry she assumed, enter the office and close the door behind himself. He walked over to Tyler and leaned down. Could he tell she had moved? She imagined if he had any suspicions, the thick carpet pile would show disturbances where she had shuffled. Tyler mentally crossed her fingers that Harry would not be so observant. She could not make out his facial expression, just his shape, but he seemed to be looking at her intently. Tyler could feel her eyelids flickering involuntarily and started to hold her breath, before realizing doing so would give away the fact that she was actually conscious. She forced herself to breathe slowly instead. After a few agonizing seconds Tyler saw Harry's outline stand up and walk away. Out of her peripheral vision it looked like he was doing something on John's desk. She thought Harry's back was to her, but due to her limited field of view she could not tell for sure. After a few moments he came back and roughly shoved her head back. Tyler forced herself to remain relaxed and listened desperately for sirens or anyone coming to help her. It remained eerily silent outside, the only sounds of her and Harry's breath. Hers slow, painfully controlled, and his fast, expectant.

Tyler felt something warm touch the inside of her left nostril. The warmness coated the inside and formed a plug. *Fuck.* Then the same on the right side. Tyler knew from copious document review that the wax stayed in the nostril for five minutes before removal for best results. Unfortunately, in this case, best results meant the entire inside of her nostril—hair included—would be removed from her nose and Tyler would quickly bleed out onto John's expensive rug.

Tyler was still desperately trying to stay still and breathe slowly as if she were unconscious, but it hardly seemed like there was a point anymore. Help was either going to arrive within five minutes, or she was going to die. She was not ready to die, and she was scared. She started to breathe faster and sensed that Harry had walked back over to her. She slitted her eyes open again. Surely it had not already been five minutes. Should she try to scream now? Was it too late? Her breathing accelerated but he did not seem to notice. Harry peered up her nose, then bent down and cut the zip ties securing her legs to the chair. He must be preparing the scene to look like a suicide. Probably there would be so much blood that he would not be able to touch her without leaving evidence after he pulled the wax out.

Tyler forced herself to stay relaxed just a few seconds longer. Surely next he would cut the zip ties on her arms. Instead, Harry stepped back again. Tyler prepared herself. He would have to cut the zip ties on her arms, then she would have to run, and hope that help would be arriving soon. The inside of her nostrils had begun to itch uncomfortable and she forced herself not to twitch her nose. Tyler started to count to herself again, and after she reached seventy-five Harry stepped back and went to work on the zip ties on her arms. When he cut the first one, she let her arm flop down to her side— partially on purpose, partially because it had become stiff sitting in the same position for hours and she could not fully control it. Tyler gathered herself mentally as he sawed at the zip tie on her left hand. As soon as it was free, she opened her mouth and started to scream.

Tyler saw Harry's surprised face and instinctually headbutted him. He tipped backwards. Tyler was momentarily stunned, the light was on in the office and her eyes had been closed so long that it blinded her, plus her head was spinning from cracking against Harry's nose. With detachment, Tyler saw that Harry's nose was bleeding. *Ironic.* She twitched her own nose, then thought better of it—she had to preserve the wax fillings until they could be melted down and removed safely. Shit, had the headbutt loosened the wax? Tyler saw Harry begin to swipe out at her legs and knew she had to move. She ran to the door and wrenched it open. Harry was up on his hands and knees, eyes glittering and blood running down his nose into his mouth and onto his shirt.

Tyler started running down the hall toward the elevator bank. Her borrowed thick white athletic socks skidded on the carpet as she rounded a corner and she almost fell. Tyler hoped she would have enough time to board the elevator before Harry made it out of the office. Or maybe she should go hide under another partner's desk. She reached the glass doors to the elevator bank and yanked at them, remembering too late that they were locked from both sides after hours for security reasons. Bitterly, Tyler thought of her badge and the guest badge sitting on the floor of John's office. She would just have to hide. She whirled around to see if Harry had caught up. Not yet.

Tyler ran into a paralegal's interior office at random. The automatic lights flicked on. *Fuck.* She ran out, sliding again on the carpet. Choosing at random again, this time Brendan's office, she slammed the light switch to the "off" position and crawled under the desk. Crouching, Tyler listened harder than she ever had in her life. She heard neither Harry nor any signs of help. Nervously, she felt her upper lip. Was that moisture blood seeping out of her nostril or sweat? It was too dark to see. Tyler's breathing accelerated.

Tyler heard thumping from down the hall, then a frustrated grunt. Then nothing. Harry must have seen the paralegal's office light. Tyler remained crouched under the desk for what felt like an eternity. She licked her upper lip, it tasted salty, so she felt hopeful that she was just sweating. Still, she heard no signs of police arriving. Tyler heard more thumping from what now sounded like two or three offices down the hall. Terrified, she curled herself into a tight ball. The thumping continued, closer now. Harry was silently inspecting every office. The silence was worse than if he had been yelling, it signaled focus and efficiency.

Tyler had somehow made it this far. She was not going to sit and wait to die under Brendan's desk. She squeezed her eyes tight, clenched her fists, then crawled out from under Brendan's desk and tiptoed out of his office as quickly and quietly as she could. As she walked out the doorway she quickly looked to the left and the right, and locked eyes with Harry, who was exiting an office two doors down from Brendan's. Harry, still silent, started running toward Tyler, who sprinted in the opposite direction, sliding again before she gained momentum. The entire office was a circular shape, so Tyler could keep running as long as she could be faster than Harry.

Without much of a head start, and without proper footwear, Tyler only made it to the corner where the hallway bifurcated to the elevator bank and out to more offices. Harry tackled Tyler by the shoulders and she hit the ground hard, with barely enough time to throw her arms out in front of her to brace her fall. Tyler tried to scream, but the wind had been knocked out of her. Harry grabbed her shoulders and flipped Tyler onto her back, then slammed her into the ground, once, twice, three times. Tyler thought she could feel the wax loosening in her nose, and her vision was starting to cloud. She lay dazed on the ground as Harry pulled the plastic bag holding the chemical-soaked cloth out of his pocket. She weakly tried to put her arms up to block the cloth's approach, but he batted them away. As the cloth closed over her mouth, she heard an enormous crash.

Finding her last ounce of strength, she pushed Harry's arm to the side and screamed.

Harry looked up at the sound of the crash, then jumped up and started running. Tyler, still reeling from the tackle, lay on the ground and watched as four pairs of legs went running by her.

"Stop, police!"

Tyler started sobbing in relief.

Still lying on the ground she heard a scuffle, then, "You're under arrest," in a familiar voice followed by a recitation of Harry's Miranda Rights. Tyler slowly rolled to her stomach and propped herself up on her forearms. Detective Myer and Officer Watson were walking Harry out, followed closely by another officer Tyler did not know and Tom, who ran past them and over to Tyler with a concerned expression on his face.

"Tyler," he said and ran a hand over her hair.

Tyler only started sobbing harder. Tom helped Tyler up into a seated position. As Harry passed by, he spit in Tyler's direction, and Tom halfway stood up, but sat down again after a stern look from Detective Myer.

"Tyler, is there something in your nose?" Tom asked, reaching out.

"Don't," Tyler managed, and shook her head. A drop of blood dropped down onto the carpet, and her crying intensified.

She heard the soft "ding" of the elevator arriving, and several EMTs arrived shortly afterward. She was able to stop crying long enough to explain the situation with the wax to them, and they walked her out carefully to an ambulance and helped her onto a gurney. To her relief the blood appeared to have stopped. Tom hopped onto the ambulance and held Tyler's hand on the way to the hospital. On the way, the EMTs started an IV with fluids and a painkiller.

At the hospital, Tyler explained the situation to an emergency room doctor who appeared interested to be dealing with something other than a car accident or assault in the middle of the night. However, when the doctor tried to examine Tyler's nose, she became so panicked that a nurse quickly added a sedative to Tyler's IV, after which she observed everything around her as if through a thick, wavy glass. After the wax had been safely melted and removed, Tyler fell asleep, exhausted.

CHAPTER EIGHTEEN

Tyler woke up feeling better rested than she had in months. She looked around the strange room she was in, confused, but quickly remembering the assault in the stairwell, her kidnapping, and her narrow escape. She was in the hospital, and someone had removed her clothes and dressed her in a scratchy hospital gown. She felt filthy and exhausted, but at least she was alive. Tyler experimentally wiggled her toes, and noticed her feet were bare. She was incongruously happy not to be wearing the dirty white athletic socks anymore. Tyler noticed several vases of flowers on bedside tables. She heard a buzzing and saw her cell phone vibrating next to a cheerful arrangement of daisies. Where had her phone come from? Without checking to see who was calling, Tyler picked up.

"Hello?"

"Tyler, John Delaware here, great to hear from you."

"What day is it?" she asked. And what did he mean, great to hear from her, he had called her.

"It's Sunday afternoon, two-thirty," he replied.

"Sorry I missed the call," Tyler said. "And I guess I didn't have a chance to put together those materials for you either."

John made a confused noise on the other end of the line.

"The Saturday morning call with NSK. I slept right through it." Everything felt vaguely amusing to Tyler, and she wondered if she was still on sedatives. She looked down and saw that an IV was indeed still attached to her arm.

"Tyler, no worries!" Well, that certainly did not sound like the John she knew. "You're in the hospital still?"

How did John know she was in the hospital? "Yes," she said, drawing the word out. "Why are you calling me? How do you know I'm in the hospital? Listen... some crazy stuff has been happening lately, but I think it's over. I'll really be able to buckle down on the billing."

John chuckled and Tyler could tell it was in the same genuine fashion that she had observed with Ty. "Just making sure my favorite associate is doing well, and knocking out some emails at the same time," he replied. She heard the familiar tapping of fingers on a keyboard. This, however, did not seem to be a full response, and Tyler sat silently waiting for more of an explanation.

A nurse walked in and gave Tyler a skeptical look when she saw Tyler's cell phone clasped to her ear. The nurse turned on her heel and walked out.

"I heard that you may have uncovered an amazing new business opportunity for the firm," John continued.

Tyler shook her head, confused. Realizing John could not hear the head shake, she managed a very non-professional, "What?"

"I mean, thank god you weren't injured, or you could have been a plaintiff yourself! Imagine! We have to think about how to position this to the client immediately. We're on the ground floor, if we move fast we can avoid NSK shopping around. You'll be a great face to have on the case. I'd love for you to join me at the pitch tomorrow. Of course, you don't need to say anything. In fact, better that you don't unless I specifically tell you to. Say, did you have any injuries during the assault?" John sounded like he hoped she might. "We can make it a video call to really add to the urgency."

Before Tyler could process what John was talking about the nurse walked back in with Detective Myer and Tom.

"Who are you talking to?" Detective Meyer asked. "Family? Is someone going to come visit?"

"I'm speaking with John Delaware," said Tyler, annoyed to be interrupted now, "And we're speaking about an important new business opportunity, so if you could just excuse me for a minute."

Tom, looking both annoyed and amused, grabbed the phone out of her hand and hung it up.

EPILOGUE

Tyler's hair was freshly cut and she had requested that her stylist add some subtle highlights—it was long and shiny from the blowout Tyler had splurged on that morning—almost as sleek as Cerene's. Tyler looked over at her friend and smiled magnanimously. Tyler could afford to do that because she was attending a department-wide happy hour that was being held in her own honor. Tyler reached out to a passing waiter and grabbed a glass of champagne. The happy hour was being held in the firm's private library-slash-bar area, but Tyler knew it was serious because every attorney in the litigation department had been invited, and because waiters and champagne had been brought in. Plus, there were passed appetizers. Consequently, the room was packed. *Take that, Ty, and your gyro buffet.* Speaking of which, where was he? Tyler saw him standing with Brendan. He caught her gaze and waved, then gave her a thumbs up. He was already sweating. Tyler smiled back and gave him a little wave.

Tyler felt a hand at her elbow and turned to Peter Parisi.

"Tyler, so good to see you, and good, you've got a fresh glass of champagne. I'm about to say a few words, come with me."

Tyler turned to Cerene. "Be right back!" she said, smiling again. She gave Cerene a brief wide-eyed look that said "can you believe this is happening?" Cerene gave her a half-smile and shook her head ruefully. She only looked a little jealous.

Peter pointed Tyler next to a podium in the corner, then collected John Delaware from a nearby conversation. Peter walked up to the podium and tapped on the attached microphone. The crowded room immediately fell silent—as always, everyone in Peter's vicinity had been subtly paying attention to where he was and what he was doing.

"Thank you *so much* for coming," Peter started. "We're here to celebrate some really exciting new business for the firm, and, dare I say, a rising star." Peter smiled over at Tyler. John, on Tyler's other side, also smiled warmly at her. She tried to look bashful, but felt fiercely proud. "As many of you probably know, we had a criminal incident here at the firm a few weeks ago. One of our young associates was assaulted, and things would have been much worse, but for the intervention of our local police force." Peter looked seriously around at the crowd. The bruise on Tyler's temple from where Harry had slammed her head into the ground had faded from purple to bluish-yellow, but was still visible. She had purposefully used no cover-up on it ahead of the happy hour, and she lifted her chin and slightly angled the bruised side of her face toward the group of lawyers. The bruise had gotten a lot of attention and sympathy the last few weeks, not to mention a seat at the business pitch to NSK with John, and Tyler would have been lying if she pretended she had not enjoyed it. She was glad the assault had not left any permanent damage, but once all evidence of the incident was over, a small part of her would miss it when she stopped receiving celebrity treatment from her coworkers.

"During the course of this assault, however, it was discovered by our very own Tyler McCarther that a product we represent—NSK's nose hair wax—was alleged to have caused a death with a limited amount of product due to a production line malfunction, and the subsequent press coverage made that public knowledge. Of course, through no fault of our own. Now, we all know NSK has been an important firm client for decades, but thus far we've been dealing with more minor injuries and we've been working through insurance companies that we all know squeeze us for every penny," he theatrically lifted up his left hand and squeezed for dramatic effect, "and, as we all know, deaths are top-dollar litigation and are not covered by general liability insurance!" Peter paused for dramatic effect. "As I mentioned earlier, I am so pleased to announce that as of last week, following an extremely compelling pitch from our own John Delaware and Tyler McCarther, Cloose & Elkman was selected to represent NSK in the pending class litigation representing the families of individuals who allegedly died after using this particular subset of the product. At our normal rates." Peter raised his glass of champagne. "Let's raise a toast to Tyler. We're so pleased you are part of our rockstar team representing NSK and thanks for being instrumental in Cloose & Elkman winning this important case."

Tyler raised her glass and looked around, from Cerene, who had succumbed to envy and was looking positively green with it, to Ty, who actually looked pleased for her and she had come to suspect was one of the few genuinely nice people working at a law firm, to John, who she gave a special smile to since she knew he would not be able to replace her for quite some time now regardless of whether he wanted to or not, to Brendan, whose face was glowing red and she was amused to see appeared to be positively sloshed, to Peter, who gave her a magnanimous head-nod, then took a sip of champagne. Tyler raised her glass up, then did the same.

ACKNOWLEDGMENTS

Thank you to my friends and family, especially my lovely husband Andrew, for supporting me throughout this process. I also want to thank my amazing therapist Robyn, for encouraging me to take time for myself and believing in me.

A <u>huge</u> thank you to my editor Michelle Krueger for cleaning up my mistakes, and doing so with such kindness and positivity, and to my fabulous cover artist Margarita Castaño who made my Instagram-able book dreams come true.

Finally, thank you to *you*, the reader. If you made it this far, I hope you loved the book and recommend it to all your friends.

ABOUT THE AUTHOR

Meredith is a novelist and attorney based in St. Louis, Missouri. She began her career at a large law firm and now practices regulatory insurance law at a nationwide carrier. Meredith is a classically trained harpist and enjoys playing in her free time. She also enjoys spending quality time with friends and family, wine and charcuterie, gossip, and pets.